A Very Lucky Christmas

A Very Lucky Christmas

LILAC MILLS

CANELO

First published in the United Kingdom in 2017 by Lilac Tree Books as
And a Sixpence for Luck

This edition published in the United Kingdom in 2019 by

Canelo Digital Publishing Limited
57 Shepherds Lane
Beaconsfield, Bucks HP9 2DU
United Kingdom

A CIP catalogue record for this book is available from the British Library.

Print ISBN 978 1 78863 578 3
Ebook ISBN 978 1 78863 274 4

Look for more great books at www.canelo.co

Printed and bound in Great Britain by Clays Ltd, Elcograf S.p.A.

For my beautiful daughter

Chapter 1

Daisy knew something was afoot. Freddie had been acting furtively (if that was the right word to describe how he appeared to have a smile playing about his lips when he didn't think she was watching, or the way he caught her gaze and swiftly looked away), and all the while he seemed to be on the verge of saying 'surprise!' or 'ta dah!', and this had been going on ever since yesterday, when he'd suggested they go out to dinner.

'Wear something nice,' he'd said, and she wasn't quite sure how to take it. Did he mean she didn't usually wear nice things, or did he want her to wear something extra nice, as in *special* nice?

Daisy settled on the latter, especially when he told her they were going to *Botelli's*, the quite upmarket and rather expensive Italian restaurant she'd been semi-hinting at going to for weeks, ever since it opened. She wondered what the occasion might be, because Freddie didn't much like going out to eat. He claimed he had enough of restaurants as a result of having to entertain clients every five minutes, and he usually wanted to eat at his house, with him doing the cooking because Daisy, he so often said, could burn water. And he usually ate off a tray on his lap, while watching TV.

She understood, she really did. He had to be sociable all day, because of his job, talking and being pleasant and entertaining, so when he came home he wanted peace and quiet, and some time and space to recharge his batteries. As a consequence, they usually spent the evenings snuggled together on the sofa, with him in charge of the remote control, until Daisy started to nod and made noises about going home, and waited for him to suggest she stayed the night. Or not, because he often didn't suggest anything. She enjoyed snuggling and flopping about on the sofa, but not all the time. It would be nice to go out once in a while, and tonight looked as though it might be a very good night indeed!

As she scoured her wardrobe, she pulled out one dress after another, adding them to the discarded heap on her bed. Her mother would have a fit when she saw the mess, but Daisy didn't care. She had butterflies in her stomach and a sense of excited anticipation, which had grown throughout the day. Let her mother shout; nothing could dampen Daisy's mood, because she had a feeling she knew why Freddie was taking her to *Botelli's*. At least, she hoped she did.

They'd been dating for just over a year, Daisy spending more and more time in Freddie's three-bed semi (built just last year, he was fond of telling her), than she spent at her own house, or rather, her mum's, because at nearly twenty-seven, Daisy was still living at home with her mum and her younger brother, though David was saving hard to buy his own place.

Daisy kept meaning to get a home of her own and, like her brother, was putting money aside every month towards a deposit, but it was so much harder for a girl, she decided, when there were all those lovely clothes, and shoes, and handbags, and other assorted stuff she simply couldn't live without. They called "buy me" and it was rare for her to ignore their insidious little voices so, as a result, she always had far less to put in the proverbial piggy bank than her brother put in his.

It didn't help that Daisy worked slap-bang in the city centre, and what else was a girl supposed to do in her lunch hour but shop? She had to pop out of the office for food, so it was only natural to browse. Each time she left the office she swore she was only going to window shop, and nearly every day she bought a little something: an eyeshadow in just the right shade of nude, a gorgeous bottle of perfume, a pair of shoes she simply had to have because they went brilliantly with the dress she'd bought last week.

Hence the mountain of clothes on her bed, some of which she'd hardly worn (okay, make that *never*, in a couple of cases), and there still wasn't anything suitable in the squashed and over-crowded wardrobe. Nothing that said "Yes, of course I'll marry you", because wasn't that the whole purpose of this special meal tonight? It must be! Daisy could think of no other reason for Freddie to fork out for a meal in such an expensive place unless he was going to ask her to marry him.

Her heart skipped a beat at the thought. Mrs Freddie Lakeland. Mrs Lakeland. Daisy Lakeland. She had a teenagery urge to write her "new" name, just to see how it looked on paper. Soon, if she was right (and she was certain she must be), she'd be writing it for real.

Ah, this might do. Not too flashy, not too understated. She held the peachy-coloured dress up to her chin and looked in the mirror. She really should have bought something new, but she hadn't managed to find anything she liked, or anything suitable. The shops were in between seasons, full of sale stuff, all shorts and little tee shirts, with the occasional splash of autumn colours on the one and only rail of new stock – and those only had jumpers and cord short skirts on them, which was lovely for a walk in the park on a chilly Sunday morning, but not for getting engaged in.

This particular dress was one she'd worn before, but not for a long time and Freddie had never seen it. She'd bought it for a friend's wedding (wedding! she squealed), and wondered if anyone would remember her wearing it when she posted photos of her engagement ring on Facebook and Instagram. Maybe, but if she angled the shot so not much of the dress showed, no one would be able to see it clearly, and anyway, the only thing anyone would really have eyes for, was the diamond on the third finger of her left hand. Oh, she hoped he'd already bought the ring, but knowing Freddie he was just as likely to propose, then expect her to choose her own, because he wouldn't want to get it wrong and risk buying something she didn't like.

She tried the dress on, relieved to find it still fitted, though she might have to eat sparingly. Anything more than a crumb would make her stomach stick out, and the dress was already quite snug. Pity – it was a shame to go to a place like *Botelli's* and not be able to stuff her face until she burst.

Her tummy did a little roll of anticipation, and she guessed she might be too excited to eat, anyway.

When would he do it? After the main course? After the dessert? He might have arranged for the ring to be hidden in the tiramisu… no, not that, because he couldn't guarantee what she'd choose, and he wasn't the alpha male type to order for her. He was far too considerate for that!

When the coffee was served then, maybe that would be when Freddie would propose. Or maybe he'd order a bottle of champagne and the ring would be in the bottom of the glass. Ooh, she hoped it would be that one, because it was so romantic.

She took great care in straightening her hair (it tended to kink halfway down its length) and applied her make-up with a light hand (she didn't want to look as though she'd dressed to go to a nightclub). She wanted to look naturally radiant, exactly like a bride-to-be should look, elegant and classy.

Almost ready, she stood in front of the full-length mirror, twisting this way and that, worrying if her bum looked big. Pah! Big bums were in, weren't they, and anyway, it wasn't *that* big. Not really. If her boobs were a bit bigger, she'd be more in proportion, so she tried hiking them up and pushing them out, but the dress wasn't very forgiving. She thought about changing her bra, but the underwear she had on was a matching set, only a shade deeper than the dress. She hoped Freddie would get a good look at it before he switched the light off – Freddie didn't like making love with the light on, though he had been known to light a candle or two when he was feeling particularly romantic, bless him!

Rummaging around in the bottom of the wardrobe, Daisy came up with a pair of shoes which would go rather well, and she had a bag somewhere, the clutch that she'd bought at the same time as the dress. One more thing – jewellery. A pair of fake diamond studs and a silver heart-shaped necklace would do the trick, but before she put them on, she removed the little gold ring her great-gran had given her. The only ring she intended to wear tonight was the one Freddie was going to present her with. She didn't want anything to detract from her engagement ring in the hundreds of photos she intended to post tomorrow.

She wondered how her mother would react to the news. The women in her family hadn't had much luck with men and her nan, especially, seemed to be allergic to them. Men made her face go all red and started her off on a rant. Only Gee-Gee appeared okay about the idea of boyfriends and marriage, but then, her great-grandmother had done things the traditional way (and more acceptable way, in those days) by getting married first then having the babies, unlike Nan who'd skipped the marriage part totally and had launched herself straight into motherhood without the (dubious) benefit of a husband.

Daisy's mum thought all men were a waste of space, her view coloured by the fact that Daisy and David's father had done a runner when the pair of them were tiny. None of them had clapped eyes on him since, though her mum had received regular payments until David left school.

So it was left to Daisy to fly the "men aren't all bastards" banner on behalf of all of the world's male population – except for David. Her brother didn't need any help from Daisy because Mum, Nan, and Gee-Gee all thought the sun shone out of his backside.

Daisy hoped everyone, her mother in particular, would be happy for her.

Full of barely contained excitement, Daisy skipped down the stairs, shouting, 'See you tomorrow,' into the living room. She had no doubt that Freddie would expect her to stay at his house tonight, and "consummate" their engagement.

Her mother grunted and waved, her attention on *Coronation Street*, and Daisy knew she wouldn't get anything else out of her. God forbid anyone who interrupted her mother when she was watching one of her soaps.

Freddie pulled up, bang on time as always. The surprise on his face when he saw Daisy scurrying out of the front door, handbag in one hand, and coat in the other, was comical. He usually had to wait a good ten minutes before Daisy made an appearance – her mother often said she'd be late for her own funeral, and Freddie would dutifully chuckle, though Daisy could see how much her tardiness annoyed him as he waited, perched uncomfortably on one of the living room chairs. Tonight, Daisy had been too excited to be late, because the sooner they got to the restaurant, the sooner Freddie would ask her to be his wife.

Eek! Daisy Jones was going to get married. She'd be a *wife*, and she almost let out a squeal, but held it in because she didn't want to spoil his surprise. She was meant to know nothing about it, but a woman can tell, can't she, female intuition and all that. Freddie even came around to her side of the car, opening the door and helping her out, and Daisy decided to believe he was being so attentive and ultra-romantic because tonight was special, and not because her dress was so tight that she had to be hauled out of the car. She must remember to practice getting in and out elegantly, because the BMW sports car was quite low slung and once they were married, she expected them to use his nice shiny car, rather than her old clapped-out hatchback. She made a note to watch some YouTube clips on how Kim Kardashian did it – or maybe not, considering the woman was forever flashing her knickers! Daisy didn't think Freddie would approve if she flashed hers; he was too up-market and too reserved for such vulgar behaviour.

The interior of the restaurant was everything she'd imagined it to be (especially since she'd Googled images of it and knew exactly what to expect). But viewing it on her phone wasn't the same as being there, and she let the elegant, understated atmosphere wash over her. The décor was all white: walls, tablecloths, chairs, and picture frames. The floor was dark, highly polished wood. The glasses and the cutlery shone and twinkled from the lights of the chandeliers, and soft music gave just the right amount of privacy. Fresh flowers were on each table, and waiters and waitresses stood discretely around the room.

One of the black-trousered, white-shirted staff took her coat, and Freddie nodded at him.

Was that a signal? Surely the proposal wasn't going to happen so soon, not before the starters?

She swallowed convulsively and followed another waiter, who showed them to their table. Once they were seated and had ordered drinks (white wine spritzer for her, because she wanted a clear head to remember every single detail of tonight), she and Freddie perused the menu.

It was all in Italian.

Daisy recognised some things, but most of it was gobbledygook.

'What are you having?' she asked Freddie.

Tonight he looked particularly handsome in a subtle sort of way. Daisy wouldn't call him a hunk, but he certainly had hunk tendencies. He liked to go to the gym, and he visited the barber every few weeks (she suspected he had a facial and a manicure while he was there, but she didn't hold that against him – it was nice to see a man taking care of himself, and male grooming was getting to be a big thing, wasn't it) and he always dressed nicely. Even his scruffs were clean and non-holey and fitted well, unlike her tattered and shabby lounging-about-the-house gear. Taller than Daisy by a good few inches, Freddie was slim with good shoulders and a suspiciously hair-free chest, leading Daisy to suspect he had a sneaky wax while he was at the barber, and he was clean-cut with an open, honest face.

That was what had attracted her to him in the beginning – his face. Her gaze had slid over him at first glance, but when he'd spoken and she was forced to give him a second glance, she'd also given him a third. He really was quite attractive in an English-gentleman kind of way. But it was his voice she liked best, well-modulated and slightly husky, it had the power to make her go weak at the knees. The rest of him wasn't so bad, either. Quite lovely, in fact!

'I fancy the *salmone affumicato* to start and maybe the *vitello al Romana* to follow,' Freddie replied, after a long pause.

'Sounds good. I'll have the same,' Daisy said, having absolutely no idea what she was ordering, though the *salmone* sounded a little like salmon. At least, she thought, if they ate the same things, then one of them wouldn't stink of garlic and the other wouldn't be trying to hold their breath when they kissed.

'How was your day?' he asked, stretching his hand across the table to reach to hers.

'Oh, same old, same old.' She didn't want to think about work. Right now, work had ceased to exist. All she wanted to think about was their future together. She wanted to talk about it too, but couldn't until he'd popped the question, because she wasn't supposed to know, she reminded herself, stamping down on her nerves.

Would he get down on one knee?

Ooh, she really hoped he would. Maybe she could discretely pop to the loo and ask a waiter to take a photo at the appropriate moment…

'I've landed a new client today,' Freddie said, stroking the back of her hand suggestively.

Her boyfriend wasn't known for displays of affection, especially public ones, him being a little reserved and all that, so Daisy relished the romance of it and he only let go of her hand when their starters were placed in front of them.

Thank goodness it was salmon, and though she wasn't totally in love with it when it was smoked, at least it was something she could eat, and it wasn't squid or chickens' feet, or something equally hideous.

They chatted about Freddie's job for a while and Daisy told him that Gee-Gee, her great-grandmother, was having to finally move into an old people's home because Nan couldn't cope with looking after her anymore.

'She'll still come to Mum's for Sunday lunch though,' Daisy said, as the plates were cleared away. 'Maybe we could have her round to ours at some point.'

Oops! She'd almost given the game away. There was no "ours" at the moment, but once they were married there would be, and she couldn't wait. She desperately wanted to put her own touch on his house. That picture hanging above the fireplace in the lounge needed to go for a start. She didn't like abstract, and every time she looked at it, she was reminded of a piece of Lego.

'Hmm?' Freddie hadn't been listening. He'd been too busy staring at one of the waiters, she noticed, who responded to Freddie's gaze with a slow wink. Daisy pretended she hadn't seen anything, but her excitement ratcheted up a notch, and she waited with her heart in her mouth for Freddie to get out of his seat and go down on one knee.

The main course arrived instead.

In between that and the dessert, Daisy decided to visit the ladies' loos, and as she passed by the winking waiter (he'd stopped winking now), she hesitated, before gathering her courage and whispering, 'When he does it, can you take a photo? I'd give you my phone, but he might notice.'

'Excuse me?'

'A photo?' She mimed holding a camera up to her face and clicking the shutter.

The waiter gave her a slightly horrified look.

'Oh, yes, right, I'm not supposed to know, am I?' she babbled. 'It doesn't matter. There'll be plenty of time for photos later, I expect.' She glanced swiftly back at the table, relieved to see that Freddie was engrossed in his phone. Maybe *he* was going to ask them to take a photo, though she doubted it – he wasn't really a photo type of guy, often shying away from her attempts to take selfies of them together, and he positively objected to her sharing any photos of himself on Facebook.

She dashed to the loo, fluffed up her hair and applied some more lipstick, then returned to the table.

'I don't fancy a pudding,' Freddie told her as she slipped back into her seat, 'but you feel free to have one, if you want.'

Dessert was the last thing on her mind in terms of actually eating it; she would only be interested in another course if there was a diamond ring hidden in it. And if he wasn't pushing her to have one, then clearly this wasn't the way he intended to produce the ring.

'I'm okay,' she said, 'though a coffee would be nice.'

Freddie called the waiter over. The man seemed rather hesitant and had a frown on his face, but it cleared when Freddie ordered two coffees.

'I've got something I want to ask you,' he said, when the waiter left.

Here it comes. Daisy was so nervous she felt sick. She tried to keep her expression neutral, aiming for a slightly quizzical look, holding in the big grin which struggled to get out. Get on with it, she thought, before I give the game away.

'We've been seeing each other for about a year now,' he said.

'Yes, yes we have.' She nodded enthusiastically.

'And I thought it was about time we took our relationship to a new level,' he continued, reaching across the table to grasp her hand once more. Twice in a night! Lucky her!

It's about time. It so definitely *is*, Daisy thought.

'…so I thought, I *wondered*,' Freddie cleared his throat, then looked past her shoulder and nodded.

This was it. This was her moment. He was going to do it!

'Could we have the bill, please?' he asked, as the waiter approached their table.

Was that a code word, she wondered, wishing he'd just hurry up.

'I wondered if you would…,' he hesitated, '…move in with me?' he finished in a rush.

'What?'

'Move in, cohabit, live together. That is, if you want to, if you're ready. No worries, if you're not.'

'Move in.' Daisy's voice was flatter than a pond on a windless day.

'Yes. There's plenty of room for two, and I wouldn't expect you to pay half of *everything*. What do you say?'

Daisy forced a smile onto her face and some enthusiasm into her voice, disappointment washing over her.

'Lovely,' she said and clapped her hands.

Chapter 2

'Deck the halls with boughs of holly
Fa-la-la-la-la, la-la-la-laa,
Go to Tesco, grab a trolley
Fa-la-la-la-la, la-la-la-laa.'

Yeah, that would work, Daisy thought, then sang the verse again, substituting Sainsbury for Tesco, then Waitrose, and finally Asda. Any of those supermarkets would do, though maybe not Morrisons because there were one too many syllables to fit.

She tapped her fingers on the steering wheel, admiring her newly painted Christmas nails (red with white snowflakes), and wished the traffic would get a move on. What was the holdup, anyway? If she wasn't home soon, Freddie would beat her to it, and she'd have no chance of smuggling her purchases into the house, and even less chance of hiding them.

She started singing again, the words popping into her head almost at random, though the method seemed to work for her.

'Fill it full of lots of goodies
Fa-la-la-la-la, la-la-la-laa,

Tinsel, turkey, and some puddies
Fa-la-la-la-la, la-la-la-laaah!'

Was puddies an actual word? Did it matter? The jingle was catchy enough, and if they showed a Christmas pudding at the same time the puddie word was sung, then—

Oh, who was she kidding? The big supermarkets had their own marketing departments, full of people who were paid a lot more money than little old Daisy Jones. And even if they didn't, they could afford to hire the big guns, like *Saatchi and Saatchi* (her heart gave a lurch at the idea of working for such a prestigious company) and wouldn't look twice at her pathetic offering. Not that any of the supermarkets would ever get to hear it. This one was for her ears only.

She sang the jingle again, happy with it, thinking it was "their loss" and "I'm wasted at *Caring Cards*", and her heart did another little lurch, but this time it had more to do with unease than anything else. She'd heard the rumours (who hadn't?) that the company was being squeezed more than usual by their competitors, and since the arrival of ecards on the internet (designing one's own cards online was a "growth strand", apparently), the company was well and truly struggling.

The traffic moved, finally, and Daisy ground the car into gear and bunny-hopped for a few feet until she got into her stride. Freddie hated the way she drove and told her so frequently. She was so glad he wasn't sitting in the passenger seat right now and giving her The Look.

Her mind turned to work again. Maybe it was about time she considered looking for another job, but she wasn't sure what else she could do, and perhaps she shouldn't have skipped out of work early, but what the hell, she could think up silly verses just as easily at home as she could in the office. She'd proved that very thing just now, thinking one up in the car, though she was pretty certain *Caring Cards* wouldn't be using her *Deck the Halls* jingle anytime soon.

As she sped along the short dual carriageway leading out of the city centre, she tried to push Christmas songs out of her head (an incredibly hard task, considering every shop and radio station had been blaring them out for at least the last two months), and concentrated on her new task.

Caring Cards was thinking about branching out into musical greetings cards and they'd decided Daisy was the best person to make it happen. Hence the reason for Daisy hijacking the *Deck the Halls* carol. She didn't have a musical bone in her body and she had no idea where to start. Did they expect her to make up her own tunes, or just supply the words to someone else's music?

She pulled off the dual carriageway and negotiated the twists and turns leading into their estate. The place was like a rabbit warren, with crescents, drives, closes and greens in abundance, and all of them were named after animals. Their cul-de-sac was rather charmingly called Red Deer Close, and as she drove into it her head was bursting with random songs and ideas.

Should she, could she, use existing tunes, or were they subject to copyright? And how long did said copyright last? Would *Caring Cards* have to pay royalties if they used someone's music, even if they changed the words?

Daisy foresaw a whole host of problems. You'd think the company would have looked into all this before asking her to come up with jingles, wouldn't you, she mused, but oh no, they had these bright ideas and expected them to magically happen. Besides, who were they going to get to sing the stupid things anyway? Not her – had any of them *heard* her sing? Actually, they had, last Friday at the company's Christmas knees-up, and it hadn't been pretty.

Daisy drove up to her little house and gave a sigh of relief. Freddie's car wasn't there, though a blue Ford was pulled up alongside the house, almost blocking the entrance to their drive. Freddie would be furious if he couldn't get his car in the drive when he got home, and he was annoyed enough that the station was too far to walk, so if someone had the temerity to park awkwardly, Freddie's strop would be astronomical. You'd have thought the builders would have allowed for the fact that every house had at least two cars. Bloody hell, she was starting to sound like her mother, all moany and grumbly about domestic crap!

She clambered out of the driver's seat, then pulled it forward to reach the parcels on the back seat. There were quite a few of them. Had she really bought this much? At least they weren't all for her – she'd managed to purchase all of Freddie's presents and most of her family's. The only person she was stuck on who to buy a present for was Zoe. Just what *did* you get the woman who had everything? Especially when whatever her sister-in-law bought was exclusive, expensive, and far too nice for words.

Bags hanging off each arm, her handbag on her shoulder, and her keys in her teeth, Daisy staggered up their very short drive, taking only five lumbering steps from the car to their front door, and she still managed to drop something.

Muttering curses, she freed up one hand and found her house key, stabbing it in the lock, then fell in through the front door, scattering bags everywhere.

'Damn!'

She scrambled to her feet, rubbing her bruised knees, and reached for the nearest bag, then paused.

'Hello?' she called, positive the faint noise she'd just heard had come from upstairs.

Silence.

She must have imagined it. That was the problem with these new houses – walls as thin as paper – and being semi-detached meant that she and Freddie could often hear the couple next door arguing. Then making up. Noisily. Freddie usually resorted to turning the volume on the TV up to full and waiting half an hour, claiming that burst eardrums were better than grossed out ones.

Daisy gathered up the various bags and their spilt contents, and carried them into the kitchen, glancing at the clock. Nearly four. Freddie would be at least another hour, possibly two, if there were leaves on the line, or there was the wrong type of rain, or one of the other silly excuses for the train to be late. She had time for a quick drink before she tackled the clothes-hiding and the present-wrapping.

Hot chocolate with a splash of Bailey's Irish Whisky would get her back into the Christmas spirit. She'd had plenty of it before she'd hit the shops, but it had soon been swiftly drained out of her by the forced cheerfulness of the decorations, and the glum and harried expressions on her fellow shoppers' faces.

While she waited for the kettle to boil, she wandered into the living room to stare critically at the tree. She'd bought a natural one this year, much to Freddie's disgust (he hated the mess the fallen needles caused) and the smell of pine filled the room, competing subtly with the aroma of berries and spice from the plug-in air freshener. She breathed deeply. Lovely.

Without even looking at the tree, the scent alone would make her think Christmassy thoughts. Add the glitter and sparkle of the decorations on the tree, and the lights which Daisy insisted be left on all the time, and the scene was satisfyingly festive. Not too overdone, but enough to show visitors that Christmas had well and truly arrived at 10 Red Deer Close.

Before she returned to the kitchen, Daisy couldn't help walking over to the tree and kneeling down. Freddie, Mr Organised, had already placed several immaculately wrapped parcels under the drooping lower branches (she made a note to remember to water the poor tree), and it took all of Daisy's willpower not to give each one a good shake and a sniff. He'd even put ribbon around them, topped off with matching bows.

What was that? Daisy stopped feeling the presents and cocked her head. It sounded like a creak, from directly overhead, but Freddie definitely wasn't home yet, so it must have come from Mandy next door. Sometimes, when their neighbour's door banged, it sounded like their own front door.

The kettle clicked off and Daisy walked back into the kitchen, trying to make her mind up between the laced hot chocolate she'd promised herself, and the half-full bottle of Prosecco which she'd just remembered was chilling nicely in the fridge.

The wine won. She'd have a glass and get changed into her slouchy clothes, and hide her "me" purchases from Freddie, before she tackled the present wrapping. Freddie's would have to be wrapped first, because she didn't want to risk him walking through the door and seeing the beautiful watch she'd bought him, or the new lamb's wool jacket in a soft tan colour.

The wine bottle was less full than she remembered it being, but she shrugged and poured a large glass, emptying the bottle, then took a hefty swig. The cool bubbles hit the back of her throat and she sighed in bliss, the sigh deepening as she kicked off her shoes to release her aching toes.

I wish every day could be like this, she thought, taking another sip. Mornings in work, and afternoons spent shopping. She'd even treated herself to lunch out: a coffee and a sandwich. She could get used to this. Half days suited her, especially when Freddie was in work, and he had no idea what she'd bought. 'This old thing? I've had it ages,' didn't work on Freddie. He knew what was in her wardrobe better than she did, so she had to resort to saying she'd found that dress/jacket/handbag/pair of boots in one of the numerous charity shops in town, or telling him the item cost a fraction of what she had actually paid.

They were supposed to be saving up for a place of their own (owned jointly that is, and not just by Freddie as was the case at the moment), something a little more substantial and not in the middle of hundreds of similar houses. So Freddie kept a close eye on expenditure, though he happily treated himself to the occasional Ralph Lauren sweater, and Daisy never uttered a word. She didn't feel she could, not when he earned more than double the wage she brought home.

Taking her glass of wine with her, she grabbed the "me" bags and trundled up the stairs, with the intention of stashing her ill-gotten booty in the never-used spare room, and drip-feeding them into the wardrobe, one sneaky item at a time.

But first, she wanted to change into something a little more *elasticated*. The waistband of her work trousers was digging uncomfortably into her stomach – the result of too many pre-Christmas parties (plus the daily mince pies Joyce brought into work and insisted on everyone eating).

She dropped her parcels on the landing by the door to the spare room, which was always kept firmly closed because there was nothing spare about that room – it was full to bursting with assorted junk, more like the "dump-it-in-and-shut-the-door-quick" room, and went into their bedroom. The state of the bed gave her a brief flash of annoyance and dismay. She'd left earlier than usual this morning, wanting to get as much done as possible before absconding for the rest of the day, leaving Freddie with the duvet pulled up to his chin and his eyes tightly shut. He hadn't even bothered to straighten the duvet when he'd gotten out of it. And he'd left a couple of glasses on the bedside table, and—

Hang on…

Daisy picked up one of the glasses, kicking a scatter cushion out of the way, and sniffed at the contents of the glass.

Wine?

Before breakfast?

Was her boyfriend a secret lush?

And what was that smell? The unfamiliar aftershave (if that's what it was, and not some new cleaning product – Freddie had a habit of buying the latest item on TV guaranteed to make your home smell fresh; he was responsible for the berry and spice plug-in in the living room) mingled with an almost animal aroma. It reminded her of the way their bedroom smelled after a good session in bed. Not that they'd had a good session, or even a not-so-good session, lately. They hadn't "done it" for a long time, if she was honest. A quick jump in the sack now and again, often over far too quickly, was all she and Freddie had managed in months.

Daisy opened the window to air the room out, then picked up the duvet from the floor and flung it on the bed.

She froze.

Those were not Freddie's shoes. They were far, far too big, for one thing…

Daisy picked up a scatter cushion and aimed it at the bed, then she froze again.

The shirt which had been hiding under it wasn't his, either. Neither were the scruffy jeans.

Another noise. This time the creak of a floorboard and a kind of rustle.

It came from the spare room.

Freddie was home, after all, but what was he doing in there with the door closed? Maybe he was wrapping another present for her, but… something nagged at her, something wasn't quite right, and although she knew he'd be cross if she walked in on him mid-wrap, she put her hand on the handle and—

'Fucking hell!'

The spare room was full of junk, and some of that junk was sported by two naked men. One of them was Freddie.

Chapter 3

The stranger had his hands clasped over his manhood, but his hands weren't doing a terribly good job. Freddie would have been equally as naked if he hadn't made a grab for one of her summer dresses as soon as Daisy opened the door.

'It isn't what you think,' her boyfriend said. He looked mortified, embarrassed and as guilty as sin.

'What am I supposed to think it is?' she asked.

She was calm, surprisingly so, considering. There was a part of her which even now hoped she'd jumped to the wrong conclusion. Maybe this was a colleague from work, and they were... *what?* What could they possibly be doing together which meant they had to be naked...?

'Er... um...,' Freddie said. 'I don't know.'

'Then tell me.'

Freddie hung his head.

Daisy wished he had his own clothes on, and not her lovely Laura Ashley flower-print tea-dress wrapped around his nether regions. She *liked* that dress, but she'd never wear it again, not after what it was currently rubbing up against.

'Fucking, dahling,' the stranger drawled. 'Freddie and I were doing it. In your bed.'

'Carl, there's no need to be so...' Freddie swallowed. He reminded her of a small boy who'd been caught cheating in class and was about to be sent to the head-master.

'Honest?' Carl finished for him.

Daisy's mouth was wide open. In *her* bed? Screwing in the bed she shared with Freddie? The one she snuggled into every night, feeling safe and loved? That bed?

Ew.

'Freddie, is it true?' Her voice was little more than a whisper.

Freddie said nothing.

Daisy wondered, rather hysterically, if *Caring Cards* had a card for *this* occasion. Maybe that should be her first attempt – the sorry-you-came-home-and-caught-your-man-bumping-uglies-with-another-bloke jingle.

She wondered how well it would sell.

Carl took Freddie's hand in one of his, exposing his not-inconsiderable manhood. He's a big fella, Daisy noticed absently, in more ways than one, and the old adage regarding the correlation between the size of a man's feet and the size of his appendage, came to mind. In this instance it was true, she noted.

Freddie couldn't look her in the eye. 'Yes,' he said finally, as the silence stretched out.

'You and *him*?' Daisy asked, seeking clarification.

She thought she could cope with a woman, but this bloke? How the hell was she supposed to compete with that, she wondered, as Carl flashed his assets at her.

Please put them away, she pleaded silently. Wasn't there another dress in there? She'd willingly sacrifice any dress she owned if it meant she didn't have to look at his dangling manhood for a second longer.

Actually, she didn't have to look. She could simply go downstairs and wait for him to leave.

'How long had this been going on?' she demanded. 'No, don't tell me, I really don't want to know. What am I to you, Freddie? A front, so people don't know you're gay?'

His voice was so low Daisy strained to hear his reply. 'Maybe.'

'Did you ever love me?' Tears threatened, though whether they were sad tears or angry ones, Daisy couldn't tell. It was too early to say how badly her heart was broken. At the moment, disbelief was riding her hard. Freddie – gay? There must be some mistake.

He'd certainly not been gay when they'd had sex, had he? He'd loved her curves, her womanliness. He'd certainly not had any trouble responding to her. In the beginning, during the so-called honeymoon period, he'd been as randy as a butcher's dog. He hadn't been able to get enough of her.

What had changed?

Had she put him off women? Was it her fault?

'It's not you, it's me,' Freddie said, in a subdued voice. 'I can't help being attracted to men.'

'Do you love him?' Daisy demanded.

Without warning, she burst into tears. Not wanting to give either man the satisfaction of seeing her cry, she fled downstairs and into the kitchen.

All her dreams, all her plans had fallen down around her ears. A bigger house, a wedding, a family – none of that would happen now, and she had no idea what to do next. Staying in this house wasn't an option. Staying in a relationship with Freddie was impossible. So where did that leave her?

She was wiping her eyes on a sheet of kitchen roll when she heard muted voices from the hall, then the front door clicked shut. The sound of a car starting up made her wonder if Freddie had left, along with Carl. A part of her hoped he had, for how was she supposed to face him after what had just happened?

Freddie sidled into the kitchen, looking apprehensive. He looked so sorrowful and contrite that she wanted to wrap her arms around him and tell him everything would be alright – but it wouldn't, would it?

'You didn't answer my question,' she said, sniffling and reaching for another piece of kitchen roll to blow her nose.

'What question?'

She knew Freddie was stalling – she could read him like a book. Except, she'd missed out the "I prefer men" chapter, hadn't she? She obviously didn't know him as well as she'd thought she did.

'Do you love him?' she repeated.

'I'm sorry.'

'Is that a "yes"?'

'Yes.'

'How long has it been going on?'

Freddie sighed and looked away. 'Is there any point in discussing this?'

'Of course there's a bloody point! I want to know!'

'It won't change anything.'

If Carl had been a woman, Daisy would have undoubtedly have asked questions like "is she younger than me?",

"do you think she's prettier?", and "is she better in bed?".
But none of these things applied, and she found she
had no basis on which to compare. There was only one
comparison which mattered – her absence of the correct
chromosome. It was like trying to compare a dog to a cat,
and at that moment, Daisy felt like the silliest bitch on
earth.

'Just tell me,' she demanded, her arms folded across her
chest, her chin wobbling as she tried not to cry.

'Are you asking how long I've been attracted to men,
or how long I've been seeing Carl.'

'Both.'

'All my life, and a few months.'

'You could have fooled me. Oh yeah, you *did* fool me,
didn't you? We had *sex* for goodness sake. Didn't it mean
anything to you?'

'Look, Daisy, I love you, you know that—'

'I don't know anything anymore,' she interrupted.

'—but I don't *love you*, love you. Not like two soul
mates should.'

'I thought you *were* my soul mate,' Daisy wailed. 'We've
been living together for years, we've got the same sense
of humour, we like the same things. Mostly.' Yeah, she
thought cynically, seems we really do like the same things
– MEN!

Freddie sat down heavily on one of the kitchen chairs
and put his head in his hands. 'I didn't mean to hurt you,'
he said slowly.

'But you did, though,' she pointed out. She puffed out
her cheeks in an effort not to cry and blinked, fluttering
her hands in front of her face.

'I'm so sorry. I didn't want you to find out like this.' Freddie actually did sound sorry. Not that it made the slightest bit of difference.

'How did you want me to find out? When we were walking down the aisle, when I was pregnant with our first baby? *When?*'

'I know it's crazy, right? But I love him and there's nothing I can do about it.' He looked at Daisy, begging her with his eyes to understand.

And she did understand, in a way, but it didn't make the situation any easier to bear. 'What happens now?' she asked.

'Clean break?' His tone was hopeful. 'Split everything we own jointly straight down the middle?'

'No.'

'No?' Freddie shrugged and suddenly Daisy noticed how thin he'd become, and how gaunt his face was. The secret must have been eating away at him for a long time. She experienced an abrupt and unwelcome surge of sympathy. She wanted to hate him, to rage at him, to call him every nasty name she could think of, to take a scissors to his stupid sweaters, and pour his expensive aftershave down the sink.

But all she felt was pity.

'I don't want half. I don't want anything, except my clothes, make-up, and laptop. You can keep the rest,' she said.

'What about the lamp in the living room? You love that lamp.'

'Not anymore. It would remind me of us, of *you*.'

'Oh. If you don't want anything then…?'

'Move Carl in, or go live with him I don't care.'
'What are you going to do?'
'Go back to my mother's.'

Chapter 4

Daisy took one last look around the place she had called home for the past three years, and quietly shut the front door behind her. She kept hold of her keys; she'd not packed everything and she intended to return at some point to pick up the rest of her things, but she wanted to choose a time when she knew Freddie wouldn't be at home.

At the moment, she never wanted to set eyes on him again.

Car loaded, she drove out of the cul-de-sac and headed towards her mother's house, feeling totally and utterly dejected. She'd envisioned only ever returning to the family home to sleep on one last occasion – the eve of her wedding. Look at her now, thirty-years-old and running back home to her mother with her tail between her legs.

Not that her mother would be too happy about it, but hopefully she'd not make too much of a fuss, except for giving her the inevitable all-men-are-bastards speech, which Daisy would probably get a double dose of from both her mother and her nan. Though Daisy suspected her nan had been secretly pleased when Daisy had moved out, because it meant she could move right in, which she'd done with all the speed of a greyhound chasing after a mechanical rabbit, and with the same amount of dogged determination.

Three adult women in one house, and all related to each other? It was a recipe for disaster, but she had nowhere else to go. She had some savings, admittedly, but not nearly as much as Freddie thought, and she didn't want to waste any of it on renting somewhere, not if she wanted to buy a place of her own someday. And she realised just how much she did want that – her own home. Hers. No one else's.

Throughout their three years of living together, Daisy had always been conscious of the fact the house belonged to Freddie. Not that he had ever rubbed her nose in it, but there were the occasional small remarks, and the odd comment. She didn't think he knew he was doing it.

Any other daughter would be going back to her mother for tea and sympathy, and hugs, and "there, there, you'll get over it". Any other mother would provide lashings of the above, plus kisses on the forehead, and squeezed shoulders, and ruffled hair.

But not Sandra. And not Elsie either.

'It's Wednesday,' her mother said, when Daisy rang the doorbell and walked into a bizarre version of a Christmas grotto. A low-hanging, foil decoration hung in the kitchen doorway, at exactly the right height for slapping her in the face, and the rest of the room was scattered with fairy lights, like Nigella Lawson's kitchen in her cookery show. Except Nigella had hers strung tastefully on a dresser, not wrapped around the back of the cooker, where it was a fire hazard, or dangling from the cupboards so you couldn't open the doors properly. Then there was the half-dead poinsettia on the windowsill, and masses of Christmas cards taped to the fridge with hardly a room for a pin between them.

'I know it's Wednesday,' Daisy said.

'You never visit on Wednesdays. We're just about to have egg, beans, and chips for tea. There's not enough for three.'

'It's okay, I'm not hungry.'

'Not hungry? Are you coming down with something?' Then Sandra's hand shot to her mouth and she gasped in horror. 'You're not pregnant?'

'No, I'm not.'

'That's a relief.'

Yeah, wasn't it just, considering. Then she bristled, and said, 'Would it be so bad if I was?'

Her mother gave her a look, the one she always used when she thought the other person was being particularly stupid. Then she spotted what Daisy had left in the hall. 'What's with the cases?' she demanded, eyeing them suspiciously.

Daisy had packed two, and wasn't really sure what she'd shoved in them. For all she knew, she might have brought her bikini and flip flop collection with her; very useful in December. She'd flung random stuff in, not thinking about what she was doing, just desperate to get out of that house and away from Freddie.

In a tiny voice, Daisy whispered, 'Can I stay with you for a bit?'

She was greeted with silence. Sandra froze, the oven door half open as she bent to check on the progress of the chips. Her nan paused, butter knife in the air, and both women turned to stare at her, as if in slow motion, their eyes wide and their mouths open.

33

Was it really so surprising? Relationships broke down every day.

'I knew it wouldn't last,' Sandra declared eventually, turning her attention back to the chips, which were nicely cooking in the oven. The smell of them made Daisy feel slightly nauseous.

'Did you?' Daisy said. 'I didn't.'

'I told you all men were bastards,' her mother declared.

Elsie nodded her agreement, then narrowed her eyes, as a thought occurred to her. 'You can't have your room back,' her nan said, defensively. 'It's mine, now.'

Daisy sank wearily onto a kitchen chair. 'I'll sleep in the box room,' she said. 'If that's okay?' she added, to her mother.

'It'll have to be, won't it?' was the reply. 'And what do you mean "for a bit"? How long is a bit?'

Daisy shrugged, and her mother let out a long huffy sigh, and exchanged glances with her nan. No sympathy from either of them. At least Daisy hadn't expected any, so she wasn't disappointed.

Elsie offered her a slice of bread and butter, and Daisy took it, stuffing it unthinkingly into her mouth, and chewing without tasting, hoping it would relieve the sick feeling.

'I'll make us a nice cup of tea after we've eaten,' her nan said. 'That'll make everything better.'

No, it won't, Daisy wanted to say, but her nan's faith in the power of a "nice cup of tea" was unshakeable, so she let it go.

'Go on then, what did he do?' Sandra asked.

'I don't want to talk about it,' Daisy said. She wasn't in an emotional place where discussing Freddie's sexuality

34

was an option. How was she going to break the news that her boyfriend of four years, the man who she'd shared a house with for three of them, was sleeping with another man. It wasn't a conversation she was looking forward to. Apart from the pity, Daisy suspected people would look at her with speculation, wondering what was so wrong with her that it had driven her boyfriend into a man's arms. 'Let's just say, we like different things,' she said.

'Rubbish! Liking different things is hardly a reason to come running back home to your mother, is it?' Sandra said.

'I thought you didn't expect it to last,' Daisy pointed out. 'What's with the relationship advice?'

'If it was something more serious, like he beat you, or he ran off with another woman, that would be a valid reason, not just "liking different things". We all like different things, especially men. Who likes watching sport for hours on end? Men, that's who. Who spends hours in the pub after work? Men. You won't catch many women doing that.'

Okay, now her mother was referring to Daisy's long-absconded father. Trust Sandra to bring everything back to her. Freddie did watch sport, but only now and again, and he never went to the pub after work. He took clients out to dinner instead.

Or did he? All those times when he said he'd be late, Daisy now suspected was nothing to do with work at all. All those times when she'd heard male voices and laughter on the other end of the phone, and all those times when he'd said he was playing golf with his mates, Daisy now realised it probably hadn't been golf he'd been playing, though it might well have involved balls of a different kind.

What a cliché. She was the girlfriend sitting obliviously at home, whilst her man was out screwing around. And to think she'd been reassured by all those men she could hear in the background. Freddie had even put one or two of those so-called "mates" on the phone to speak to her.

She'd never felt so stupid.

'Get back there and kiss and make up,' Sandra insisted.

'I can't.' Daisy shuddered at the thought of where Freddie's lips had so recently been. 'Why are you so keen anyway? I thought you hated men.'

'Your mother thinks Freddie is one of the better ones,' her nan interjected. 'If you've gotta have a man (and I can't see any reason why you would, but that's just my opinion and no one listens to me), then Freddie is probably as good as it gets. Are you sure he hasn't hit you, has he, because if he has…' Elsie waved a meaty fist in the air.

'No, Nan, he hasn't hit me.'

'And he's not kicked you out because you've gotten yourself pregnant?'

'No, I've already said, I'm not pregnant.'

'It's gotta be another woman!' Sandra declared with relish.

'I can honestly say, there is no other woman involved,' Daisy replied stoutly.

'Is it your fault then? Have you been with another man and Freddie found out? Poor bloke, no wonder he threw you out,' Nan said.

'I've not been with another man,' Daisy growled through gritted teeth.

Thanks for jumping to conclusions, Nan, Daisy thought, marvelling at how quickly her grandmother could change her tune. The pair of them were like a dire double-tag team. Daisy hoped they'd settle down a bit, once they got used to her being in the house.

'So you've fallen out over nothing,' Sandra concluded. 'No doubt you'll run back to him in a couple of days, but don't expect to come back here every time you have a tiff.'

Daisy narrowed her eyes. Run to her mother, run back to Freddie… her mother seemed to think Daisy was an Olympic sprinter. She was hardly running; slinking back with her tail between her legs would be a more accurate description.

'I'll take my cases upstairs,' she said, desperate for a couple of hours on her own to wallow in her misery, and to give herself time to try to come to terms with the mess her life had suddenly become.

She had a feeling it was going to take much longer than a couple of hours, as she humped her heavy cases up the stairs, and hesitated outside what had once been her bedroom. Although she knew it was childish and her mother hadn't had much of an option when Nan had suggested she move herself in (what was her mum supposed to do, say no?) a nasty little part of her wished her mum had refused. This had been *Daisy's* home. Once. But now she felt like an unwelcome guest.

It wasn't her mother's fault. Daisy realised that Sandra had assumed both her children were settled, with their own homes, and their own partners, and their own lives to lead. She'd not expected either one of them to return to the nest, especially with Daisy being thirty and safely settled with Freddie, and David having his own home (though it came via a hefty mortgage), a good job (if you enjoyed peering into people's mouths for a living), and a pretty, new wife.

What did Daisy have?

The house she'd lived in with Freddie had belonged solely to Freddie, and Daisy was just beginning to feel the first stirrings of resentment as she considered exactly how much money she had paid towards *his* mortgage, disguised as "contributing to the finances", and clearly *her* partner had never been *hers* to begin with. The only thing she had going for her, was her job, and *Caring Cards* wasn't exactly doing well, according to her colleague, Melissa, who knew everything (how did she *do* that?).

Sighing, Daisy lugged her case onto the bed, thinking that at least they didn't have a marriage to dissolve and children to console. Things could be worse, she guessed, struggling to find a silver lining in the storm clouds hovering above her head.

But the reality was, she was thirty, single, and living back at home with her mum.

Her friends, once they found out, would rally round her, but she guessed their sympathy would be heavily laced with pity and the relief that they weren't in her shoes, and the gossips at work would have a field day. She'd keep them going for weeks, months, even.

She unzipped one of the cases and started to unpack, one slow, reluctant item at a time, realising all she had to show for three cohabiting years were some clothes, shoes and toiletries. Of course, she'd bought things for "their" house, like the smoothie-maker, the scatter cushions, and the pretty art-deco lamp in the living room, but she hadn't been lying when she'd said she didn't want any of them. They held too many memories of him, of them, and the life they'd shared.

It had all been an illusion, though, hadn't it? A lie to conceal Freddie's sexuality and it had worked until he'd fallen in love.

She had the horrible thought that if he hadn't met Carl, she and Freddie might have trundled on in this fashion for years, Daisy investing more and more time and emotion in the relationship until her eggs had shrivelled up along with her hope.

Thank goodness she'd been spared that.

She was young enough to start over again with someone else, but did she want to? She feared she didn't have the stomach to do the dating thing anymore, and that she was destined to live with her mum until she was old and wrinkly and had been adopted by twenty-six cats.

Daisy came to the conclusion she hated her life. This wasn't what she'd dreamed of when she left school, full of hope and anticipation. Now look at her. Every one of her friends was either married or in a long-term relationship, and most had kids, heck, even her baby brother had gotten himself hitched before she had.

Daisy sniffled into a crumpled tee shirt, feeling very sorry for herself, indeed.

Bracing herself, she took her mobile phone out of her handbag. Time to break the news to Sara. Daisy hated the thought of her best friend hearing about it via the grapevine, and bad news tended to travel fast. She'd leave telling her family for another time, though…

'Daisy!' Sara shrieked as soon as she answered the phone. 'Are you all ready for Christmas? I've got you a lush pressie – you're going to love it!'

Daisy's heart sank – another thing she'd left at Freddie's and would have to collect were all the presents she'd bought earlier today. Was it only today? It seemed like much, much longer.

'I've got some news,' she began hesitantly, but Sara interrupted her before she had a chance to say anything further.

'Oh my God, are you engaged? That's fantastic.' Sara had a fiancé and had spent the last few months, since Andrew had popped the question, dropping huge unsubtle hints that it was about time Daisy joined her in bride-to-be bliss.

'No,' Daisy replied shortly. 'Freddie and I—'

'You're not pregnant? Oh, Daisy, that's fab! When's it due?'

'No! Now will you listen?'

'I'm all ears.'

Daisy took a deep breath. 'Freddie and I have split up.'

Silence on the other end.

'Hello?' Daisy called. 'Are you still there?'

'I'm here.'

'I said—'

'I heard.'

More silence and Daisy tried to think of a way to tell Sara what had happened. Her friend wasn't reacting in the way Daisy thought she would. Where was all the sympathy?

'Is it because he's finally come out?' Sara said, after the pause had stretched out for so long Daisy wondered if her friend had rung off.

'What!' Daisy shrieked.

'I'm sorry, I shouldn't have said anything, it's just that—'

'You *knew*?' Daisy was horrified.

'Sort of. Not really, but Andrew once spotted Freddie in a gay bar and, well… he was with someone.'

'With someone,' Daisy repeated flatly.

'A guy.'

'What was Andrew doing in a gay bar?' was all Daisy could think of to say.

'He was out with friends on a stag do, and they thought *Kitty Kats* was a strip joint. It was, but not the sort they were expecting.'

'And Freddie was there?'

'Yes, I—'

'With a man?'

'Yes, but—'

'Kissing and stuff?'

'Mmm…'

'Why didn't you tell me?'

'Look, Daisy, I'm sorry. I should have, but how do you tell your best friend that her boyfriend might swing both ways?'

'You say, "your boyfriend was kissing another bloke", that's what you say,' Daisy stated, anger building in her chest. Had everyone known, except her?

'You're right, maybe I should have.'

'There's no maybe about it.' Daisy was firm – Sara should have told her.

'My only excuse is that I didn't want to hurt you, and Andrew was half-cut. He could have jumped to the wrong conclusion.'

'That's two excuses, and his conclusion was spot on.'

Sara was crying on the other end of the phone. 'Please don't hate me,' she whimpered.

Daisy sighed. 'I don't hate you, I just wish you'd told me. How long ago was this?'

'I don't know, maybe a year?'

Sara had known for a *year* and hadn't said a word. Daisy, despite her anger, admired her friend's restraint. If Daisy had seen Andrew with another woman, she'd have been straight round to Sara's to tell her.

Daisy paused. Or would she? She put herself in Sara's position and tried to imagine how that conversation would pan out – and failed.

Her temper slowly subsided. Freddie wasn't important enough to risk her friendship with Sara. No man was.

Taking a deep breath, Daisy admitted, 'I caught him at it with another man.'

'Aw, love,' Sara sniffed, and blew her nose loudly.

Daisy held the phone away from her ear.

'That's awful,' Sara said. 'My heart goes out to you.'

Daisy appreciated the empathy, but she had a sneaking suspicion that her family wouldn't be quite as sympathetic.

Chapter 5

'No, Mum, she's not said a word.' Daisy's mother was peeling potatoes, a mound of them, and talking to Elsie at the same time, when Daisy stalked into the kitchen, catching her mother and her nan in the act.

'Were you talking about me?' she asked them, knowing full well they were.

Her mother and her nan looked around guiltily. Her nan rallied first, going on the attack.

'You should be ashamed of yourself, worrying your mother like this,' she began. 'You come back home, refusing to say what happened. She thought she'd got rid of you, and here you are, turning up again like a bad penny.'

'Thanks, Nan.' Got rid of me, indeed! Charming!

'I'm right, aren't I, Sandra?' Daisy's nan said. 'Now take our David, he's no trouble to anybody.'

Yeah, well, when you're a saint you're not going to cause anyone any trouble, Daisy thought sarcastically. Her brother was the perfect son, the golden boy, the only man on the planet who could do no wrong, hence her nickname for him – Saint David. He was another bloke she couldn't compete with.

'Now Mum, leave our Daisy alone. I'm sure she's got her reasons,' her mother said, in a rare show of solidarity for Daisy. Nan scowled at her daughter.

Not for the first time in the four days since she'd walked out of Freddie's house, Daisy almost regretted her decision to move back in with her mother. Maybe she should have stayed put and fronted it out, rather than leave Freddie to wallow in the stew of his own making, though, from what she could see, Freddie wasn't exactly doing much in the way of wallowing. She'd heard that Carl had moved in. If Freddie was doing any wallowing, he was doing it with Carl, in the bed Daisy had once slept in with Freddie, leaving Daisy to cram herself in a box room filled with crap, and trying to muck along with two very opinionated and set-in-their-ways elderly women.

Daisy envied Saint David with all her green, little heart.

'Well?' Elsie demanded.

'What, Nan?'

'Are you going to explain why you walked out of a perfectly good house and away from a perfectly good man, if you can call any man "good", to move back in with us?' Elsie was relentless.

It was time to spill the beans. The pair of them would only keep on at her until she did.

'Because he's been having an affair – *with a man*.' There, she'd said it. She wished she didn't have to, but her nan, and to some extent her mother (though her mother was more subtle about it) had been demanding an explanation ever since she'd rocked up with her suitcases, a face like thunder, and a heart to match. Besides, word was bound to get around, and they'd find out sooner or later anyway. She might as well get it over with.

'Eh, what?' Elsie said.

'You heard.' Daisy had no intention of repeating it.

'You say Freddie is doing the dirty with a fella? Well, I never!' Her nan sat back in her chair and folded her arms. 'I always said there was something fishy about that Freddie of yours. You should have listened to me.'

'You say that about every man you've ever met,' Daisy retorted, aware that the older woman had just contradicted herself − only a few minutes ago she was singing his praises.

Her grandmother generally disliked all men, except for Saint David. Her mother wasn't keen on them either. Daisy's fear was that she, herself, was speeding along the same path, to end up her mother's age, hating the opposite sex, and being a lonely spinster.

'At least that Freddie didn't get you pregnant,' her nan stated. 'Though you are looking a bit porky around the stomach.'

'Thanks,' Daisy said. 'I can't help it if I comfort eat.' Her appetite had come back with a vengeance after that first awful day, and she hadn't stopped eating since. Chocolate mostly, so her mother had taken to hiding the tin of Quality Street under the stairs. It had taken Daisy less than five minutes to find it, and now the chocolates were more than half gone, and Daisy would have to go out and buy another tin.

'Is David joining us for lunch?' she asked, to change the subject.

'He's always here for Sunday lunch.' Daisy heard the reprimand in her mother's voice. Sandra added, 'He's gone to fetch Gee-Gee.'

Daisy felt a tad guilty – she hadn't seen her great-grandmother in weeks. 'How is she?'

'Old,' was Nan's reply.

And she wasn't wrong. When David, closely followed by his wife Zoe, manoeuvred Gee-Gee's wheelchair over the doorstep and into the hall, Daisy was shocked to see how old her great-gran looked. Still, ninety-six was a good age, and at least she was lucid. More or less. Some of the time.

'Daisy,' she said gummily, holding her arms out.

Daisy leaned in for a kiss and regretted it when the old woman slobbered on her cheek.

'What are we having?' Gee-Gee asked.

'Beef,' Sandra said.

'Eh?'

'Beef.' Sandra yelled this time.

'No need to shout,' Gee-Gee said, and Daisy sniggered. Sunday lunch at her mum's house could be rather entertaining, if a little fraught.

'What are you doing here?' Gee-Gee demanded, staring at Elsie.

'I live here.'

'Why? I thought you had your own house. David, doesn't Elsie have her own house?'

'Not for quite some time now, Gee-Gee,' David said, wheeling the old lady into the living room. As he passed Daisy he whispered, 'I hear you've moved back in.'

Daisy scowled at his smug expression. It was alright for him, with his perfect life. He had no idea what she'd just been through.

Elsie soon enlightened him. ''Ere, David, guess what? That Freddie has got himself a bit on the side.'

46

Yep, that about summed it up.

Zoe let out a squeal of laughter and Daisy narrowed her eyes at the younger woman. She failed to understand what David saw in his wife, aside from the long blond hair, big blue eyes, and upturned nose.

'What?' David paused his wheelchair duties, and even Gee-Gee perked up. 'Come again?' he said.

'Daisy's young man,' Elsie said loudly, 'has been having an affair, with another man. That's why our Daisy has come back home to live.'

'Is it true?' David's eyes lit up in glee. Sibling rivalry was still alive and kicking, then.

'Yes,' Daisy muttered, her face pink. It was a wonder her great-gran didn't feel the heat coming off her cheeks and demand someone help her remove her coat (she had a habit of keeping it on, regardless of the temperature).

'That sort of thing didn't happen in my day,' Gee-Gee said, to no one in particular.

Zoe giggled again. She giggled a lot, usually at inappropriate times. Daisy thought she was a bit… vacant? dumb? dippy? Probably all three.

Gee-Gee piped up, 'That's nice, three generations of women together in the same house. Like Macbeth's witches.'

Daisy grinned, until she realised that the three witches her great-gran was referring to, was Daisy, Sandra, and Elsie. 'I don't think the Macbeth witches were related, Gee-Gee, and with you here, that makes four.'

'There's six of us. I can count, you know.'

Daisy was confused for a moment, until she realised her great-gran was including David and Zoe. 'I mean, four generations of women: you, nan, mum and me,' she added but Gee-Gee wasn't listening.

'None of you can keep a man for love nor money,' Gee-Gee said. 'There's something wrong with the lot of you. Zoe, hang on to our David, else you'll end up like this lot. Bitter.'

'I'm not bitter,' Daisy protested, then realised that she was. Very.

Four years she'd wasted on Freddie, and here she was at the other end of those years in exactly the same position as she'd been at the start of them.

Actually, that wasn't true. She was in a worse position, because during those years when Daisy thought she was happily home-making, her nan had moved into the family home, forcing Daisy to sleep in the little box room which had once belonged to her brother.

Daisy had gone from smug, self-satisfied contentment to bitterness, envy, and despair in the space of a week. And during those years, Saint David had qualified as a dentist, got married, and had bought a lovely four-bed detached house in a nice village.

At least, Daisy said to herself, I can't sink much lower than this.

Chapter 6

'What did you say, Gee-Gee,' Daisy asked her great-grandmother, after wiping the old lady's chin. She'd only been half listening, because she had been concentrating on getting the spoon into Gee-Gee's mouth without dropping anything. Mentally her great-gran might still be okay, but physically Gwenda needed a great deal of help, and being fed was part of that.

'I said, you need a dollop of good luck,' Gee-Gee repeated.

Daisy sure did; a great big, steaming pile of it. She didn't think a measly dollop would make much difference. Perhaps she should start playing the lottery, or betting on the horses – though knowing her luck at the moment, she'd lose every penny she had.

'Fetch my bag, lovely,' Gee-Gee said to Daisy, pointing to where she'd left it in the living room.

Daisy did as she was asked, hoping her great-gran wasn't going to try to foist a tenner on her, like she used to when Daisy was a child. Daisy appreciated the gesture, but she didn't want the old lady's money – the poor old thing only had her pension, and most of that went towards her upkeep at the retirement home.

Daisy watched as the frail, trembling fingers, distorted by arthritis, probed and poked in the depths of the bag, her hopes sinking when Gwenda removed a purse. From past experience, Daisy knew not to argue, but to accept the money, then try to sneak it back into Gwenda's purse when the old lady wasn't looking.

'Open it for me,' Gee-Gee instructed, her gnarled hands clutching it awkwardly.

Daisy did as she was asked, making a face at the assortment of stuff inside: coins, hairgrips, old receipts (to Daisy's knowledge, her great-gran hadn't been anywhere near a shop for years), elastic bands, but no paper money.

'There's a sixpence in there somewhere,' Gwenda said.

'A what?'

'A sixpence, an itty-bitty silver coin.'

Daisy stuck her fingers in, and dug through the various coins. Ten pence pieces, five pences, copper coins and the flash of pound coins, were mixed with money she didn't recognise. Daisy held up one of them, a coin she'd first thought was a pound, but on closer inspection, it was a flatter colour and slightly smaller. She wondered which country it came from, and how it had ended up in her great-gran's purse.

She held it up.

'That's a thruppeny bit, that is,' Gwenda said, with a wistful look on her face. 'I miss the old money.'

'Old money?' Daisy vaguely recalled a mention of pre-decimalisation money, but she hadn't taken much notice.

Sandra said, 'I remember it. You couldn't get to grips with the new money for ages, could you, Gee-Gee?'

'New-fangled rubbish. There was nothing wrong with proper money. Why did they have to change it?' Gee-Gee's expression folded into hundreds of creases as she screwed her face up in disgust.

'Because everything was decimalised in the early seventies, no more twelve this, and shillings that,' Sandra said.

Daisy remembered how, when she was younger, she'd hear Gee-Gee mutter, 'How much is that in old money,' and then doing some weird conversion on her fingers.

'I used to get a sixpence every Friday night off my old da, for helping Mam around the house,' Gwenda said. 'I want you to have it, Daisy. It's in there somewhere.'

Daisy scrabbled around some more, until she found the coin her great-gran wanted. It was small, like a five pence piece, and was remarkably similar. 'I can't take this,' she protested. 'It's yours. You should keep it.'

'It'll bring you luck,' her great-gran said. 'But only if you find it in your pudding.'

'Huh?' Daisy raised her eyebrows at her mother and mouthed, 'What's she talking about?'

'Christmas puddings,' Nan said. 'When I was a girl, she used to make her own Christmas pudding every year, and she used to hide a sixpence in the mixture. Whoever got the sixpence was supposed to have good luck all year. It never bloody worked.'

'That's because you hated Christmas pudding and never ate any,' Gwenda said.

'I remember – you were still making them right up until Great-Grandad died,' Daisy's mother declared. She turned to David. 'You never knew your great-grandad, did you? He died when you were a baby, but Daisy might remember him.'

Zoe giggled, one hand held delicately over her mouth. For a dentist's wife, she was really reluctant to show her teeth, Daisy thought. She'd actually forgotten Zoe was in the room, the woman had been so quiet.

'Have you got any brandy, Sandra?' Gee-Gee asked.

'Mum, you can't drink, not with the tablets you're on,' Elsie protested.

Gwenda replied frostily, 'I haven't had a drink since 1992.'

'What happened in 1992?' David asked.

Daisy watched him slip a choice slice of roast beef onto Zoe's plate and smile at her drippily, and she felt slightly nauseous. And rather envious, if she was being truthful. No one had ever picked out a nice slice of beef for her. Not that she wanted them to, but the offer would have been nice.

'I stopped drinking alcohol, that's what happened in 1992,' Gwenda said, and her mouth became an inverted smile. She clearly wasn't going to say anything more on the matter.

But Elsie was. 'She got drunk and demolished your great-granddad's garden shed,' she said.

Gwenda glowered at her daughter.

What was it with the women in my family, Daisy wondered. They were always bickering and trying to score points off each other.

David smiled. 'You go, Gee-Gee.'

'Go where?' their great-gran wanted to know.

'It's a saying, Gee-Gee,' David tried to explain.

'What is?' Gwenda asked.

Zoe giggled again. She'd hardly said a word all through lunch. In fact, Daisy wondered if her sister-in-law was actually able to speak at all. She also wondered what a supposedly intelligent man like her brother, saw in the air-head; apart from her prettiness, Zoe didn't have much else going for her, Daisy surmised, meanly. Then immediately felt guilty for thinking such sour thoughts. After all, she'd never really taken the time to get to know the other girl.

'Where's the brandy?' Gwenda demanded.

'I told you, you can't have any,' her daughter said.

'It's for the pudding,' Gwenda argued.

'What pudding? I've not bought any pudding. You can have a biscuit or a French Fancy.' This was from Sandra.

'I don't want any pudding,' Gwenda said.

'You just said you did! Make your mind up.' Sandra stood up, huffing, and clattered plates together.

'For the *Christmas pudding*,' Gwenda enunciated, slowly and clearly, despite her lack of teeth. She'd taken them out yet again, and Daisy guessed she'd shoved them down her bra for safe-keeping.

Daisy watched the exchange in amusement. Conversations could be quite surreal in her house. Oh dear – she was already back to thinking of this house as hers, as if she was going to be living here forever. It *had* been her house once, she supposed, as in, she'd lived there since she was born, but technically it was her mother's house, and Daisy so didn't want to be that thirty-year-old woman who still lived at home with her mother.

'We haven't got a Christmas pudding,' Sandra pointed out.

'You will have, if Miss Miseryguts there gets up off her backside and makes one,' Gwenda came back.

'Stop a minute – Miss who?' Daisy asked.

'Miseryguts.' Gwenda stared at her defiantly.

'You mean me?' Daisy queried.

'If the cap fits.' This time Gwenda smirked at her.

'I don't know how to make a Christmas pudding,' was all Daisy could think of to say.

'I'll show you,' Gwenda said.

Elsie said, 'You can't cut your own dinner up. How are you going to make a pudding?'

'Mum, don't be mean!' Sandra exclaimed.

'Well, it's true,' Elsie said, sulkily. 'She never showed *me* how to make a Christmas pudding.'

Oh God, get me out of here, Daisy pleaded silently. If she had to put up with this for the next few months, she'd be asking to swap places with Gee-Gee and go and live in the old people's home.

'I'll tell her what to do and our Daisy can do it, can't you, Daisy?' Gwenda insisted.

'Yes, Gee-Gee.'

'And I never showed you, Elsie, because you don't like Christmas pudding. How many times do I have to tell you?' Gwenda scowled at her daughter.

Elsie's face folded in on itself as she sulked. Daisy made to leave the table and let the bickering old biddies get on with it, but Gwenda had other ideas.

'Is that corner shop still open?' she asked.

Sandra nodded.

'Right, my girl, I need brandy (unless Sandra has drunk it all and if she has, you'd better add that to the list), plain flour, that sugar that's not dark, but not white. Oh, what's it called?' Gwenda wrinkled her nose up as she thought.

'Muscovado?' Zoe piped up.

'That's it! Eggs, butter, mixed dried fruit, raisins, candied peel, almonds, oh, and brandy,' Gwenda said. 'Did I say brandy?'

'You did, Gee-Gee,' David said, then added, to Daisy, 'I'll come with you to help you carry it. Will you be alright on your own Zoe-poo?'

Zoe-poo? Ug. Daisy made gagging noises. Of course she'll be alright – she was being left with three elderly ladies for about half an hour, what could possibly happen? Actually, maybe he had a point.

Zoe, predictably, giggled, and this time she added a simper to it. Daisy had never seen anyone simper before. It took a certain skill.

She stuffed her feet into her boots and shrugged on her coat, grabbing an umbrella from the stand in the porch on the way out. Christmas was less than a week away, but the weather was being predictably British – wet and gloomy, with not a festive snowflake in sight. At least the outside matched her inside – she felt like a drizzly December afternoon, all miserable and glum.

'I'm sorry about Freddie,' David said, as the pair of them stomped down the street. It was only three in the afternoon, and already the streetlights were on. Daisy debated whether to put the umbrella up and risk poking her brother in the eye, or put the umbrella up to purposely poke her brother in the eye. She did neither, pulling her hood over her head instead, to keep off the worst of the fine mist.

'You really didn't know?' David persisted. He liked a good bit of gossip, did Saint David. Now if anyone had told her that her *brother* was gay, she might believe them. He was too perfect to be a typical beer-swilling, football-ogling bloke, then she mentally apologised for stereotyping gay men and straight alike. She was just being mean.

'No,' she said curtly, stuffing a lock of hair back beneath her hood. It immediately popped back out again.

'What are you going to do now?' he asked. 'You can't stay with Mum forever.'

'Why not?' Daisy was indignant. It wasn't as if she was scrounging off their mother. Daisy paid rent (albeit a small token amount) and a sum towards food and bills though she might have to consider upping it, what with the amount she was eating at the moment.

'Because the pair of them will drive you mad,' her brother said, linking his arm in hers. 'You could always move in with me and Zoe for a time, if you need to,' he added.

Aw, that was so sweet of him. But they were newly-weds, and Daisy was well aware what that meant. Not only were they blissfully happy, in a shiny new house, but they were probably at it like rabbits too. Her brother meant well, (though Daisy sometimes had the feeling he was rubbing her nose in it), but all his generosity served to do, was to highlight what she *didn't* have. Thanks, David, I owe you one…

Anyway, as tempting as the offer was, she didn't think she could put up with Zoe for more than an hour or so before she tried to bash some personality into that pretty head of hers. Daisy would take her chances with her mother and grandmother, thanks all the same.

Chapter 7

'Mary Berry, eat your heart out,' Daisy cried, reaching for an orange from the fruit bowl on the kitchen table. She'd never mixed and grated so many ingredients in her life, and was feeling rather pleased with herself.

'Everyone's got to stir it and make a wish,' Gwenda instructed from her place next to the fridge, where she oversaw proceedings with the same attention to detail and determination as a premenstrual woman on the hunt for chocolate.

Daisy lifted the bowl off the worktop and placed a wooden spoon in her great-gran's clawed hand. Gwenda clutched it with difficulty and Daisy winced. The old lady's arthritis was much worse than the last time she'd seen her, and Daisy put it down to the damp and dismal weather. Her own hands ached in sympathy, but it might have had something to do with all the grating she'd done. Daisy wasn't used to cooking. If anything more than a simple open the box and stick it in the microwave was involved, then Freddie always used to do it. He was a good cook too, and she imagined him lovingly preparing steak with all the trimmings for Carl, and she let out a small sigh.

Gwenda gave the mixture a stir as best she could, and Daisy took the spoon from her and passed it around so everyone could have a go.

'You've forgotten the sixpence,' Gwenda said. 'It won't work without the sixpence. You've got to put it in, Daisy, and make a wish.'

The sixpence sat gleaming on the counter (Sandra had scrubbed and disinfected it to within an inch of its life), and Daisy picked the tiny coin up with trepidation. Goodness knows how many germs it might still be covered in. It had probably been sitting in Gee-Gee's purse for years, and Daisy imagined all the grubby fingers that had handled it in the past, and she grimaced. Perhaps she should put it in boiling water for a few minutes first, to make sure any lingering nasties were dead.

'Hurry up,' David said as he and Sandra wrestled Gwenda into her coat. 'They're expecting her back at five-thirty.'

'There's plenty of time, and what are they going to do to her if she's late? Lock her out? Ground her?' Sandra chuckled. 'I used to ground Daisy all the time.' She gave her daughter a steely stare. 'It didn't work, did it?'

'It did!' Daisy protested.

'I never had to ground David,' Sandra pointed out, and Daisy heard the unspoken criticism in her mother's voice – perfect David, with his perfect job, perfect house, and perfect wife, had never once been grounded and look at how well he'd turned out. Blah, blah!

Maybe she could write a ditty for that too. It could start off with, "When you're not good enough…"

'Put it in,' Gwenda urged.

Daisy did as she was told and gave the bowl another stir.

'Make a wish,' her great-gran instructed, 'else there's no point in making the bloody thing.'

Daisy, still stirring, wondered what to wish for. Were multiple wishes allowed, or just one per coin? Could she fool it by joining two wishes together? She wanted to wish for a man who'd love her the way she wanted to be loved, with his body, heart, and soul (the way she would love him), but she also wanted the assurance of marriage and children. And a home of her own. And maybe a mother-in-law who wasn't a total dragon (a couple of her friends had mothers-in-law to rival Daenerys Stormborn's dragons in *A Game of Thrones* – fearsome and able to burn you to a crisp with their dislike.

Start with the basics Daisy, she told herself. You don't get the marriage, the babies, or the mother-in-law (dragon or no dragon) without the man first.

'I wish…' she began, closing her eyes because it seemed the right thing to do.

'Don't say it out loud,' Gwenda warned, 'or it won't come true.'

I wish for a man to love me, Daisy said silently, and who I love back, she added, just in case the wish decided to land a stalker on her (she'd seen enough films to know how this sort of thing could seriously backfire).

She stirred the mixture one last time and opened her eyes, images of Alexander Skarsgard lingering in her mind. 'What now?' she asked Gee-Gee.

'You want to steam it over a pan of boiling water,' Gwenda said.

Daisy noticed the old lady was wearing her coat again (though that didn't necessarily mean anything), and David was wheeling her towards the door.

'Aren't you going to stay until it's cooked?' Daisy asked. What if something went wrong? And how would she know when it was done?

'Not on your nelly! It'll take hours,' Gwenda said. 'Eight of 'em.'

Oh? Never mind, it sounded easy enough. She'd put the pan on to boil just before she went to bed, and it should be just about cooked by the time she got up for work in the morning.

Then she thought again.

Eight hours? Boiling water? There was no way she could leave the pan to bubble away unsupervised, which meant Daisy would be up half the night.

'Can't it be left until next Saturday?' she asked, a yawn already forming in her throat at the thought of it.

'No,' her great-gran, her nan, and her mother all chorused.

Zoe giggled.

Gwenda left, after issuing some final instructions and Daisy settled down to pan-watch until the wee small hours.

'This had better be worth it,' she muttered crossly, as she clambered off the sofa for the twenty-forth time and trundled into the kitchen to check the level of water in the pan. The theme tune of *The Antiques Roadshow* followed her out. With only one TV in the whole house, Daisy was forced to watch whatever rubbish her mother and her nan had on, and she seriously thought about subscribing to Netflix, so she could watch something decent on her laptop. Even *The Walking Dead* would be preferable to the soaps that pair were addicted to, and Daisy hated zombies.

She decided she might as well do some work and get a head start on tomorrow. With Christmas only a week or so away, Daisy was finding it hard to think of anything other than Christmas tunes and if *Caring Cards (A Card for Every Occasion)* was determined to go down the musical card route, she could use the opportunity to come up with something Christmassy ready for next year.

She still couldn't get the *Deck the Halls* tune out of her head, though, and she hummed it, whilst trying to think of words to rhyme with holly. Brolly, Molly, Polly, dolly, lolly, folly... hmm. Maybe not.

'Nice to see you getting into the festive spirit,' Sandra said, wandering into the kitchen to prepare the nightly ritual of hot cocoa and biscuits. Daisy eyed up what remained of the brandy instead.

'I'm working on some Christmas stuff,' she said. 'The company wants to branch out into musical cards.'

'What have you come up with?' her mother asked.

Daisy thought for a moment, then she sang:

> '*Deck the halls with boughs of holly*
> *Fa-la-la-la-la, la-la-la-laa,*
> *Buy some gifts, spend all your lolly*
> *Fa-la-la-la-la, la-la-la-laa*
> *On lots of things that no one needs*
> *Fa-la-la-la-la, la-la-la-laa*
> *Then spend the next month just eating beans*
> *Fa-la-la-la-la, la-la-la-laah!*'

'That's not very Christmassy, is it?' Sandra said. 'I don't think it'll be very popular.'

'I'm not feeling very Christmassy,' Daisy replied.

'No, my love, I don't expect you are.' Her mother lifted a couple of mugs out of the cupboard and put a pan on the stove. 'You can stay here as long as you like. This is your home, after all, and I mightn't say it often enough, but I do love you and I hate to see you so unhappy.'

'Oh Mum!' Daisy began to cry, tears welling up and trickling down her cheeks.

Her mother gathered her into her arms and patted her back. 'There, there, it'll be alright. In a while, you'll realise it's all for the best. There are plenty more fish in the sea.'

Her mum was a great one for clichéd platitudes, but Daisy found it comforting all the same. She knew her mother was right, but it didn't stop the ache in her chest.

'He was wrong for you, Daisy-doll, but one day you'll find someone who is right.'

Wrong didn't go anywhere near describing her and Freddie's relationship, but how hadn't she seen it? How could she have fooled herself into thinking Freddie loved her? As a *woman*? As a partner? She had no doubt he cared for her, but not in the way she needed, or wanted, to be cared about.

Daisy saw their relationship for what it was – a sham, a lie, an illusion. She'd bought into the whole fairy-tale, happily-ever-after-ending in the same way a gullible buyer bought a used car from a man in a shiny suit with a good line in sales talk. She hadn't thought she needed to look under the bonnet to check the engine, she'd just driven the thing and took it at face value.

Well, not anymore. Never again would she accept a man for what he appeared to be. Next time (if there ever was a next time), before she gave her heart away, she'd make sure the man in question deserved it and he had no rattley bones hiding in his closet.

Talking about closets, Daisy wondered if Freddie had told his parents yet. Now *that* was going to make for an interesting conversation, considering his mother had made endless hints that she expected grandchildren soon. For a second there, Daisy actually pitied Freddie. His mother could at best be described as a force of nature, and at worst, a harridan. No wonder the poor man had tried to deny his real self for all those years.

She pulled away from her mother, sniffing loudly and wiping her eyes with the back of her hand.

'It hurts now, but give it time,' her mother repeated. 'Get some distance, and you'll realise you never really did love him. Not true love.'

I *did* love him, Daisy went to say, then paused.

Did she really?

Yes she was hurting, and yes she was heart sore, but she wasn't devastated. She wasn't looking at the future and wondering how she could live in it without Freddie at her side. Instead, she was wondering how soon she'd be able to scrape together enough money to put a deposit on a little place of her own. She certainly wasn't contemplating the end of the world because her boyfriend had dumped her.

Her mother was staring steadily at her, waiting for the penny to drop. And drop it did, with a ruddy great clang.

Daisy didn't miss *Freddie* – what she missed was having someone to share things with, and she wasn't talking about the electricity bill or taking turns to put the bins out. She missed having someone to laugh with, and to snuggle up with at night, and tell her worries to. But it didn't necessarily have to be Freddie. It wasn't him she missed, but the idea of him. She missed playing happy families and being able to say she lived with her boyfriend, but she wasn't pining for Freddie himself.

Did that make her as bad as he was? Had she, too, been living a lie by not being honest with herself? Had she been guilty of holding back as much of herself in their relationship as Freddie had?

Perhaps that's what had drawn him to her – he may have sensed she wasn't giving all of herself, which gave him carte blanche not to either.

An abrupt stab of envy lanced her in the chest.

Freddie was in love. He was happy. He'd found what he'd been looking for and it had given him the courage to be true to himself.

She realised she wasn't jealous of Carl, because she'd never really wanted Freddie at all. What she'd wanted, and still did want, was a man she could give herself to, heart and soul, one who'd give the same back to her.

Yeah, good luck with that, she thought.

Chapter 8

Daisy crept into Red Deer Close like a really bad spy on a not-so-secret mission. She was aware she could only look more suspicious if she was sporting a fake moustache and a false nose. Her only hope was that neither Freddie nor Carl would be at home, and if they were, neither of them would look out of the window.

Her other hope was that the rest of her possessions hadn't been left out for the bin men to take.

She puffed out her cheeks when she realised that Freddie's BMW was absent and so was the blue Ford. Of course, Freddie's car hadn't been on the drive on CITA (Caught-In-The-Act) Day, either, but when she managed to think clearly, she'd realised he must have left it somewhere so as not to risk Mandy next door making a comment about Freddie being home, and dropping him in it. Daisy guessed her ex must have been sneaking about for weeks, before finally getting caught.

Gripping her keys so hard they dug into the palm of her hand, she parked on the drive and got out, looking around for witnesses. Technically, she was aware she shouldn't be entering the house without asking Freddie's permission first, and if one of the neighbours spotted her she might be challenged if they knew she no longer lived there.

She shoved the key in the lock, turned it, and was relieved when the door swung open. She'd half expected him to have changed the locks.

'Hello?' she called.

Silence. No Freddie. No Carl.

Just a pile of boxes stacked neatly in the narrow hall.

She opened the nearest. It appeared Freddie had erased every little sign of Daisy ever inhabiting his house – he'd even rounded up the box of tampons which had been on a shelf in the bathroom cabinet.

She wondered just how soon after she'd left, that Carl had moved in, as she eyed the boxes sadly. At least it saved her the bother of finding all her stuff and packing it into the plastic bags she'd brought with her.

Defiantly, she did a quick tour of the house anyway.

The downstairs was immaculate: no used mugs on the little side-table next to the sofa; no crumbs on the kitchen worktop next to the toaster and no dirty dishes in the sink. It seemed to her that even the windows sparkled, and she guessed Carl had cleaned them.

Upstairs was much the same. Even the toilet seat and lid were demurely down. She opened the cabinet door. Nothing of hers was in there, though she did do a double-take at the selection of cosmetics on display. Carl owned more than Daisy did, and they were all expensive brands – no supermarket specials for Carl!

In the bedroom, the wardrobe was divided into clothes she recognised (Freddie's) and those she didn't (Carl's).

Daisy had taken an instant dislike to him, but she found it difficult to say whether it was the circumstances under which she'd met him (Daisy suspected she would instantly hate anyone she caught in bed with her boyfriend

– though technically the pair of them had been standing upright in the spare room), or whether it was Carl's brashness which was responsible for Daisy's aversion to him. Daisy had ongoing issues with the way Carl had been so in-her-face, as if the whole situation had been one of Daisy's making.

That was the real beef Daisy had with him – Carl was the "other woman". He'd knowingly hooked up with a man who was already taken, and whether Carl was male or female made no difference (or mostly, no difference) to Daisy. Cheating was cheating.

And the same went for Freddie.

After cramming the boxes into her car (she honestly hadn't realised she had so much stuff) Daisy walked slowly back into the house she had once lived in, went into the living room and took a long, slow look around.

It didn't feel like her home anymore. She didn't know why, because everything looked the same, yet there was an unidentifiable subtle difference in the ambience of the house, as if it knew she had left, and she was no longer welcome.

With tears welling in her eyes, Daisy closed the front door gently, and posted the house key back through the letter box.

She knew she'd never need it again.

Chapter 9

"Deck the halls with—"

'Argg! Turn it off!' Daisy shouted. If she heard that carol one more time, she was going to explode.

'I thought you liked it,' her mother said, stabbing at the off button on the ancient CD player.

Daisy took the "best" cutlery out of the drawer and stated, 'I did. Now I don't.'

The song had played non-stop in her head for the past two weeks. It was the tune she associated with Freddie and Carl in their semi-naked glory. Even though she was on the way to forgiving Freddie, she wasn't quite there yet and she didn't want to be reminded of it.

Only one more day to go, and the whole sorry Christmas thing would be all over. The TV would stop showing Christmas movies, the various shows would take down the fake trees and the tinsel, and stop playing Christmas songs on a loop. Instead they would be showing adverts for summer holidays and the upcoming New Year's sales, and at work she'd be roped into helping to ship out the vast quantities of Valentine's Day cards.

She had one day to get through, then she could put this year behind her and concentrate on the new one.

The table looked lovely, even if she did say so herself. Determined not to rain on anyone else's parade, she'd gone all-out to make Christmas Day an enjoyable one, starting with Bucks Fizz and parma ham with scrambled egg on seeded toast for breakfast. Elsie had grizzled a bit (she'd wanted a cup of tea and cereal) but a glass or two of the bubbly stuff had soon sorted her out.

They were holding off opening any presents until the rest of the family arrived, and David and Zoe were picking Gee-Gee up, as usual, after spending Christmas morning with Zoe's parents. Daisy, remembering previous Christmases, thought there was most definitely a silver lining to the dark cloud hanging over her – at least she didn't have to spend any time with Freddie's family.

Her phone rang.

'Hello?'

'It's me,' Freddie said.

Think of the devil and he'll appear, Daisy mused, recalling one of her nan's old sayings.

'I just wanted to… you know,' he rambled.

'Wish me a Happy Christmas?' Daisy failed to keep the sarcasm out of her voice, even though she tried. She might have realised (too late) that she didn't love Freddie as much as she should have, but the sting of rejection was still sharp.

'Er… yes, I suppose.' A pause followed, which Daisy had no intention of filling, until Freddie eventually asked, 'How are you?'

'How do you think?' She certainly wasn't going to make this easy for him, either.

'I'm sorry I missed you when you picked up your things.'

His voice was so familiar, it hurt to hear it. If only things had been different; if only *they* had been different.

'Are you really sorry?' Daisy asked. 'Because I'd bet my left arm that you're glad you didn't have to see me, in case I made a scene. I posted the key through the letterbox, by the way.'

'I saw it, thanks. And yes, I am sorry. I still care for you, Daze.'

Daisy–Daze, that's what he used to call her. He should have called her Dippy Daisy, because she'd been so gullible.

In time, she would come to terms with what he'd done, but not right now. It was too soon, too raw, and forgiveness of an abstract Freddie was a different kettle of fish to forgiving a contrite Freddie who was on the other end of a phone. She decided to be honest with him, even though the time for honesty should have been when they first met.

'I care for you, too,' she said quietly, realising that she did and probably always would.

'I never wanted to hurt you,' he said.

She understood that, but he had hurt her, all the same, and it would take a while for the pain to fade. She knew it would fade eventually, it was dissipating already, morphing into hurt pride and annoyance with herself for not seeing what was now so obvious. But it hadn't completely gone yet and she knew she had to give herself time.

'Merry Christmas, Freddie,' she said softly, before ending the call, feeling the prick of tears in the back of her eyes.

'Who was that?' her mother asked, coming into the little dining room carrying a jar of cranberry sauce.

'Just a friend,' Daisy said, taking the jar from Sandra and putting it in the centre of the table.

Her mother gave her a shrewd look, but didn't pursue it. 'Everything is almost ready. David can carve the turkey when he gets here. I've taken it out of the oven to rest.'

The smell of roasting meat was mouth-watering. Daisy was starving, as usual. Not for her the loss of appetite due to heartbreak, but instead, she found herself eating everything and anything. Except sprouts. And cabbage. Broccoli was a bit take-it-or-leave-it too. But the sight of the mound of roast potatoes being kept warm in the oven made her almost swoon.

Her mother slapped her lightly across the back of the head when she caught Daisy trying to steal one.

'Anyone would think you hadn't been fed for a week,' Sandra complained, pushing her daughter away from the open oven door and checking to see if any potatoes were missing.

Daisy nearly burned her fingers trying to hide the offending roastie behind her back. Then she really did burn her mouth when she stuffed the potato in whole as soon as her mother's attention was diverted by a peas-boiling-over crisis.

'Here, take the wine in, and try not to drink any of it before the others get here,' Sandra instructed, thrusting a bottle of white into Daisy's hand.

Daisy seriously debated whether to have a quick swig straight from the bottle to cool her burning mouth, but a glare from her mother changed her mind.

'Merry Christmas!' David called, as the front door banged open and her brother wheeled Gwenda into the hall. Zoe, as usual, followed silently behind, an inane smile on her face.

Daisy vowed to play nice. It wasn't Zoe's fault the girl was a bit silly and vacant, though Daisy was surprised David chose to marry someone like her in the first place. She thought he would have gone for someone a bit more intellectual. Or at least, someone who did more than giggle.

'Daisy, help your great-gran. David, come and carve the turkey. Zoe, take Elsie another glass of sherry – she's in the living room, hoping all the work will get done by magic – then pour one for yourself.' Sandra barked orders, and everyone jumped to do her bidding.

Once the food had been brought to the table and they were all seated, Daisy noticed her mother relax a little, Christmas lunch successfully accomplished, and she glanced around at the smiling faces of the rest of her family, and realised that all of them, except one, were female. Last year Freddie had been with them, and Daisy felt a little sorry for her brother, who was now the only man in a room full of women – four generations of blood relatives along with his wife. God help him!

Gee-Gee sat at one end of the table, her wheelchair pushed as close as was practical, and David as the honorary (read *only*) male head of the family, sat at the other. Zoe sat next to him, with Zoe, her nan and her mother opposite. This week, Elsie had the job of feeding Gee-Gee, with Daisy chipping in to help.

With the crackers pulled and the wine poured, the family settled down to enjoy their meal. Enough food was on the table to feed a small army. Daisy dug in with enthusiasm. As she shovelled a forkful of turkey and stuffing into her mouth, she noticed how David kept putting his knife down and squeezing Zoe's knee under the table. Daisy was tempted to tell him to leave the woman alone for five minutes, but she held her tongue when she saw Zoe's face.

Something was definitely amiss with her brother's wife, Daisy thought. The younger woman was paler than usual; she was normally all long golden hair and translucent skin, but today she looked positively wan. Plus, Zoe was only picking at her food. The dark circles under her eyes made her look rather unwell. Daisy wondered if the girl had had too much of a good time last night and now had a humungous hangover. Zoe seemed the type to do a party justice, being blond and giggly, and Sandra had mentioned that Zoe's parents were having a few friends, as well as Zoe and David, over for a couple of drinks. It looked like Zoe had downed more than a couple.

Without realising, Daisy saw she had cleared her plate. Groaning, she pushed her chair away from the table slightly, surreptitiously undoing the button on her trousers, and almost crying with relief as the pressure on her over-full stomach eased.

Two helpings of roast potatoes, another of veg, and a whole turkey leg plus what she'd piled on her plate at the start of the meal, had left her with an aching belly. She estimated she must have eaten her own share plus Zoe's, and there was still plenty of food left over. She suspected they'd be eating turkey in some form or another for the next week, and guessed that by day three she'd be pleading for beans on toast, or a pizza – anything but turkey!

Her glass was empty, and she reached for the bottle of wine and refilled it, then offered to top up Zoe's barely touched drink. For once Zoe didn't giggle, placing a hand over the top of the glass instead.

All the more for me, Daisy crowed, though she did think it rather mean of her sister-in-law not to take a turn with the driving, and let David have a drink or two, considering the woman was so hungover she clearly couldn't face alcohol today.

David didn't appear to be any the worse for wear – he'd eaten as much as Daisy – and even Gee-Gee, with her sparrow-like appetite, had managed to polish off a decent portion.

Daisy helped her mother clear the table, glad for a chance to stand up. She really shouldn't have eaten so much, and when Gee-Gee said, 'Bring on the Christmas pudding and I hope you remembered to make brandy sauce,' Daisy wanted to disappear off to her room for a lie down and never think about food again. There was no way she'd be able to force another morsel down her throat.

'And there are mince pies, and cheese and crackers if anyone wants them,' her mother announced.

Daisy caught Zoe's eye, thinking Zoe looked as green as Daisy felt. She really shouldn't have had that last "pig-in-the-blanket", but she simply hadn't been able to resist the sausagey-baconess of it, and when it was covered in rich gravy it was heaven on a fork.

Zoe gave Daisy a pallid smile, but before Daisy could think of anything to say to her sister-in-law, David cried, 'Look,' and pointed to the window.

Snowflakes were falling thick and fast from a heavily laden sky.

Sandra clapped her hands. 'Oh, how wonderful. Now I really do feel like it's Christmas.'

'They didn't forecast snow,' Elsie pointed out, 'and let's hope we don't get too much because our David has still got to take my mother back, and get home himself. I bloody hate snow. Nasty slippery stuff.'

'I need a wee,' Gee-Gee said, and all thought of snow was banished by the complexity of getting a very old, wheelchair-bound lady safely into the small downstairs loo and back out again.

Daisy let her mother and nan sort that one out. She rolled up the sleeves of her rather itchy and very silly Christmas jumper (it had a flashing Rudolf nose on the front and strategically placed grey-brown antlers over her boobs, which looked suspiciously like hands) and tackled the washing up.

By the time everyone returned to the dining room, Daisy's lunch had gone down enough for her to consider some Christmas pudding. Just a little bit, not too much, but enough to keep her great-gran happy.

Sandra made the brandy sauce and Daisy took centre stage as she carefully carried the flaming pudding into the dining room, images of accidentally setting the curtains alight popping into her head. What idiot had started the stupid tradition of pouring neat brandy onto a pile of cooked fruit and setting it on fire anyway? Someone who sold sprinklers or smoke alarms for a living, probably.

'Ooh,' Gee-Gee exclaimed. 'It looks lovely. Did you make a wish?'

'Yes, Gee-Gee, when I put the sixpence in, remember?' Daisy replied.

'What did you wish for?'

Elsie said, 'Don't tell, Daisy, otherwise it won't come true.'

'Since when did you believe in sixpences?' Gwenda demanded. 'You're too miserable to believe in anything!

You've never been the same since that man of yours did a runner.'

'Pudding anyone?' Daisy asked, seeing the very real possibility of the once-civilised meal deteriorating into a verbal mud-slinging match. Exactly the same thing had happened last year, except Elsie had started it first. This year it appeared to be Gee-Gee's turn.

'I'll have some,' David replied, gamely, as he held out his hand for a bowl.

Zoe shook her head, and Daisy thought the girl didn't look at all well.

'Gee-Gee?' Daisy asked, praying she'd managed to head things off at the pass.

'And whose fault was that?' Elsie demanded.

'Gee-Gee? Pudding?' Daisy tried again, hearing the slight sound of desperation in her own voice.

'Yours, that's who!' Elsie continued. 'You frightened him off.'

'If your daughter had come home at eighteen and told you she was up the duff, you'd frighten off the bloke who'd got her that way, too,' Gee-Gee said.

'Nan? Pudding?' Daisy pleaded, looking at David for help when Elsie failed to respond. David had his head down and his gaze on his own bowl, and was pretending he was deaf.

Daisy saw her sister-in-law kick him on the shin, and he looked up at his wife in confusion. Zoe waggled her eyebrows at him, and jerked her head at the combatants.

'Oh, er, right. Now?' David asked.

Zoe nodded.

'We was going to get married, before you went and interfered,' Elsie stated.

Daisy decided she'd done all she could, and it was best to keep out of it and let the two old biddies have their slanging match, so she turned her attention to her own dessert and spooned some of the pudding into her mouth. Her eyes widened in surprise. It was actually quite good, and the brandy sauce set it off nicely. Why hadn't she eaten Christmas pudding before now? Why hadn't she *made* it before now?

David clinked his spoon against the side of his glass. Everyone ignored him.

'Bah!' Gwenda fired back. 'He got what he wanted from you, then he took off like a rat up a drainpipe when he saw the size of your belly. And who ended up looking after you and your baby, eh? Me, that's who!' Gwenda tried to poke herself in the chest with a distorted finger.

'I didn't ask you to!' Elsie cried, snatching up an empty bowl and angrily dolloping a generous helping of Christmas pudding into it.

'We're pregnant,' David said.

'Yes, that's right, David,' Gwenda said. 'Your grandmother got herself pregnant.'

'It takes two, you know,' Elsie retorted. 'I didn't do it all by myself.'

'No, but you had to raise the baby all by yourself, didn't you?' Gee-Gee's face creased into a smirk.

'I thought you just said *you* raised the baby,' Elsie countered.

'Pregnant?' Sandra repeated.

'Keep up,' Gwenda grumbled. 'Of course, your mother was pregnant. How do you think you got here?'

Daisy shot a swift glance at Zoe, who was staring down at her hands as they twisted in her lap. No wonder her sister-in-law was upset. Daisy's family was enough to upset a gang of football hooligans on the way to a match. This sort of squabble tended to happen quite often between the three women, which was possibly one of the reasons why Freddie always found some excuse or another to avoid Sunday lunch at Sandra's house.

'I'm not talking about Mum,' Sandra said.

'Who are you talking about, then?' Elsie asked, and Daisy, sensing she'd missed something important, hurriedly shoved the last spoonful of pudding into her mouth.

'Zoe, my lovely wife,' David said, 'is expecting a baby.'

Daisy tried to swallow the mouthful of pudding and speak at the same time. She took a breath, felt something hard hit the back of her throat and swallowed convulsively. It was stuck. She tried to swallow again, but it didn't budge. When she tried to take another breath, she realised what had happened.

That bloody sixpence!

Chapter 10

'What do you mean "pregnant"?' Elsie asked at the same time as Sandra cried, 'How lovely!'

Daisy, meanwhile, carried on quietly choking.

She couldn't breathe. It was stuck in her windpipe, a solid lump, going neither up nor down.

She slapped the table, and the three older women joined in with Daisy's apparent delight, began to clap and cheer.

'Woohoo, our David's going to be a daddy,' Sandra shouted.

'I hope it's a girl,' Elsie said.

'A boy would be lovely,' Gee-Gee chimed in, and mother and daughter glared at each other.

'Daisy?' Zoe asked. 'Are you alright?'

Did she bloody look alright? She was choking for God's sake. Maybe even dying.

Her sight dimmed, her chest was on fire, and her head felt really woozy. Suddenly Daisy was very, very frightened, indeed; her lungs hurt as she struggled for breath and her eyes felt as though they were going to pop out of her head.

'Daisy!' Zoe leaned closer. The rest of Daisy's family were too busy congratulating Saint David on his prowess in the bedroom, to notice they would soon have a one in/one out situation on the family front, if someone didn't get her some medical attention fast.

Sodding hell! What a way to go – choking to death on a silver sixpence.

A massive blow on the back sent Daisy face first into what was left of the Christmas pudding.

She came up coughing and spluttering, drawing deep breaths into her beleaguered lungs, pudding all over her face and in her hair. It took few seconds to realise she could breathe properly again. It also took a few seconds to realise something else.

She'd swallowed the sixpence.

And to think, when she'd stirred it into the pudding, all Daisy had been worried about were a few little germs. The damned thing had almost suffocated her.

'Are you okay now?' Zoe asked, and Daisy nodded, uncertainly.

'You're such a messy eater, Daisy Jones,' her mother said, noticing Daisy for the first time since David had made his announcement. 'Go and get yourself cleaned up, you're a disgrace.'

Daisy took another deep, welcome lungful of air, and announced, 'I think I'm going to die.'

'Don't be so melodramatic. It's just a bit of Christmas pudding.' That was from Elsie.

'That "bit of Christmas pudding" almost killed me,' Daisy proclaimed, and Zoe nodded her agreement. 'I think I've swallowed that sixpence.'

Silence.

Everyone stared at Daisy.

'Right.' David, with his saintly disposition, took charge. 'Let's get you to A&E.'

'She doesn't need to go to Accident and Emergency. It's an itty bitty sixpence. It'll come out the other end in a day or so,' Gwenda said. 'What is it they say these days? Drama Queen, that's it. Our Daisy's a drama queen.'

'I nearly choked on it,' Daisy said, banging her fist on the table. 'If it wasn't for Zoe, I would have died.'

Zoe, with big blue eyes and a solemn expression, nodded again.

'You let a pregnant girl save your life?' Elsie cried. 'You should be ashamed of yourself.'

David pushed away from the table and stood up. 'Daisy, get your coat.' He turned to the rest of the family. 'We won't be long, but I do think she needs to get checked out. It could have damaged her trachea, or it might become stuck in her bowels.'

Great, Daisy thought, stuck in my bowels – what a truly disgusting way to go.

'Will you be alright?' David asked Zoe.

Zoe nodded. Her sister-in-law had gone from giggles to nods, and she still didn't say much. Not that Daisy blamed her; the other women more than made up for Zoe's silence. It was a wonder anyone else could get a word in edgeways with that lot squabbling and cackling.

Daisy got to her feet, on slightly wobbly legs. 'Thank you,' she said to Zoe. 'Oh, and congratulations.'

Zoe smiled and Daisy followed David out into the cold, snowy afternoon.

It was only three o'clock but it seemed far later. The sky pressed down on her and the street lights were just coming on. Neither Daisy nor David spoke on the short journey to the hospital, Daisy because her throat hurt and she had nothing to say, and David because he had to concentrate hard on driving. It had more or less stopped snowing, but the stuff that had fallen lay in a slushy, slippery blanket on the roads and pavements. Few other drivers were brave enough or stupid enough to venture out, but some vehicles had left tracks on the road, and David stuck religiously to them, driving slowly with extreme caution. It would have been quicker to walk.

Daisy wanted to yell at him to hurry up, before this thing inside her exploded, or gave off radioactive waves to rot her from the inside out, or ripped her bowels apart, but she said nothing, not wanting to disturb her brother's concentration, because it would be just her luck to have an accident on the way to the hospital.

Talking of luck, that sixpence hadn't been too lucky for her, had it? First, it had tried to choke her, and when that failed, it was now going to block up her innards or something equally horrible. Not only that, but just at the moment when she'd popped it into her mouth, David had announced he was going to be a father.

She was pleased for her brother, but at the same time envy poked Daisy in the stomach. No wonder Zoe had looked peaky, was off her food and had refused any alcohol. The woman was pregnant, having a baby, up the duff, as her great-gran so eloquently phrased it.

Daisy would donate a kidney to be in her sister-in-law's shoes. Longing, so strong it caught her breath, rose up in her chest. It should be her, Daisy, who was expecting a baby, her and Freddie. They'd been a couple much longer than David and Zoe. Two years longer. It should have been Daisy's turn.

But there *was* no Daisy and Freddie anymore, was there? And Daisy's brother was proving how charmed his life was, by becoming a parent before her.

Lucky, lucky Zoe.

'Are you alright?' David asked, risking a quick glance at her face.

Daisy wished people would stop asking her that, when she clearly wasn't alright. 'How far along is she?' she wanted to know.

'Nearly twelve weeks. We were going to leave it until after we'd opened the presents, but with Nan and Gee-Gee kicking off...' he ground to a halt.

'I'm really pleased for you,' Daisy said, and she found she meant it, despite her envy and her longing. She was going to be an aunt! 'You'll be a great dad,' she added.

'Do you think so?' David looked worried, petrified almost. 'We've talked about it, and had fun...' he coughed, 'er... making it, but now that it's actually happened...' He risked another quick glance at Daisy. 'I'm scared. What if he or she doesn't like me?' He sounded worried, just like he used to when they were kids, and Daisy had tried to talk him into doing something he thought he might get told off for.

'Of course the baby will like you. It'll love you, you'll be its dad. Anyway, it won't have any choice, I think it's hotwired into babies, or something, that they have to love their parents.'

'Thanks,' David said dryly, pulling into the hospital's car park then into a space. The place was surprisingly empty. Maybe the weather had put people off.

Always the gentleman, David helped her out of the car, and Daisy stood on uncertain legs whilst he fed the parking meter. The cold seeped through her shoes, and when she wiggled her feet they felt wet too. She looked down, and realised she still had her slippers on. Could the day get any worse?

A&E was equally quiet inside, she noticed as they took a seat in the waiting room. A couple of families were there with children sporting an assortment of injuries, an old man with his wife, and a youth with blood on his face – the usual varieties of festive casualties. It wasn't long before Daisy's name was called.

'Do you want me to come in with you?' David asked.

'You'd better,' Daisy threatened. 'They might do anything to me in there – I want a witness.'

They followed a nurse through a security door and into the treatment area where she showed them into a cubicle.

'Doctor will be with you shortly,' she said. 'In the meantime, I need to take some details.'

The list of questions was endless, and when they got to the part about what happened, Daisy had a sneaking suspicion the nurse was trying not to smile.

'You must see this all the time,' Daisy said. 'People swallowing things.'

'It's normally young children who swallow coins,' the nurse said, and Daisy felt like a right idiot. 'Is this gentleman your next of kin?' she continued, glancing at David.

Daisy shrugged and nodded. He'd be better in an emergency than her mother, and he was right here if she had to be whisked into theatre for an operation, and something needed to be signed.

'Name?' the nurse asked.

'David Jones,' Daisy replied, watching the nurse write it down. 'What happens now?'

'Doctor will be with you shortly,' she said, and left.

Was that a good sign or a bad one? If the nurse wasn't prepared to, or allowed to tell Daisy anything, maybe it was because it *was* serious. Maybe the sixpence was poisonous or—

'Hello? I'm Dr Hartley.' A man in a white coat pushed through the curtains surrounding the cubicle. 'Daisy Jones?'

Daisy nodded and her heart did a little flip of excitement. This man was scrummy. Tousled dark hair, closely-trimmed beard, and the bluest eyes she'd ever seen on a bloke. She couldn't really tell, but she thought he might be fit under that white coat.

Damn! Why couldn't she have met him when she didn't have a coin leaking toxic chemicals into her stomach and when she wasn't wearing her bunny slippers.

'And you are…?' the doctor asked her brother.

'David Jones.'

'Right.' The doctor turned his attention back to Daisy. He had long, black eyelashes, she noticed. 'What can we do for you?'

'We were having Christmas lunch and my nan and great-gran were arguing, and to shut them up David said he was having a baby. Not him having it, obviously—'

'Can I stop you there, a second? What about swallowing a coin?'

'Oh, yes, right. My great-gran wanted to put a silver sixpence in our Christmas pudding because, according to her, it brings good luck, and she thought I could do with some. Well, she's right actually, I do need some good luck because—'

Dr Hartley held up a hand. 'I don't mean to be rude, but I've got other patients waiting. Are you telling me you swallowed a coin in a pudding?'

'Yes.' Daisy nodded. 'Am I going to die?'

'Yes.'

Daisy looked horrified.

'Everyone dies at some point, but I'm fairly sure you won't be pushing up *daisies* any time soon.' The doctor chuckled at his own joke, and Daisy narrowed her eyes at him.

'Will it make me ill?' she asked, hoping for a bit of sense this time.

'Unlikely.' He took her face in his hands, and she tried not to jerk away as a bolt of electricity shot through her at his touch. Oh my!

'Does that hurt?' he asked, turning her head this way and that, whilst staring deeply into her eyes, and stroking a thumb down the side of her neck.

'Um… no.' It actually felt nice, really nice. He had strong hands with long fingers and neatly trimmed nails.

'Open your mouth for me,' he said.

Daisy opened her mouth, hoping she didn't have a piece of carrot or something equally offensive stuck in her teeth. He tilted her head to the side, peering down her throat, then dropped his hands to his sides, and peered intently at her. He then reached towards her again and lifted a strand of her hair. His quizzical look almost made her faint, as his lips turned up into a smile.

'If I'm not mistaken, Daisy, you have Christmas pudding in your hair.'

'Oh, yes, um.' Yuk. She hadn't had time to get it all out of her hair before David had ushered her into the car. 'I sort of fell face first into it when Zoe slapped me on the back. Zoe is—'

'Is the slap relevant?'

'Yes. You see, I was choking on the sixpence and couldn't breathe. I really thought I was going to die, then Zoe thumped me, and I started breathing again, and that's when I realised I'd swallowed it.'

'Let's quickly check you over,' he said, and Daisy had the irreverent thought that she'd be happy letting him check out anything he damned well pleased.

'Are you having any difficulty swallowing?' he asked.

Daisy swallowed. 'I don't think so.'

'Any problems with your breathing now?'

Daisy inhaled and let it out again. 'No.'

'Any pain or discomfort in your throat?'

'It's a bit sore.'

He asked her to open her mouth again, and he peered inside, shining a light down her throat.

'I'm reluctant to do anything more invasive at this point,' he said. 'There may be a small amount of swelling, but nothing to worry about, but if you have any difficulty breathing, come straight back to A&E.'

'Is that it?' Daisy asked. 'What about the sixpence?'

'It should pass through your digestive tract in a matter of days. Are you regular?'

'Eh?' She so didn't want to be discussing her toilet habits with this man, doctor or not.

'Your bowel movements, are they regular?'

Daisy shrugged, trying not to be too embarrassed. 'I suppose so.'

'My advice is to check your stools until the coin makes an appearance.'

'Yuck, that's nasty!'

David let out a snort. She could see he was trying not to laugh.

The doctor sent her a professional smile. 'I'd like to make sure it's not in your oesophagus before you leave, but under the circumstances, I don't want you to have an x-ray.'

He shouted for a nurse, who popped her head in through the curtain. Daisy could have sworn she heard the words "metal detector".

She heard right.

'This is a metal detector,' the doctor said, holding up a thick black wand. 'Lie down on the bed,' he instructed.

She lay down and he waved it over her chest to just below her rib cage. It beeped immediately, and the doctor swiftly moved the machine away. The whole thing was over in a couple of seconds.

'The coin is in your upper digestive tract,' he said. 'It will slowly move through it over the course of the next few days, and you should expel it as a matter of course.'

Expel it. He meant poop it out. Gross. And if he thought she was going to fish around in the toilet, looking for it, the doctor had another thing coming.

'Keep a close eye on your stools,' Dr Hartley added, 'because if it's not expelled you'll need to come back. Give it a week to ten days, and of course, if you are at all anxious, then pop back in.'

Davie stepped forward and offered the other man his hand. 'Thank you, doctor.'

'You're welcome,' Dr Hartley said. 'Make sure you keep a close eye on her, and bring her straight back if you're at all worried about her.'

'Oh, er, right. I'll tell our mother.'

The doctor gave David a confused look. 'If that's all?' he said.

Daisy and David took the hint and left.

Chapter 11

'How are you feeling?' David asked as they made their way to the car.

'Stupid,' Daisy said. 'So much for a lucky sixpence. The damned thing nearly killed me.'

'Look on the bright side, it could have done exactly that.'

Daisy grimaced at the thought of being remembered as that girl whose boyfriend cheated on her with a bloke, and who then choked to death on an old coin. Everyone would be laughing their way to the cemetery.

'Oh bugger, look at that,' her brother said, as they stepped through the sliding doors and out into a night filled with thick, white flakes falling from a leaden sky. 'I'm never going to get Gee-Gee back to the old people's home in this. I don't even know if we can make it back to Mum's. We might have to walk.'

The idea of tramping over two miles in sodden, freezing slippers was unbearable, and Daisy burst into tears. It appeared the sixpence was intent on killing her – choking hadn't worked, so now it was aiming for death by hypothermia or pneumonia instead.

David hovered at her elbow, and when she saw the concern in his eyes, she cried even harder.

'Let's give driving a go,' he offered, when she pointed wordlessly to her feet and he realised what she was wearing on them.

Daisy skidded and slipped towards the car and by the time she'd plonked down into the passenger seat her feet were soaked and her teeth were chattering. Saint David, ever the considerate one, turned the heating on to full and aimed the blasts of air at her legs.

She knew she really must stop calling him Saint David, but she couldn't help feeling a little resentful towards the brother who seemed to have everything that Daisy herself wanted, and was an honestly nice person into the bargain. Maybe if she was more like him, she'd have better luck, and not have to rely on a murdering sixpence.

David eased the car out of the car park and onto the main road. Thankfully the gritters had been out, but the snow fell faster than the rock-salt melted it, and the tracks of earlier vehicles were quickly filling up.

Perhaps not hypothermia then – maybe a car accident. She just hoped David wouldn't be hurt; he had a wife and an unborn baby to think of.

Daisy prayed silently to God, Lady Luck, Fate, or whoever was listening, "take me, and only me", and her heart was in her mouth when the back wheels skidded as the car negotiated a roundabout. 'Spare my brother...'

'What?' David asked.

Oops, she didn't realise she'd said it aloud. 'Nothing.'

Feet pressed firmly on the floor, "braking" when she thought David should slow down, Daisy gripped her seat-belt in one hand and the door handle in the other, bracing for an imminent impact.

None came, and when David finally eased the car into a parking spot outside their mother's house and switched the engine off, Daisy leaned across and gave her brother an impulsive kiss on the cheek.

'What was that for?' he asked, warily.

'Because you're my brother and I love you,' Daisy said, wondering what on earth had gotten into her, even as the words left her lips.

'Love you too, Daisy-chain,' he said, and her eyes filled with unshed tears. It had been many years since he'd called her by her old nickname, and she remembered sunny school holidays when they'd picked daisies out of the lawn to make those unending chains.

Life had seemed much simpler then.

'Thanks for coming with me, and sorry for spoiling Christmas Day,' she said.

'It was the least I could do for my sister,' he replied, his fingers touching his cheek where she'd kissed him, and a warmth filled her heart.

It soon dispersed when they entered the house.

'Still alive, I see,' Sandra said dryly, spotting Daisy trotting up the stairs to change into a pair of dry socks.

And when she came back into the living room, David had already told everyone about the hospital visit, including what she was expected to do to determine the reappearance of the coin.

The laughter increased as soon as her family saw her.

'I take it you're all laughing at me,' Daisy said with a scowl. 'Thanks a lot.'

Sandra, slightly red in the face with mirth, bit her lip and disappeared into the kitchen, returning a minute later with a pair of rubber gloves, a bowl, and a wooden spoon.

'Here, you can use these,' she said grimly, handing them to Daisy. 'I don't want them back. And make sure you wash your hands thoroughly.'

What was she, three-years-old? She always washed her hands. Ew!

'Can I tell everyone we've got a real-life shit-stirrer in the family?' Elsie asked, almost doubled up with laughter.

'Mum! Don't be so crude,' Sandra said, but she was almost wetting herself too, as she stood there cross-legged and practically cross-eyed.

Daisy growled, and stuck her nose in the air, trying to ignore them. There was no point leaving the room, they'd only catch her later. Might as well let them get it all out of their systems now.

'I want regular updates, mind,' Gee-Gee said, 'because I want that sixpence back. It's my last one.'

Daisy shuddered.

'That's nasty,' Elsie said, and for once everyone else agreed with her.

'I'll get you another one off the internet,' Daisy said through gritted teeth.

'It won't be the same,' Gwenda protested. 'That sixpence was the last one my da ever gave to me.'

'You shouldn't have put it in the pudding, then.' Daisy pointed out.

'I wouldn't have, if I knew you were going to swallow it.'

'Believe me, I didn't mean to.' Daisy huffed. Not only was she having to check for hidden treasure whenever she went to the loo, but she was also now expected to fish it out, give it a rinse, and hand it back.

Words failed her.

But they didn't fail her great-gran. 'David, I think it's time to take me back. I don't want to still be here when our Daisy goes poo-mining.'

Poo-mining? Charming!

'That might be a bit of a problem, Gee-Gee,' David said, after he'd stopped laughing. 'It's snowing a blizzard out there.'

Everyone took a minute to think about that, then Sandra heaved out a sigh. 'You're going to have to stay here, then. All of you. Mum will have to sleep with me, David and Zoe can sleep in Mum's bed, and Gee-Gee can have Daisy's.'

'Where will I sleep?' Daisy asked, plaintively.

'The sofa.'

Daisy rolled her eyes. The day was going from bad to worse.

She helped her mother put fresh sheets on all the beds after the family belatedly opened their presents. Once supper was done and the rubbish the TV showed on public holidays had been watched and commented on, it was up to David to carry Gwenda up the stairs (or was it "stagger", because for such a little thing, Gee-Gee weighed a ton, as David pointed out several times).

'What are they feeding you in that home?' David puffed, half-way up the stairs, and having to stop for a breather.

Both Sandra and Elsie were poised behind him, in case he dropped the old lady, or fell backwards, though what use they were going to be if he did, baffled Daisy. The most likely scenario was that everyone would fall down the stairs, resulting in a load of broken bones and another trip to A&E. And it would probably be Daisy, because the way her luck was going, they'd all land on her.

She shuffled back a step or two, then lost interest when David summited the landing to a round of applause, and she joined Zoe in the living room.

'Congratulations,' she said, belatedly, and Zoe smiled her thanks.

'I'm going for the first scan next week,' the younger woman told her, and that was the most Daisy had ever heard her say.

Having little, or no clue regarding pregnancy and childbirth, Daisy said, 'Can you find out what it is then?'

Zoe shook her head. 'I don't think so. Anyway, we want it to be a surprise.' She ran a hand tenderly over her still-flat stomach.

Daisy thought about her own not-so-flat tummy and tried to suck the flab in. Anyone comparing the two women would think Daisy was the pregnant one, not Zoe. She discreetly undid the button on her trousers once more, and breathed a little easier. Her New Year's resolution was to join the gym.

David, duty finished for the moment, came into the room and sat next to his wife on the sofa, putting an arm around her, and Daisy watched enviously as Zoe snuggled into him. David whispered in her ear, and Zoe giggled.

Daisy missed having someone to cuddle with, someone to snuggle on the sofa with and whisper sweet nothings in *her* ear.

Oh, who was she kidding? Freddie had never been a sweet-nothings kind of guy. Or maybe it wasn't her he wanted to whisper them to.

After the rest of the family had turned in for the night, Daisy spread the spare duvet on the sofa and lay under it, watching a re-run of White Christmas, thinking this must be the worst Christmas she could ever remember having, and except for the wonderful news that her brother was about to become a dad of course, the day couldn't have been any worse. Thankfully it was almost over, only another hour to go, and Daisy could forget all about it until next year. And to think, she used to love Christmas!

Daisy found herself looking forward to being an aunt. She vowed to be the best aunt in the world, a fun aunt, the sort of aunt who her niece or nephew would love to be around. After all, this might be the closest she'd get to having a child of her own, with the way her love life was going. Daisy intended to let him, or her, stay up past their bedtime, feed them popcorn and chocolate on the sly, and take them ice-skating (not that Daisy had ever been on an ice-rink in her life). She'd let them—

'Elsie?'

Daisy sat up.

'Elsie?' Gee-Gee's mournful voice floated down the stairs. 'Sandra?'

Daisy waited for her mum or nan to get up to see what her great-gran wanted.

'Anyone?' The voice sounded desperate.

Daisy let out a sigh and pushed the duvet off. Everyone was obviously fast asleep or, more likely, ignoring Gwenda, in the hope that someone else would see to her. Clearly that someone was going to be Daisy.

'What is it, Gee-Gee?' she whispered, pushing open the bedroom door.

Even though the bed was a single, Gwenda looked tiny in it, like a child, and Daisy had a brief flash of how David's son or daughter would appear in it, when he or she slept over. Without the wrinkles, of course, and the wispy white perm.

'I really wanted your mother or your nan,' Gwenda said.

'They're asleep, so you've got me instead. What do you need, Gee-Gee?'

'The toilet.'

'Righto,' Daisy said, taking a deep breath and letting it out in false bravado. 'Let's get you out of bed, shall we?' This wasn't a task she particularly relished, and she hadn't been called on to take her great-gran for a wee all that often, the job usually falling to Sandra or Elsie, but she knew she could do this.

She pulled the duvet back, revealing Gee-Gee's skinny, wrinkled knees and helped the old lady swing her legs over the side of the bed. Then she heaved Gee-Gee's top half up until she was sitting upright.

They both paused for a breather for a moment, before Daisy hoisted her great-gran into a standing position, one arm under the other woman's armpits and thinking David was right, that Gee-Gee did weigh as much as a small pony.

She waited until Gee-Gee had steadied herself, then the pair of them shuffled painfully slowly towards the bathroom.

Here comes the bit I really don't like, Daisy thought, as she helped her great-gran hike up her borrowed nightie and pull her knickers down. Then she lowered the old lady carefully onto the toilet seat, while trying to keep her gaze averted, as much for Gee-Gee's dignity as for Daisy's sanity.

Daisy tore off a couple of sheets of loo paper and handed them to Gwenda.

'I'm going to need more than that,' Gee-Gee announced.

'Oh?'

'And I'm going to need you to do something else for me.'

'Anything, Gee-Gee. What is it?'

The old woman still had her dentures in – she probably wanted Daisy to put them in a glass for her, and Daisy tried not to show her dismay at the thought of cleaning another person's teeth.

'I'm going to need you to wipe my arse,' Gwenda said. 'I've got to do a big jobbie.'

Oh, the gods must be laughing at Daisy – *could it get any worse*, indeed!

It could, and it did, as Gee-Gee let out a tremendous fart, followed by hideous plopping sounds.

Ew.

Chapter 12

'And have you been, you know… grubbing around looking for it?' Melissa asked, wiping the tears from her eyes. Her face had gone an odd shade of purple.

Daisy didn't think the story was that funny, but Melissa had laughed so hard she'd snorted coffee through her nose and had nearly gotten them thrown out of the café.

'Yes,' Daisy replied, stiffly.

'I've never heard of anyone shitting silver before,' Melissa chortled.

'Don't be so crude,' Daisy said. 'Anyway, it hasn't made an appearance yet.'

'How long has it been?'

'Three days.' Three long, rather disgusting days. 'It was so embarrassing,' Daisy said.

'I bet they see that sort of thing every day,' Melissa said, stirring the coffee dregs in her cup.

'Yeah, but I was still mortified.' Daisy grimaced. 'Dr Hartley said—'

'Dr Hartley?' Melissa interrupted.

'The guy who examined me.'

'Is that really his name? I bet he wished he was a heart doctor,' she chortled.

'He could have my heart any day,' Daisy muttered. 'And any other part of me, for that matter.'

'Oh, he was cute, was he? No wonder you were embarrassed.'

'I suppose, but he was more interested in my bowels than my face.'

'So he should be – he's a doctor!'

'That's not what I meant, and you know it. Doctors are men, too.'

'Yes, but you were also his patient and I don't think that kind of thing is allowed.'

Daisy sighed. 'I expect you're right. Besides, Freddie has put me off men for life.'

'Don't give up on love just because of one bad experience,' Melissa protested. 'Go on, tell me what this doctor of yours looked like.'

'You know the guy out of *Grimm*?'

'The one who turns into a kind of wolf-thing?'

'No, not him, the other one, the Grimm himself, David Giuntoli. Think of him with a beard. Dark hair, blue eyes, all intense and… doctory.'

'Dr Hartley,' Melissa crooned. 'Dr Loveheart, instead of Burkhardt.'

'Doctor Rummage Around In Your Poo, you mean.'

'The fact that you fancy him proves you've not lost your mojo,' Melissa pointed out.

'Just because I look, doesn't mean I want to touch,' Daisy said.

'Oh, but you do, my lovely. I can see it in your eyes. They've gone all gooey.'

'It's not goo, it's realising what the time is. We'd better get a move on or we'll be late back and the Grumpmeister will have a good reason to be grumpy.'

'Do we have to? I'm still in Christmas mode.'

It was that dead time (work-wise) between Christmas and New Year, when people were still recovering from the last round of festivities while gearing up for the next lot. She had no idea why the company insisted on opening the offices. Surely the management could tell they'd get little or no work out of their employees until January. But needs must, as they say, and if she wanted to keep her job then she had to return from lunch. Anyway, look what happened the last time she'd had a half day – Freddiegate.

'Yes.' Daisy was firm. 'I want to be paid at the end of the month, and I've now got a deposit on a house to save for.'

'Okay, since you put it like that…'

The two women were back at work in record time, though Daisy thought her calf muscles might take a while to recover from the mad dash. Even so, Grumpmeister, a.k.a. Simon, their manager, was staring fixedly at the clock.

He pointed at Daisy and jerked a thumb at his office.

'Great, a meeting with the most miserable man on the planet. Just what I need,' Daisy muttered, throwing her bag under her desk and stomping in the direction her boss had indicated.

She hated these meetings, especially when it was only him and her. He usually picked one of these little tête-à-têtes to lay some new task on her, like the musical card fiasco which he expected her to magic out of thin air. She wrote poems and little verses, not music, for goodness' sake!

She slunk in through the door and took a seat. Grumpy was already perched on his chair on the other side of his desk. Perched was an unusual position for him – he normally slouched back, his arms folded, with a scowl on his face. Today, he looked nervous. He was leaning forward, fiddling with a pad and pen, and the skin under his left eye kept twitching. Daisy stared at the little tick in fascination.

'I know what you're going to say,' she said, before Grumpy had a chance to open his mouth. 'And no, I haven't come up with much yet. But I will. I just need some time to get to grips with it. This is a whole new thing for me.'

'It's shelved,' Simon said.

'Shelved? That's um… er…' If she said "great", he'd know she hadn't wanted to do it in the first place. If she said, "that's a shame", or appeared too disappointed, he might decide to unshelve it and give the project back to her.

'Yes, shelved,' he repeated. 'You'll go back to doing what you did before.'

Not that she'd actually stopped doing what she was doing before, because she hadn't had much of a go at the musical cards. 'Oh, good,' she replied.

'For the time being.'

'The time being?' What was that supposed to mean? Did they have something else in mind for her?

It appeared they did. The powers-that-be on the floor upstairs where the accounts and senior managers had their offices, had something quite radical in mind for Daisy Jones.

'We are going to have to let you go,' Simon said, steeling his hands under his chin (or should she say "chins"?), and looking solemn.

'Go where?' A trip would be nice, even if it was only for a day. Any old excuse to get out of the office, eh?

'Go, as in, made redundant,' Simon clarified.

Daisy sat in stunned silence. Surely she couldn't have heard him correctly?

Simon began rabbiting on about severance pay, redundancy packages, and proposed end dates, but Daisy wasn't really listening.

'There's been a considerable downturn in the sales of traditional cards since the rise of the ecards.' He said the last four words as if they were a title of a sci-fi film – "The Rise of the Ecards, coming soon to a cinema near you."

'We have yet to confirm all the details, and HR will be in touch in due course,' he carried on, speaking faster, obviously eager for this terrible ordeal to end.

Caring Cards didn't have a Human Resources Department – they had a woman called Joyce.

'HR?' Daisy asked. 'As in Joyce, from upstairs? Joyce who does the wage slips? That Joyce?'

'Yes, Joyce.'

'When…?' Daisy swallowed, still in shock. Her hands trembled and she shoved them under her thighs, hoping that sitting on them would stop them shaking. 'When am I supposed to go?'

'As I said, the date hadn't been determined yet. It's TBC,' Simon replied, almost airily.

'TBC?'

'To be confirmed. It's not official yet, but I wanted to give you a heads-up, so you know where you stand.'

Daisy sat for a moment, trying to get her numb mind working. Something Simon said didn't make sense. 'Am I, or am I not, being made redundant?' she asked.

'Yes,' he said.

Okay then.

'And no,' he added.

Oh? 'Which is it?'

'Both. Look, I'm going to be honest with you, here. The situation could go both ways. We're facing a redundancy situation if the market doesn't improve. Upstairs has given us three to six months to turn things around. If there's no improvement in that time, then redundancies will have to take place.'

'Redundancies?' Daisy emphasised the plural.

'It's not only you who'll be affected,' Simon said huffily. 'Other people's futures are on the line too.'

'Will you be speaking to Melissa?'

Simon went red. 'I expect so.' He squirmed in his seat.

Daisy narrowed her eyes. If this was a first-in, last-out thing, then by rights Melissa should be the one sitting in the hot seat and having this conversation with Simon, considering both of them did roughly the same job. Daisy was more senior, and was paid a little more than Melissa, so, on the one hand, it would be cheaper to get rid of Daisy in terms of salary, but Daisy had worked at the company for much longer than Melissa, and any redundancy payment would be more. Daisy had far more experience, and even if she did say so herself, she was better at it.

Then the penny dropped. Simon had most likely been told to give Daisy the "heads-up," as he'd put it, in the hope that she'd jump ship before she was pushed.

Bitterness flashed through her. She'd worked for *Caring Cards* (or Uncaring Cards, as they should now be called), since she'd left school at eighteen. She'd given them the twelve best years of her life, and look at the thanks she'd got – a vague, undisclosed redundancy package. And *that's* why Simon had told her, because they were hoping she'd find another job and leave, so they could save themselves paying her anything. The mean bastards!

She'd show 'em. There was no way she was going to forgo any redundancy pay-out. It probably wouldn't be much, but it might be enough to give her the deposit she so desperately wanted. Added to the little she had already saved, she could maybe think about a small semi in Warndon Villages, a series of interconnected estates on the outskirts of the city. She would be one step closer to buying her own home.

Then another thought struck her. How was she going to get a mortgage without a job? She wasn't, was she?

Catch twenty-two.

Not giving Simon a chance to say anything further, Daisy stood, and said, 'If that's all, I've got work to do,' and stalked back to her desk with her head held high, trying not to let anyone see how upset she was.

Unlocking her computer, she heard Melissa whisper, 'Is everything okay?'

'No, it bloody isn't,' Daisy snapped, immediately regretting her outburst. It wasn't Melissa's fault; the other girl couldn't help that the company decided Daisy was the one they wanted to let go.

'What's wrong? Has he said something to upset you?'

'You could say that. He told me I'm about to be made redundant.' Daisy had a fleeting thought about whether she should share the information with her colleague, but Simon hadn't told her it was confidential, had he? And besides, Melissa had a right to know, because hadn't Simon said he would be speaking to Melissa too? Though, why would he, when the company couldn't do without a verse writer?

'Oh Daisy, that's awful. When?'

'Simon couldn't give me a date, but he said it's on the cards.'

'What are you going to do? Look for another job?'

'I think that's exactly what they're hoping I'll do, so they can get out of paying me anything.'

Melissa gasped. 'They wouldn't!'

'They would, but I'll show 'em. I'm not going anywhere until they've paid me what I'm owed.'

Melissa glared at Simon's now-closed office door.

No wonder he hadn't left it open; he didn't want to witness any fallout – the coward. Not that Daisy intended to oblige him. She wouldn't give him the satisfaction, so instead of working on the next round of Father's Day cards as she was supposed to be doing, Daisy Googled job sites instead. It wouldn't hurt to look, to see what jobs were out there.

After a while, she sat back, despondent. There didn't appear to be much call for unemployed greeting card verse writers.

'Daisy?'

She looked up to see Melissa standing behind her, with a strange almost self-satisfied expression on her face. It certainly hadn't taken her colleague long to work out that with Daisy gone, they had to keep Melissa on. Daisy didn't blame her for being relieved that her job was safe.

'Found anything?' the other girl asked.

'Not really.' Daisy wondered how long it would be before the news spread around the office. Melissa, bless her, was a bit of a gossip, but at least it spared Daisy from having to explain things twenty different times to twenty different people. No doubt the office would soon be giggling to the news of Freddie's sexual preference, and Daisy's coin-swallowing trick, too.

She sighed and clicked out of Google. 'Not that I was planning on leaving until they sorted out the redundancy,' she said, 'but it looks like even if I wanted to get out of this shitty company, I couldn't.'

'Shh,' Melissa said, shooting a swift glance around the office. 'Simon will hear you.'

'Let him,' Daisy said. 'After all, what is he going to do – sack me?'

Chapter 13

'You're sacked,' Simon said.

'Eh? What did you say?'

'Sacked, as in, get your things and leave. You'll be paid until the end of the week.'

'What do you mean "sacked"?' Daisy wailed.

'Fired,' Simon said, leaning back in his chair, folding his arms, and gazing at her with a self-satisfied expression.

'Don't you mean "made redundant"? We've already had this conversation.'

'No, I mean sacked.'

'But you can't sack me,' she said, close to tears for the second time that day, and this time she didn't try to hide it.

'Yes, I can.'

'Why?'

'For inappropriate use of the internet.'

She had no idea what he was rabbiting on about. Was he accusing her of looking at porn?

Simon noticed her blank expression and explained, 'For job hunting on company time.'

'It was only for a few minutes,' she protested. 'And everyone uses the internet. I have to use Google for my job.'

'For your job, yes, but not for the purpose of changing your job.'

'This is a joke, right?' she pleaded. 'Tell me it's a joke.'

'No joke, you're to leave at the end of the day.'

Daisy's eyes brimmed with tears, and they spilt over to trickle down her cheeks. 'You're really sacking me?' she whispered.

'Yes, I am.' You've contravened the company's internet policy, which states, and I quote, "no employee will use the company's internet for personal use".'

'You booked your last holiday in work, and you're always on eBay.'

'I'm not,' he replied, calmly, with no change of expression.

'You are, I've seen you.'

'But *I* haven't been caught,' he said, 'and if you try to make trouble I'll deny everything. It'll be your word against mine, and I know who management will believe.'

'You bastard!'

'Calling me names won't help, not if you want a reference.'

Daisy, about to call him something far worse, snapped her teeth together with a click. She had to have a reference, she simply *had* to, otherwise getting another job would be downright impossible.

Defeated, she got to her feet, turned to leave, then paused and walked back into Simon's office.

'Can I go home *now*?' she asked in a small voice. 'I can't stay here another minute.'

Simon didn't speak for a moment, taking a quick look at the other staff in the office beyond his own. They were all trying desperately to hear what was going on.

'Okay,' he said, pretending to be reluctant, but Daisy saw the gleam of relief and satisfaction in his eyes.

'Thank you,' she said, quietly. There was no point in saying anything else. She knew the company's rules, she'd broken them, and she'd been caught. They had every right to dismiss her. The fact that everyone else did their personal stuff on company time and using company resources, wouldn't hold any water. She needed that reference.

It was actually very good of them to provide her with one under the circumstances, because they were well within their rights not to.

As she slunk out of Simon's office she wondered if Simon, or another manager had spotted her screen by sheer bad luck, or if someone had shopped her. Melissa had seen what she'd been looking at, but there was no way her friend would blab. It must have been bad luck – one of the pitfalls of working in an open-plan office was the lack of privacy. She'd been so engrossed in her job search that the Queen could have strolled past, and Daisy wouldn't have noticed. She did, however, have an inkling she might know who had split on her – Stacey, the marketing officer. Her job was to source out new clients, but she fancied herself as being creative, often spouting ideas, hoping someone would take her up on one of them and recognise her talent.

Daisy had very few belongings at work, apart from her coat, scarf, gloves, and bag. It took her all of thirty seconds to go through her desk drawers to check there was nothing she wanted to take with her. There wasn't, except for a bundle of receipts she'd stashed in an envelope – reminders of the items she'd bought and not confessed to Freddie

("What? This old thing? I've had it ages/Sara gave it to me because she can't fit in to it/picked it up in a charity shop…").

When she lifted her coat off the rack of hooks, Melissa appeared at her side.

'What's the Grumpmeister got you doing now?' the other girl asked brightly then hesitated when she saw Daisy's expression. 'Is everything alright?'

'Simon sacked me,' Daisy whispered, not wanting the others to hear, though they could clearly tell that something was up and would find out for themselves soon enough anyway.

'He did *what*?' Melissa exclaimed, lowering her voice when Daisy shushed her. 'Why?'

'Job hunting on company time,' she replied, wrapping her scarf around her neck.

'That's terrible. As if *he* doesn't do stuff like that all the time.'

'*He* didn't get caught. *I* did.'

'Can he do that?'

'Apparently.'

'Are you going to do anything about it?' Melissa asked.

'Like what?'

The question gave Melissa pause. She shrugged. 'I don't know', she said, 'but there must be something.'

'I honestly don't think there is.' Daisy was ready to go, her bag slung over her shoulder, and her coat on.

Melissa leaned in for a hug. 'You'll keep in touch, won't you?' she said.

'Of course, I will,' Daisy replied, hugging her back.

'Promise?'

'Promise.' Daisy meant it at the time, but once again the gods were about to teach her a lesson – don't make promises because you never know if you will be able to keep them.

And for the last time, Daisy walked out of *Caring Cards*, attempting to hold her head up while keeping her tears at bay, and failing miserably.

Which was why she ducked back inside and headed for the comforting solitude of the ladies' loos, to give her time to compose herself and wait for her mascara to stop running down her face.

Mindful that someone might walk in at any moment, Daisy went into a cubicle, locked the door and put the toilet lid down, then she sat on it and wept.

First Freddie, then the Christmas Day debacle, and now this.

What more could go wrong?

She was about to find out, and by the end of the day she would seriously begin to wonder if someone up there was having a sick joke at her expense.

At last her crying jag began to abate, subsiding into hiccuping sniffles. She felt washed out, drained, an empty shell of herself, and she leant back, resting her aching head on the wall behind her. At least she hadn't broken down in the middle of the high street – the melt-down had been in private, and though there may be a few more episodes to come, she had a feeling this was the worst. She hadn't really cried over Freddie, and she supposed it was overdue. Combined with the terrible news today, it had all become a bit much.

She gave her nose one final blow, wiped her eyes with a fresh tissue, and took a deep breath.

Time to face the world again.

A door opened and the click of high heels on the tiled floor made Daisy decided to wait until whoever it was had left. She's simply couldn't face any more questions, so she sat there listening to the sound of perfume being sprayed and lipstick being applied.

Then…

'Hiya, it's me.' Melissa's voice was low and sultry.

Daisy stopped breathing, hoping her friend didn't realise she had an audience. Saying goodbye to her once had been hard enough and she didn't want to go through it a second time in less than fifteen minutes.

'Yeah, she's gone. I can't believe Simon actually had the balls to do it.'

Who on earth was Melissa talking to? Daisy gave a mental shrug – she knew what a gossip Melissa was, and she didn't hold it against her. Daisy would probably do the same in Melissa's shoes, and she realised she was going to be the topic of the day for a while yet.

'Nah, meek as a lamb.' A pause, then Melissa laughed, and it wasn't a nice laugh, either. 'I don't think she'll make any trouble. I asked her before she left, and she didn't think there was anything she could do. If only she knew. But thank God she doesn't.'

Another pause and Daisy fervently wished she knew who was on the other end of the phone, and what it was Melissa was thankful Daisy didn't know.

'I know she could go to ACAS and claim unfair dismissal, but believe me, she won't. She slinked out of here with her tail well and truly between her legs. You've heard the last of Daisy Jones.' This time Melissa's laugh sounded downright mean. 'Now, do I get that promotion you promised me, snookums?'

What promotion? Who *was* Melissa talking to?

'Okay, I love you too,' Melissa was saying, her voice breathy and flirty once more. She giggled. 'I look forward to playing secretary to your big, powerful boss, Mr Dearborn, sir.'

Too much info, Melissa – hang on, Mr Dearborn? *The* Mr Dearborn, the new MD?

Daisy realised she was right, and as soon as she did, everything slotted into place.

Melissa had ratted her out to the MD because she was having an affair with him, and because he'd offered her an incentive.

The lying, scheming, two-faced cow!

Then something else Melissa said pinged on Daisy's shellshock radar. ACAS? Did Melissa mean the Advisory, Conciliation and Arbitration Service? Unfair dismissal? Daisy searched her mind trying to remember the details of the contract she'd signed when she first started with *Caring Cards*. She vaguely recalled something about verbal warnings, written warnings, and gross misconduct. But which one of those categories did her misdemeanour fall under?

There was only one way to find out. She had a copy of the contract at home somewhere, and as soon as she got in through the door, by gum she intended to find it.

Not wanting to give Melissa (or Mr Dearborn) any inkling that she was anything other than a meek lamb to the slaughter, Daisy waited until Melissa left, then waited some more, just to make sure. She didn't want her so-called friend to witness her leaving the premises for the second time. As she splashed cold water on her blotchy face, Daisy had a new determination in her eyes.

Sacked indeed? She'd see about that!

Chapter 14

The house was blessedly empty when Daisy stepped into the hall. She wanted to find that contract first (luckily she had thought to take a photocopy of it, all those years ago), and she intended to have her ducks all in a row before her mother shot a barrage of questions at her.

But first, she had some business to take care of, and she retrieved the rubber gloves, bowl, and spoon from her bedroom with distaste.

Nada. Nothing. Zilch.

She disinfected the utensils and her hands about twenty-three times, then pressed a hand to her stomach. It felt a bit swollen, and she hoped it wasn't the result of a silver sixpence festering inside her. Lord knows what poison the damn thing was leaking into her innards.

It took her about an hour of rooting through assorted letters, papers and stuff she had no idea as to why she'd kept, but it must have seemed like a good idea at the time. Daisy eventually found what she was looking for, snatching the contract from the file and waving it triumphantly.

'Ta dah!' she squealed, before remembering that she didn't know what it said, and she might not have anything to be triumphant about. She had just started to read it, when the insistent and stupidly loud ring of the house phone broke her concentration.

'Go away,' she muttered, knowing it wouldn't be for her, and nodded when it stopped.

It started again.

Daisy rolled her eyes and tried to ignore it, but when it stopped again and her mobile rang instead, she answered it.

'Daisy?' It was Zoe and she sounded strange.

Mind you, Daisy had hardly heard the other woman say more than a handful of words, and two of those had been "I do", when her sister-in-law had said her vows, so for all Daisy knew, this could be her normal speaking voice.

'I'm sorry to bother you in work, but I didn't know who else to call. My parents are on a cruise and your mum doesn't answer and—'

'Slow down,' Daisy said, and uncrossing her legs; she'd been sitting on her bedroom floor, leaning against the bed, surrounded by files and boxes, but now she sat up straight.

'What's wrong, and where's David?' she demanded, and unease squirmed deep inside her.

'He's at a conference in London and his phone is switched off,' Zoe said. 'Oh, Daisy, can you come? I'm at the hospital.'

'Why?' Daisy asked, but she thought she already knew the answer.

'I think I'm losing the baby.'

'Stay there. Don't move,' Daisy shouted, leaping to her feet, her legs cramping as pins and needles shot down her calves. 'I'll be there as soon as I can,' she cried, hopping around her bedroom, wondering what she'd done with her car keys. They were here somewhere…

The call ended, and Daisy flew out of the door, never so thankful in her life that she had no one to ask permission of, and that the snow was a slushy memory. How she made it to the hospital without having an accident, Daisy didn't know, but she pulled safely into a space and ran from the car.

Poor Zoe, she thought, as she dashed into the A&E waiting area. Poor David. Please tell me this isn't happening.

'Zoe Jones,' she panted at one of the admin staff. 'She's pregnant.'

With infinite slowness, the woman behind the bullet-proof glass checked her computer. 'Oh yes,' she said. 'Doctor is with her now.'

'Can I see her? How is she? Is the baby okay? Please tell me it is.'

'When Doctor has finished examining her, he'll be out to speak to you. Please take a seat.'

'But she asked for me,' Daisy protested. 'She just called, not half an hour ago. Ask her, if you don't believe me.'

The woman gave her a seen-it-all-before smile and pointed at the seat. 'Doctor will be with you soon,' she repeated. Daisy could tell there was no budging her, so she plonked down in a chair and nibbled on her nails.

After five minutes, the skin around her index finger started to bleed, so she stopped biting and started phoning instead.

There was no answer from anyone.

'Pick up,' she muttered, cursing her mother for forgetting her mobile – again.

If only she could speak to Zoe she might be able to find out where David was, and ring the conference venue direct.

She tried Zoe's mobile, but it went straight to answerphone.

Shit!

It looked like Daisy was going to have to deal with the situation on her own, though nothing in her thirty years had prepared her for something like this.

Finally, the door opened and a man in a white coat peered through it. 'Zoe Jones?' he called.

'She should be in there,' Daisy replied, pointing at the half-open door behind him.

'She is,' the doctor said. 'I was asking if there was anyone with her.'

No, you weren't Daisy thought, as she stood up to follow him. He'd said Zoe's name, not hers, and she hoped Dr Hartley didn't recognise her.

Trust it to be him.

'How is she?' Daisy asked.

'Comfortable,' he said noncommittally.

Daisy knew that comfortable could mean anything from having lost the baby, to Zoe still being pregnant. *Comfortable* told her absolutely nothing at all.

'Has she…?' Daisy trailed off as she trotted behind him.

Dr Hartley said nothing, stopping outside a cubicle and pulling aside the curtain. It was empty.

Daisy let out of small cry, followed by a sob and then, 'Oh God.' She slapped a hand to her mouth.

'You can wait here,' Dr Hartley said. 'I'm sure she'll be glad to see a familiar face.'

'Oh.' Daisy took her hands away from her mouth. 'Okay. Thank you.'

'We'll know more after the ultrasound,' he said, and this time he sounded almost sympathetic.

Daisy nodded.

Dr Hartley turned away then paused. 'And how are you?' he asked, over his shoulder. 'Any change?'

Daisy shook her head, mortified.

He gave her a chuckle. 'Any change,' he repeated, then. 'See what I did there? Change, as in "have you got any change"?'

Daisy saw, and she wasn't amused. She glared at him and he shrugged, abruptly losing the brief flash of humour (if you could call it humour) and his expression sobered. 'How are you feeling?' he asked, and glanced at her stomach.

'Fine,' she said. 'I think, though my tummy is a bit bloated,' she added.

He gave her an odd look. 'It would be, wouldn't it?' he said.

Would it? She knew swallowed coins could do *some* damage but why hadn't he warned her about it? She placed a hand on her tummy and pressed in a bit. It felt decidedly squishy and flabby. Once this sixpence was out of her, she'd simply have to find some time to go to the gym.

Oh yes, she remembered, she had plenty of time now, didn't she, just when she couldn't afford the membership fee. Typical.

'When is it due?' he asked her.

'Five to ten days, you told me,' Daisy replied, wondering how he could have forgotten, since he clearly remembered the incident.

'Not the coin, the baby,' he clarified.

'Oh, in about six months.' Surely Zoe would have told him how far along she was.

'Early days then,' he said. 'Congratulations.'

'Thank you,' she said, taking hope. He must think the baby was okay to say that. She couldn't wait to tell Zoe.

'As I said before, any problems, any at all, come straight in. Don't wait to go to your GP.'

'I won't,' she said, wondering if he was talking about Zoe, or about her.

'We can't be too careful when you're pregnant, can we?'

Daisy realised that he was still talking about her sister-in-law. 'I'm sure David will take good care of her,' she said.

'David is…?

'Her husband.'

'*He's* the baby's father?'

'Of course.'

A noise distracted him and he pulled out his bleeper, frowning when he looked at the screen. 'Can you get hold of him?' he asked.

'His phone is switched off,' Daisy explained. 'He's at some kind of dental conference.'

Another frown, this time directed at Daisy. 'He's the man who brought you in on Christmas Day?'

'Yes, that's him.' Her reply was cautious. What was it with all these questions?

'Zoe must be a very understanding lady,' he said, and Daisy could have sworn there was a note of reprimand in his voice.

'He doesn't go away all that often,' Daisy said, feeling the need to stick up for her brother.

'Ah, here she is,' Dr Hartley said, as the curtain was pulled aside and a porter wheeled Zoe into the cubicle. Daisy marvelled at the way the doctor's whole demeanour changed the minute he saw Zoe. Gone was the stern, slightly forbidding man he'd been for the last few minutes, and in its place was a man full of concern, and more than a little solemnity.

That wasn't good. Hadn't he just told her everything was okay?

'Zoe,' he began, his tone sending a child chill down Daisy's spine. 'I've got the results of your ultrasound, and they're rather mixed, I'm afraid.'

Zoe's eyes welled up and her chin wobbled.

'I want to admit you,' the doctor said.

'Is the baby alright?' Zoe demanded, her hands on her stomach.

'You were carrying twins,' he said. 'You've lost one of them. The other foetus is still viable.'

'Twins?' Zoe asked her voice catching.

'It's not uncommon to miscarry one,' the doctor said, 'and I know how upsetting this must be for you, but the other baby looks fine. I want to keep you in, run a couple of tests. But the most important thing is to keep you calm and rested.' He shot Daisy a look full of significance as he said the last.

Daisy nodded frantically. She could do that. She could help look after her sister-in-law, especially now, since she didn't have anything else to do.

'I'll look after her,' Daisy offered.

'Is that wise?' Dr Hartley countered, and Daisy was confused, and more than a little hurt. Just because she'd been unlucky enough (or silly enough) to swallow a foreign object, it didn't mean she couldn't look after Zoe.

'Under the circumstances,' he added, glancing at Daisy's stomach.

'Oh?' Daisy's heart plummeted to her feet. There must be something the doctor hadn't told her, like the coin was leaking some noxious substance into her body, which was coming out through her pores or something. He obviously thought there was a risk to the baby.

Zoe lay in stunned silence, tears trickling unchecked down her cheeks.

Poor thing – what awful news. Two babies, and only one still alive. Daisy put a hand on Zoe's shoulder and gave it an ineffectual rub. How long does it take to recover from something like this, if one ever did, she wondered? David would be devastated.

Zoe must have been thinking the same thing. 'I must tell David,' she said.

'We'll get hold of him,' Daisy promised. 'Where is the conference being held?'

'I've got it written down somewhere,' Zoe said, staring around her frantically.

She looked even worse than she had on Christmas Day, with her pale face and huge eyes, and dark circles beneath them. Her long blond hair hung limply and Daisy absentmindedly brushed a stray strand away from the other woman's cheek.

Zoe subsided against the pillow. 'It's at home,' she said. 'I tacked it to the fridge.'

'I'll try him on his mobile again,' Daisy said, and stepped outside into the corridor.

This time her brother answered, but Daisy, to her eternal shame, had hoped he wouldn't. How was she supposed to break news like this to him?

'Hi, Daisy? What's up?'

Daisy never called him during the day, knowing he was usually with a patient (actually, she hardly ever called him at all), so it was no surprise he jumped to the conclusion there was something wrong.

'It's Zoe,' she said. 'I've got some bad news.' She took a deep breath and ploughed ahead before her brother had a chance to say anything. 'She was having twins. She lost one, David. I am so sorry.'

A muffled sound came down the airwaves, followed by, 'How is she?' after a pause, during which Daisy simply knew he'd been crying.

'She's okay, and the other baby is fine,' she said. 'Zoe is still pregnant, David. You're still going to be a father.' She understood this was little consolation to him now, but she had to try to give him any comfort that she could. 'They're keeping her in, and she's got to take it easy,' she added.

'I'll be there as soon as I can,' he promised, and Daisy went back inside to try to comfort his wife.

Dr Hartley was taking a blood sample and Daisy looked away, suddenly squeamish. Zoe was lying on the trolley, her eyes closed, tears still dripping into her hair. She looked so young and so helpless, and Daisy vowed to take care of her, if it was the last thing she did.

She waited until the doctor finished and had put a cotton wool ball on the tiny wound, securing it with a plaster, before she said to Zoe, 'I managed to get hold of him. He's on his way.'

She turned to the doctor. 'Can I stay with her until he arrives?' she asked.

Dr Hartley looked up, his eyes meeting hers. His were such a startling blue and they gazed into hers with such intensity that it made her shiver.

'It's up to Zoe,' he said, 'though I would be inclined to say no. I don't know the dynamics of your personal relationships, but I'm seriously concerned that my patient isn't subjected to any undue stress right now.'

'I promise I won't do anything to stress her,' Daisy said, resisting the urge to add "cross my heart and hope to die".

'Zoe?' he asked.

'I want her to stay, please.' Zoe was so quiet, Daisy could hardly hear her.

'You can stay until her husband arrives,' the doctor said. 'But I want you to leave as soon as he gets here. What you do outside of this hospital is your own concern; it's Mrs Jones,' (he stressed the word *missus*), 'who is my main concern.'

Daisy wondered what on earth he was talking about and she was about to ask, when Zoe struggled into a sitting position.

'Are you sure the baby is okay?' Zoe asked.

'I'm sure,' the doctor said. 'Did you see it on the screen when you had the ultrasound?'

'No, the screen was turned away from me.'

The doctor nodded and muttered, 'Of course.'

'But I did hear a heartbeat,' Zoe added.

'Do you want to listen to it again?'

Zoe's nod was emphatic. Daisy wanted to hear it too, to reassure herself, and David, when he arrived.

The doctor called for a nurse, and after a quick conversation, a machine was wheeled in. The doctor rubbed gel over Zoe's rather flat stomach and placed a wand on it.

A steady rapid thump, alarmingly fast, filled the cubicle.

Zoe closed her eyes and smiled. It was a tiny frightened smile, but at least it was a smile. 'Thank you,' she said quietly.

'My pleasure.' The doctor turned to Daisy. 'Do you want to listen to yours?'

'Er... no thanks. I think my heartbeat is fine.'

'Not *your* heartbeat,' the doctor said. 'Your baby's.'

'What?' Daisy, for want of a better word, was gobsmacked, and she started back until she was brought up short by the cubicle wall.

Oh my God! No wonder her tummy was bloated. No wonder she'd been so hungry (her friend, Wendy, had been ravenous during both of her pregnancies). And no wonder Dr Hartley hadn't wanted her to have an x-ray. The doctor had seen what she hadn't.

She was pregnant.

Chapter 15

How the hell was she going to break the news to Freddie? More to the point, how was she going to break the news to her mother? And her nan would be livid. At least Mum had a ring on her finger before she'd had kids, even if the man who'd put it there was nothing but a waster who had absconded once the reality of having a wife and children had sunk in.

Were all the women in her family doomed to play the same broken record over and over again?

She thought of the little soul developing inside her, and prayed it was a boy.

Her, a *mother*? She couldn't believe it. This wasn't the way she'd imagined her life would play out (she'd expected marriage to come first), and here she was lacking a man, as well as the wedding. But… she was going to be a mother. She'd have a little person to nurture and love, and to guide and teach. If it was a girl, she'd dress her up in ribbons and tutus, take her to ballet lessons, have princess-themed birthday parties, braid her hair and—

Reality struck with the force of a wrecking ball on a pre-fab house. The truth was, she'd be a single mother, with no home, and no job, and little prospect of getting either. An employer would take one look at her round belly and say "thanks, but no thanks".

Daisy felt sorry for the little mite she was about to bring into the world. What kind of a future would it have? And she also felt scared, not just because of the problems she faced, because although she'd always imagined herself being a mother, the reality was terrifying. She might be nearly thirty, but she still felt about fifteen, twenty at a push, on a good day, when she was seriously trying to adult.

She really wasn't ready for this.

'Well?' Dr Hartley was staring at her enquiringly, when Daisy came out of her shock-induced fugue.

'I'll pass,' she said. She needed to get her head around being pregnant first. Time, that's what she needed, and a lottery win wouldn't go amiss, either. Neither would a double vodka, but she suspected she wouldn't be drinking alcohol for the foreseeable future.

Get a grip, she said to herself, as her mind went off on a tangent again. She had a grieving sister-in-law to consider, and the last thing the poor girl needed to hear was the news of another woman's pregnancy, especially since Daisy felt so ambivalent about it.

The doctor's piercing blue eyes drilled into hers, and Daisy blushed furiously. She put a finger to her lips, pointed to her stomach, and shook her head.

He shook his in return, and she couldn't quite fathom his expression. Was it disbelief? Disgust? Disdain? He must think her a dreadful mother for not taking the opportunity to listen to her own baby's heartbeat when offered it, but this news was such a shock, such a bolt out of the blue that—

'Daisy?' Zoe's voice was weak.

Daisy jumped. 'I'm here,' she said, hoping Zoe hadn't heard or seen the odd exchange between her and the doctor.

'How long will David be?' her sister-in-law asked.

Daisy pushed thoughts of babies (her own baby) out of her head and tried to focus on the woman who needed her now.

'A couple of hours. Three at the outside, if the traffic is bad,' she replied.

And it probably would be bad at this time of year, and who in their right minds held a conference between Christmas and the New Year, anyway? What a bloody stupid time to have it, when most normal folk wanted to be at home with their families, nursing their hangovers.

'Is David supposed to be staying overnight?' she asked Zoe.

'No, it's a one-day thing,' Zoe said, her eyes still closed. 'I was going to go with him and spend the day in London, but I've been feeling so ill lately,' she added with a shudder.

Daisy shuddered, too, imagining poor Zoe on her own in the centre of London, and suffering a miscarriage. It didn't bear thinking about.

'I'll arrange for you to be admitted,' Dr Hartley said to Zoe. 'You,' he glanced at Daisy, 'can stay with her until she's sent to the ward. Then I expect you to leave.'

What was wrong with this guy? Her sister-in-law had just been given terrible news and Dr Hartley (Dr Heartless, more like it) wanted Daisy gone. Surely, rather than being distressed, Zoe would be comforted by having a family member with her? Unless, Daisy was toxic because of that sixpence, and if she was, what damage might it be doing to her own unborn child?

'Can I speak with you?' she asked the esteemed doctor, *sotto voce*.

He jerked his head, in a follow-me gesture, and they stepped outside the cubicle. Conscious that the curtained little boxes were far from soundproof, Daisy took the doctor's elbow and led him down the corridor.

A bolt of electricity travelled through her hand and up her arm when she touched him, and she gasped. He shook her hand off, and the feeling dissipated, leaving Daisy to wonder if she'd imagined it.

'Did I cause Zoe to lose her baby?' she asked, without preamble, 'and will the coin hurt mine?'

'The coin? No, it'll have no effect on your baby. As for Mrs Jones, stress may have contributed to it,' he said. 'We'll never know.'

Daisy's heart plummeted to her feet. This was all her fault. She'd caused Zoe more than enough stress on Christmas Day with her near-choking experience. It wasn't fair that by saving Daisy's life, Zoe lost one of her babies.

'I didn't mean to,' she murmured, wondering how she was going to live with herself. If only she hadn't put that bloody sixpence in the pudding. How stupid had she been?

'I doubt many people do,' was the doctor's dry response.

'She was there when it happened,' Daisy said.

'I bet that was cosy.' Another dry remark.

'I wouldn't describe it as cosy; she saved my life. Do you really think the stress of seeing me almost choke to death made her miscarry?' Daisy put a hand to her mouth.

The doctor blinked. 'I thought...' He cleared his throat. 'It could have been a contributing factor, and under the circumstances...'

'What circumstances?' What the hell was the man on about?

The doctor glared at the zipper on her rather-tight jeans.

'Oh, that. No.' She shook her head emphatically. 'She doesn't know about my baby.' Daisy almost choked again at the thought of a little human inside her.

'What about her husband? Will he say anything?' Dr Hartley asked.

'Hardly!' How could he, when Daisy had only found out herself. No one knew.

'I'd like to keep it that way, for a while,' Dr Hartley said, 'until Zoe's pregnancy is a little further along. Twelve weeks is a common time for a less-viable foetus to be lost. Can you do that for her?'

'Of course I can.' At the moment, keeping her secret wouldn't be much of a hardship, certainly not until she'd come to terms with the situation herself. And she needed to tell Freddie first, before she spread the (good?) news. As the baby's father, he had a right to know, but how he'd react was anyone's guess.

'Who's your doctor?' Dr Hartley asked, abruptly.

Here goes, she thought, anticipating rounds of surgery and hospital visits. 'I'll need to make an appointment, won't I?'

'You haven't seen your GP yet?'

Daisy couldn't believe the handsome, sexy man (yeah, she could still admire a good-looking bloke, even if she was in the "family way" – it was a bit like admiring a nice painting, even if you didn't want it hanging above your fireplace) could look more disapproving of her than he already did.

'How could I have?' Daisy said, 'when you only just told me I was pregnant a few minutes ago.'

'*I* told you?'

'Yes, you did.' For a doctor, the man had an appalling memory.

'*I* didn't say you were pregnant.'

'You did, too! You asked if I wanted to listen to my baby's heartbeat.'

'That's because I thought you *were* pregnant. Aren't you?'

'You tell me.'

'How can I tell when I haven't examined you?'

'I thought you could tell by looking at me,' Daisy said.

'Hardly,' he said, echoing her. 'I would never presume to think a woman was pregnant – it could lead to all kinds of problems.'

Daisy sighed in frustration. 'Then why did you presume I was? Is it because I've got a fat stomach?'

'See, that's the kind of problem I'm talking about, and no you haven't got a fat stomach. Zoe's husband told me.' He practically sneered when he said the word "husband".

'He didn't.' Daisy was absolutely, positively certain.

'He did.'

'When?' she demanded, crossing her arms.

'When you came to A&E on Christmas Day.'

Why would David say such a ridiculous thing – wait a minute. Daisy thought back, trying to recall the conversation. She closed her eyes, then opened them again slowly.

'He didn't say *I* was pregnant,' she said. 'He said Zoe was.'

It was Dr Hartley's turn to close his eyes. She noticed the little pulse at the base of his throat and had an insane urge to kiss it.

'I think I may have got the wrong end of the stick,' he said, after taking a deep breath and opening his eyes to stare earnestly at her. 'I was under the impression that David had announced you were having a baby, then you choked on the coin. Isn't that what happened?'

'Not quite. He did say he was having a baby, but I'm not the one who is pregnant.'

Or was she? It would explain a lot – her bloated stomach, her insane appetite – and now that she'd been given a glimpse of potential motherhood, she was strangely reluctant to let go of it.

'But you *are* having an affair with him,' Dr Hartley said.

Daisy choked for the second time in less than a week. Gasping for breath, she cried, 'Water,' and the good doctor rushed off to get her some, making her sit down before giving her the plastic cup.

When she stopped spluttering, she scowled at him. 'I can't believe you thought *that*. It's disgusting!'

'I wouldn't call him "disgusting", he's quite a good-looking guy.'

'He's my brother!'

Another deep breath from one of the medical professions finest, when what she'd revealed sunk in.

'My apologies.' He managed to look sheepish and haughty at the same time. 'That would explain why all three of you have the same surname.'

It most certainly would. 'Do all doctors jump to the wrong conclusions, or only you?'

'You *did* list him as your next-of-kin.'

'You should have checked.'

'You're right, I should have. I can only apologise, it was coming to the end of a very long shift and—' He stopped. 'I'm sorry,' he said again.

Daisy thrust the empty cup back at him. 'If you don't mind, I'd like to get back to my sister-in-law.' She emphasised the last word. 'I expect she's wondering where I am.'

'Of course, can I say again how sorry I am, it was an honest mistake.'

'It was a stupid mistake,' Daisy countered. She couldn't believe it. The insufferable man! She was prepared to forgive him for thinking her and David were husband and wife when they'd rocked up on Christmas Day, but to then think she was David's mistress and that he had gotten both her and Zoe pregnant at the same time... He was like something out of one of the soap operas her mum loved.

'Bet you watch Eastenders,' she muttered, pushing past him. 'Or Jeremy Kyle.'

As she marched off down the corridor, Daisy was furious, both with him and what he'd made her think. Clearly she wasn't pregnant. It had all been a figment of Dr Jekyll's fevered imagination. Wasn't it?

Hurried footsteps sounded from behind her, and the doctor grabbed hold of her arm. 'I don't blame you for being angry,' he said. 'I would be too. But can I give you a word of advice?'

She stopped and glared at him. He removed his hand, but the heat of his fingers through her blouse lingered on her skin. She crossed her arms. 'What?'

'Take a pregnancy test,' he said. 'Sooner, rather than later.'

'Why?'

'Because you didn't seem too surprised when you thought you *were* pregnant,' he said.

And deep down, she hadn't been, had she…

Chapter 16

Call it karma, call it fate, or you could say the gods were bored and wanted a small diversion, but someone once told Daisy not to tempt fate (more than one person, more than once actually, and it was a phrase she'd used herself, so she should have known better) but both of the times she'd been to the hospital in the past few days, she had thanked her lucky stars that she hadn't had an accident getting there.

David wasn't so lucky.

He'd become caught up in a five-car pile-up on the motorway south of Worcester, a couple of hours after Daisy phoned him, and it was Dr Hartley (of all people), who came to tell her.

'Can I have a word?' he asked Daisy, sticking his head through the curtain.

Zoe had yet to be moved to a ward (a lack of beds apparently, and Daisy had heard the nurses saying there'd been a couple of emergency admissions), and Daisy was trying her best to console the grieving girl. Unsuccessfully, she might add, so she was grateful for the diversion, even if it was the doctor from hell who was providing it. At least she had finally managed to contact her mum, who was on her way, and Daisy looked forward to handing over the bedside-sitting duty to Sandra.

'I'll only be a sec. Probably more paperwork,' Daisy said, while Zoe nodded blankly, too immersed in her sorrow to pay much attention to what was happening around her.

'Well?' Daisy demanded. 'Come to accuse me of sleeping with anyone else?'

He didn't rise to the bait, but instead led her down the corridor until they stood in the exact same spot as before.

'It's about your brother,' he began, and his expression was one of pity.

It chilled Daisy to the bone.

'He's been involved in an accident on the motorway—' the doctor said.

'Is he dead?' Daisy shrieked.

'Hush, no, he's sustained a nasty injury to his leg, hopefully nothing that an operation, a pin, and several months of physio won't fix. He's also sustained some minor cuts and bruises.'

'An operation?' she demanded.

'He's broken his leg in three different places. It will require an operation to insert a pin into the bone, but the prognosis is good.'

'Is he here?' Daisy looked around her as if she expected to see her brother limping down the corridor.

Dr Hartley nodded. 'He was brought in a half an hour ago by ambulance. He's being prepped for theatre as we speak. I did the initial examination,' he added.

Yeah, based on previous experience, Daisy didn't hold out much hope that the doctor would recognise a broken leg if it jumped up and bit him.

'Can I see him?' she asked.

'That's why I came to get you. He's worried about his wife and he wants to see her.'

Zoe! What was Daisy going to say to her?

As if the doctor had read her mind, he continued, 'I don't think it's a good idea to tell Zoe until he's out of theatre and we know exactly what we're facing.'

'I've got to tell her *something*. She's expecting him to arrive any minute.'

Dr Hartley thought for a moment. 'Tell her the traffic is abysmal?'

Right, that was really going to work. 'She'll want to speak to him. I've been trying to ring him for the past half hour.'

No wonder he hadn't answered. David had been busy having his leg smashed to smithereens. It never rains but it pours, Daisy thought, recalling another of Gee-Gee's sayings.

'Bad signal, battery dead…' the doctor said. 'I'm sure you'll think of something.'

'She'll have to know eventually,' Daisy pointed out.

The doctor gave her an odd look. 'Of course she will. I'm not advocating keeping it from her forever, just for the next few hours, until he's out of surgery.'

Daisy had a go at reading between the lines. 'Do you think it might not go well?'

'All operations carry a risk.'

'Don't tell me that,' she pleaded, wishing she hadn't asked.

He patted her on the shoulder. 'Your brother had a narrow escape, others involved in the accident weren't so lucky. David is alive, and the outcome looks good, but I wouldn't be doing my job properly if I didn't point out the potential risks.'

'I want to see him.'

David looked awful. She hadn't known what to expect, but seeing her once-healthy, robust brother lying on a trolley, his face pinched and grey with pain, one eye black, dried blood around his nose, and looking older than his twenty-seven years, made her want to weep.

But she held it together because she had to. He needed her to be strong, for him and for Zoe, at least until her mum and nan arrived to share the burden.

The sheer terror in his eyes squeezed her heart.

'Zoe is okay,' she said. 'Sad, but okay, and the baby is fine.'

'The one we lost isn't,' her brother replied, shortly, and Daisy heard the anguish in his voice.

'No, it isn't,' she said quietly. 'I'm so sorry.'

'So am I.'

Nothing Daisy could think of to say was going to make even the tiniest dent in her brother's grief, so she said nothing else, leaning forward to kiss his forehead instead.

'Time to go, David,' a cheery nurse said, bustling around the bed. 'We're going to take you to theatre, my lovely, okay?' She checked a chart on the end of the bed, and glanced at Dr Hartley for confirmation.

'Take him up,' the doctor said, then spoke to David. 'You're in good hands with Mr Smythe, he's an excellent surgeon.'

'I want to see Zoe.' David struggled to raise his torso off the bed, but fell back in pain. 'I want to see my wife.'

Dr Hartley stepped closer and leaned over the other man. 'We haven't told your wife about your accident,' he explained. 'I don't want to upset her any more than she already is. I'll bring her to see you personally, once you're out of theatre,' he promised.

Daisy gave her brother one last peck and let the orderly take him. 'Please keep him safe,' she murmured.

'We will,' Dr Hartley said.

She hadn't been talking to anyone in particular, she had been speaking to karma (who wasn't being particularly kind at the moment), but she let it go, saying instead, 'That damned sixpence has brought nothing but trouble.'

'Excuse me?'

'It was supposed to be lucky. Yeah, *bad* luck.' She ignored the fact that the run of bad luck had started before she'd even put the coin in the pudding. It had started when she came home to find her boyfriend shagging another man.

But whatever the luck, why was the sixpence targeting her family? Surely the bad luck should stay remain with her, and not migrate to everyone she cared about? Was it haunted?

This was day four of Sixpencegate, and she fervently prayed things wouldn't get any worse.

Chapter 17

Daisy offered to go to her brother's house to fetch the essentials needed for a couple of nights in hospital, and wished she knew her sister-in-law better, as she stared around the bedroom. She felt like a burglar, or an unwanted guest, having been upstairs in this house only once before, and that was when David and Zoe had shown her, Mum, and Nan around when they'd purchased it. The couple had been given the keys the day before, so the place had been empty and rather soulless. Now it was so obviously Zoe's domain that Daisy felt uncomfortable being here on her own.

Quickly, she gathered what she thought the patients might need, stuffing the items into two separate bags, while trying not to think of the couple's misfortune and grief. All the while, she couldn't help but wonder about her own situation. Was she, or was she not, pregnant?

Giving in to impulse, she darted into the spotless en-suite and opened the cabinet above the sink. It was unlikely but you never know… ah. Found one! Not one, but several pregnancy testing kits sat neatly on the top shelf, and underneath was a whole pile of ovulation kits. She realised Zoe and David must have been trying to get pregnant for some considerable time. Daisy imagined each barren month must have brought its own share of misery, when Zoe realised she hadn't caught. Zoe had been going through her own version of hell, and probably David had too, if his joy on Christmas Day, when he finally shared their good news, had been any indication.

She picked up one of the little boxes and held it, imagining Zoe's impatience and desperation, her sister-in-law not wanting to wait until her period arrived, but wanting to know as soon as possible after ovulating whether she was, in fact, pregnant. She also imagined Zoe's despair when no little blue line appeared next to the test one, and Daisy thought back to her own relief when the exact same line had failed to develop that time when she'd thought she might be pregnant several years ago. She also thought she'd been doubly careful since that scare, but had she?

She thought about her own lack of trying, and how she could be pregnant without even knowing, as shame stole over her. Zoe and David had tried for what might have been some time, and now they'd lost one of their precious babies.

Daisy's tears finally came, and she perched on the edge of the bath crying for the nephew or niece she'd never get to know, for her brother and sister-in-law's pain, and for David's near miss with death.

She only regained control when she reached for yet another handful of loo-paper and spotted the test kit still clutched in her damp hand. She knew what she had to do.

Her fate was going to be decided by a little stick of plastic and the magic it contained. It seemed like this week was one for discovering secrets in toilets. She knew how she felt about Melissa's nasty little secret (Daisy made a mental note to go back to reading the contract when she had five minutes), but she had no idea how she felt about the little human who may, or may not, be growing inside her.

For a brief moment, she didn't want to know. If she ignored it, she could pretend everything was the same as it had been this morning, when she was getting ready for work, in happy ignorance about what the day held in store for her. If she didn't do the test and she *was* expecting a baby, then she could apply for jobs with impunity, able to say that she honestly hadn't known she was pregnant once she started a new position.

Tempted though she might be, she understood how unethical it was. Anyway, if she was indeed pregnant, she had a responsibility to the baby, and needed to make an appointment to see her GP in the next few days. Soon, Daisy could be listening to her own child's heartbeat, and the thought filled her with an odd mixture of excitement and trepidation. More trepidation than excitement, if she was honest.

Though she'd used a pregnancy test before, it was a long time ago and each brand may be different, so she peeled off the cellophane and read the instructions carefully.

Pee on stick. Wait two minutes. One blue line = not pregnant. Two blue lines = oh shit!

Her stomach felt distended and bloated, and when she put the leaflet down and pressed against her flesh with slightly trembling fingers, it felt firmer than usual. She stopped pressing, terrified of harming anything which might be in there.

She read the instructions again, just to make sure, then she dropped her knickers, took her future in her hands, and peed on the stick.

It was the longest two minutes of her life. For the first ten seconds she gazed fixedly at the two little windows. For the next ten she gazed out of the real window, counting in her head. The sky was a dull December gunmetal grey, heavy with the promise of more rain to come. The sky is pregnant, she thought slightly hysterically. Zoe pregnant, sky pregnant, me pregnant. Or am I?

She risked a quick look. One line, the test line, had emerged, faint but clearly there. She scrutinised the other window for several long seconds.

Nothing.

She looked away again this time catching her reflection in the mirror above the sink. The woman staring back at her was a frightened stranger.

She looked at the test again.

Still no second line.

How long had it been? She'd forgotten to keep counting and she hadn't thought to time it, using her watch.

She started over: one, two, three...

Seventy-five.

One hundred and thirty-six.

Five hundred and ten.

Still no second line.

Daisy Jones wasn't pregnant.

A wave of relief, then sadness, followed by relief again, swept over her.

She didn't know whether to fist pump the air and do a happy dance, or whether to curl up in a ball and cry.

She did neither. Wrapping the evidence in one of those bags for used sanitary towels, Daisy went downstairs and stuffed it in the kitchen bin, taking care to shove it down deep. Then she picked up David's and Zoe's overnight things, and returned to the hospital.

All the while, the only thought in her head was "not pregnant, not pregnant, not pregnant".

Chapter 18

Zoe wasn't a good patient. Neither was David, but at least he was still in hospital, though his consultant was making "discharge soon" noises. If Daisy thought she had her work cut out now, it was going to be twice as bad when David came home. Daisy, being out of work and considered by her mother to be at a loose end, was the nominated carer, a task she wasn't particularly relishing. And today was only day one. In fact, Zoe had been home from the hospital for less than two hours, and Daisy had already caught her trying to make up the bed in one of their spare rooms.

Daisy had sent her back downstairs with a flea in her ear, and strict instructions to sit on the sofa until Daisy had finished putting fresh sheets on the bed in which she was to sleep for the next week or so.

After that, they'd see, wouldn't they? It all depended on Zoe's GP. At present, the younger woman had been told to take it easy and rest, but when Daisy carried an armful of bedlinen into the kitchen, she caught Zoe chopping vegetables.

'What did I tell you?' Daisy demanded, whipping the carrot away and nearly getting her finger sliced off as she did so.

'I can't just sit there,' Zoe protested. 'I'm going to go mad.'

'I don't care if you go doolally, you're going to put your feet up. Or do I have to call David?'

'No,' Zoe replied hastily, 'don't do that. I'll be good, I promise.'

'I'm not doing this to be mean,' Daisy pointed out. 'I'm doing it because I care.'

The other woman's eyes filled with unshed tears. 'You're so good to me,' she said.

And Daisy felt like a heel. She had never been good to her sister-in-law in her life. All she had done was make fun of her (silently – she'd not shared her thoughts with anyone) and mostly ignored her, and because Zoe was so unassuming and quiet, she often faded into the background like an unused armchair.

Now that Daisy was getting to know Zoe a little better, she couldn't understand why she had thought the other woman so dull. Yes, she was reserved, but then who wouldn't be when faced with an overpowering Elsie and a very capable and loud Sandra. Gee-Gee, not to be outdone, could be a force to be reckoned with, too.

Again and again, the phone rang, with people wondering how Zoe was, asking if she was okay and offering their help. Daisy was impressed with the sheer volume of friends her sister-in-law had.

Daisy could count hers on the finger of one hand, and her friends had been suspiciously silent since she and Freddie had split up. Daisy hoped it was because they simply didn't know what to say to her, and not because they were laughing behind her back. It was also an odd time, in between Christmas and New Year, when family commitments come first, so she gave them the benefit of the doubt. Then there was the other issue, that many of her friends had been Freddie's friends too, and maybe they didn't want to appear to take sides.

'What are you making?' Daisy asked, gently prising the knife from Zoe's reluctant fingers.

'I thought I'd do chicken in a mushroom and parmesan sauce.'

'I can do that,' Daisy said firmly. 'Sit down and let me put this load of washing in the machine, then you can supervise.' Daisy would definitely need supervising – she had absolutely no idea where to start.

Zoe obediently sat, watching Daisy work and Daisy was conscious of her sister-in-law studying her every move.

'David might be home tomorrow,' Daisy said, trying to make conversation.

'I hope so. Will you take me to visit him later?'

Daisy saw an opportunity and jumped at it. 'I will, if you have a lie down after lunch.'

Zoe thought, then nodded. 'But only if you let me phone work first.'

'Don't blackmail me, lady,' Daisy warned, with a smile.

'You started it.'

'I did, didn't I.'

Zoe, Daisy discovered as they talked, worked in a solicitor's office as a paralegal, and Daisy could imagine her sitting at a desk, her blond hair in a bun and glasses perched on her nose.

It surprised her, having never before been able to imagine Zoe doing anything other than hanging off David's arm and giggling. Anyway, she'd never seen Zoe with her hair up, and the other girl didn't actually wear glasses.

'Do you enjoy your job?' Daisy asked suddenly, surprised that she really did want to get to know David's wife better.

'Yes, I do. It's hard work, but interesting. And I'm good at it,' Zoe declared, almost defiantly, and Daisy had the sinking feeling Zoe might have guessed that Daisy thought of her as a bit of a bimbo.

'What qualifications do you need?' she asked. She hadn't had much time to think about her jobless position since she'd been unceremoniously sacked, but as soon as the world had moved past the madness of New Year's Eve and returned to normal, she intended to start looking in earnest. The problem was that writing verses for cards wasn't exactly a skill which was in great demand in the Midlands, and that was all she had ever done.

'I've got a law degree,' Zoe said, to Daisy's immense surprise.

'Have you? Didn't you want to become a lawyer?'

'No thanks. I'm happy doing what I do. The hours are good and so is the pay, and when David and I got married we talked about having a family, with me staying at home to look after the children.' Her face clouded when she said children, and Daisy hastily changed the subject.

Sort of. She brought it around to her problems – not for any selfish reason, but to take Zoe's mind off her own. 'I've been given the sack,' she announced.

Zoe looked shocked. 'Poor you! Let me give you a hug.'

The other woman was a hugger, and Daisy had often seen her hug Sandra and the other two Macbeth witches, who comprised the rest of the women in Daisy's family. It was only Daisy who had never been on the receiving end of one of them, and Daisy realised she only had herself to blame. Zoe must have accurately read Daisy's body language and kept her distance.

Zoe stood up and Daisy put the knife down and walked into her sister-in-law's embrace. It was surprisingly comforting. They patted backs for a while, then Daisy pulled away, embarrassed.

'When?' Zoe asked.

'The morning you went into hospital.'

'It wasn't a good day for you, was it?' Zoe said quietly.

'It wasn't a good day for you, either, but at least David is on the mend now, and you've got your little one to think of.'

Zoe's tears were close to the surface and Daisy could have kicked herself. She wasn't doing too good a job of preventing her sister-in-law from becoming stressed, was she?

'I know,' Zoe said, 'and I'm so grateful. I'm a lucky lady.'

Daisy seriously doubted the luck aspect, unless it was *bad* luck. And there was still no sign of that dratted coin. She ought to eat more roughage – that should get things moving.

'Got any prunes?' she asked.

Zoe blinked at her, bewildered. 'I don't think so. It's not something we ever buy. Is this for your sixpence problem?'

Something in Zoe's voice made Daisy smile. The other woman was laughing at her, but not in a nasty way, in a sympathetic way. If only she knew the trouble the blasted little coin had caused.

'I'll get some next time I go out,' Daisy said. 'In the meantime, I want you to go lie down while I finish preparing dinner.'

Zoe walked slowly out of the kitchen, but before she disappeared into the hall she said, 'Feel free to use the laptop.'

'Eh?'

'Job hunting. I'm sure you'll find something. A lady with your talents is bound to get snapped up.'

Daisy gave her a rueful smile. 'My talents consist of thinking up silly rhymes to sing to the tune of *Deck the Halls*,' she said.

'Are you joking?' Intrigued, Zoe came back into the kitchen and sat down again.

'Nope. The last thing they asked me to do before they sacked me, was to look into musical cards, and since it was Christmas and carols were playing everywhere, I couldn't get the damned tune out of my head.'

'What did you come up with?'

Daisy started to hum, running the words through her mind. 'Here's one,' she said and started to sing…

> *'Deck the halls with boughs of holly,*
> *Fa-la-la-la-la, la-la-la-laa*
> *Don't forget you'll need a brolly*
> *Fa-la-la-la-la, la-la-la-laa*
> *Cause all the weather does is rain*
> *Fa-la-la-la-la, la-la-la-laa*
> *Time to move abroad to Spain*
> *Fa-la-la-la-la, la-la-la-laah'*

'Did you just make that up?' Zoe asked.

'Yep. Pathetic, isn't it?'

'I think it's quite good.'

Bless her, Zoe really was a sweetie. Daisy finally understood what her brother saw in her.

'It's awful,' Daisy said. 'Not exactly what *Caring Cards*
were looking for.'

'Is that why they sacked you?'

'I didn't get a chance to share it with them. No, they
sacked me because of the rise of ecards, I think, not that
they actually said so.' Daisy blushed. 'They caught me job
hunting on company time.'

'That's not usually a sackable offence in the first
instance, unless you've been disciplined before?'

Daisy shook her head. 'Nothing official. I've had the
odd pointed look from my manager for being late, but no
one has ever said anything. But just before that, and the
reason why I was looking at a job site in the first place,
was because Simon pulled me into his office to tell me
that they were thinking of making me redundant.'

'Did he actually say that, were those the words he
used?'

Daisy looked at her sister-in-law closely. Something
had changed. Zoe wasn't Zoe anymore. Okay the thought
was silly; of course Zoe was still Zoe – she hadn't been
taken over by aliens or anything – but she seemed less
Zoe-like, or rather, less like the Zoe Daisy thought she
was.

'Yes,' Daisy said. 'Simon said I was going to be made
redundant, and that a date hadn't been set yet. He said he
was giving me a "heads up", and I actually thought, stupid
me, that he was being kind, giving me a chance to look

for another job. Then I realised the company was hoping I'd leave before they had to officially make me redundant, so saving them having to pay me any redundancy.'

'What happened then?'

'I went back to my desk, decided I wasn't going anywhere until they gave me my redundancy payment, then I did a quick hunt on the internet, just to see what was out there.'

Zoe leaned forward, resting her elbows on the table. 'Could your line manager have reasonably expected you to do that? Look on the internet, I mean.'

'I don't know. Why?'

'Does *Caring Cards* have an internet policy?'

'No idea. But there was something about using it for personal reasons in the contract I signed when I first started.'

'Have you got a copy of it?'

'Yes, that's what I was reading when you phoned.'

'Can I see it?'

'I suppose so. Why?'

'I may be shooting in the dark here, and it may come to nothing, but I think you have a case.'

'For what?'

'Unfair dismissal.'

Was there such a thing? Daisy had never heard of it, but then she had never been sacked, either.

'Let me look into it,' Zoe said.

'You're supposed to be resting.'

'I can read and rest at the same time, and it will give me something to do. I'll go insane if I have to sit here twiddling my thumbs. Besides, I want to repay you for everything you've done.'

Heel time again, except now Daisy felt even worse. After all, she had done nothing to help and might even be responsible for Zoe's miscarriage, stupid though it sounded. Remind me never to say it out loud, Daisy told herself.

A thought occurred to her. 'What sort of law does your company practice?' she asked.

'Employment law.'

Chapter 19

Daisy put the chicken in the oven and logged onto the computer, after Zoe had been persuaded to go upstairs. Daisy fervently hoped her sister-in-law was doing as she was told and wasn't reorganising her underwear drawer, or something. The two women had agreed that they would swing by Sandra's on the way to visit David in hospital so Daisy could pick up the contract.

She didn't expect to see many jobs (wrong season for job hunting) but she had to start somewhere. At least she'd be able to finish the search she had started on her last day at *Caring Cards*.

There were plenty of jobs for carers (no thanks, she'd been grossed out enough this Christmas already, what with scrabbling about in her own poo, and wiping her great-gran's bottom), lots of bar work (she'd do it at a push, but it meant standing on your feet for hours on end and dealing with drunks, and she wasn't sure if she was cut out for that).

One by one she scrolled down the list: waiting staff (ditto the on your feet for hours on end bit, but with rude customers instead of drunken ones), taxi driver (she could get lost going from her house into the city if she wasn't careful), receptionist (she could do that, maybe), nurse (no qualifications), social worker (she had enough problems of her own without trying to solve other people's), forklift truck driver... and so on.

Out of the two hundred or so jobs on the website, there was absolutely nothing she thought she could do, or stood a chance of even being considered for.

The whole experience was a sobering one. She was officially unemployed and seemingly unemployable. She might have to wait on tables, or serve behind a bar after all, and whilst there was nothing wrong with any of these jobs, she really didn't think she had the temperament for them. For one, she wasn't at all gregarious, and she didn't particularly like meeting with, and talking to people, and for another, she worked better when she was left to her own devices, with the minimum amount of supervision. She hated having anyone breathing over her shoulder, and at least Simon used to let her get on with it, as long as she churned out the verses. On a good day (and she was proud to say, she had more good ones than bad) she could produce upwards of twenty verses. Not all were chosen and many required redrafting after Simon had scrutinised them, but Daisy was still prolific and she was *good* at it. He was stupid to let her go in favour of Melissa. Then, Daisy hadn't been screwing the MD, had she?

She made a face at the thought. Aaron Dearborn, from what she'd seen of him, had struck her as a bit of a wise guy, a shark, a would-you-buy-a-used-car-from-this-man type of bloke. He was too smarmy, and too sure of himself, for Daisy's liking, but he must have something about him to have gotten so far up the corporate totem pole. For the life of her, she couldn't think what. Neither could she see what Melissa saw in him, apart from the high-paying job, the company car (a Jag), the handmade suits, and the suave arrogance.

There was also the issue of his wife.

Was Melissa aware he had one, and if so, did she care? Daisy suspected not, though she did know that her former colleague would need to tread carefully; he'd already gotten rid of one employee by nefarious means (Daisy) so what was to keep him from getting rid of Melissa when he tired of her, or the risk became too great? Oh yeah, a little fact that Melissa was bonking him and could tell his wife. That might stop him, alright.

Concentrate Daisy, you've got a CV to write.

Having no inkling where to start, she downloaded a typical template, and stared at it. She could do the name, address, and phone number bit, and even her current (past) employer. She could fill in her school details and qualifications, but it was the rest of it which had her stumped. Significant achievements? What significant achievements? Hobbies? Okay, she could fill that bit in too, but she didn't think watching TV and going out for meals was particularly riveting to a prospective employer.

Daisy Jones, on paper, sounded as boring as Daisy Jones in the flesh.

What if she put "studying for…"? But for what? A degree? A BTEC in administration? That sounded good, but they would most certainly want proof, and even if they didn't, they'd probably ask her about it, and bluffing wouldn't be an option.

She typed "enjoys fine dining" instead, then added, "training for a marathon", before having second thoughts and deleting it. Training to win a gold in couch potato would be more accurate. "Carer to my brother and his wife"? Er, no. It made her sound as though she had ongoing responsibilities which might affect her commitment to a job.

"Volunteering at an old people's home"? That might work. She often called in to see the other residents, to have a quick chat when she visited Gee-Gee. Unfortunately, she rarely visited her great-grandmother, relying on old lady being at Sandra's every Sunday, though over the past year or so Daisy had usually only managed to pop in for the occasional lunch.

However, it looked good on paper, or at least, better than "can list all the plot lines in *A Game of Thrones*". The main reason for her watching the series was because she had a bit of a fan crush on Jon Snow – but then, who didn't? Freddie had often said how good-looking the character was, in a moody kind of way. Freddie's interest made more sense now.

She fudged her way through the rest of the document, though by the time she'd finished it the CV looked more like a work of fiction than a factual document. She'd amended her role at *Caring Cards* slightly to incorporate more administration and secretarial duties, confident she could wing it if she had to. After all, how hard could it be to type up a letter, or organise a meeting?

She returned to her job hunt feeling a teensy bit more confident.

Ah, here was one.

"Office Junior sought for builders' merchants. Duties include filing, answering customer queries, sending out invoices", blah blah blah. The "make the tea" part was hidden three paragraphs down, and that was the one thing she was certain she could do well. She'd even provide cakes if it meant she got the job. But the golden words were, "no experience necessary". The salary wasn't fantastic, a measly one pound over the minimum wage, but it would serve to give her the experience she so desperately needed.

She drafted a quick covering letter to her email, attached her CV and pressed "send", and wondered how many more jobs she would have to apply for before she finally landed one – she suspected it might be a few.

By the end of the session, Daisy had applied for a PA to the managing director (not a hope in hell), librarian (she still wasn't sure what a CILIP qualification was, or whether a GCSE in English literature was a reasonable substitute – anyway, how complicated could putting books on shelves be?) plus loads more.

The reasoning behind Daisy's throw-a-CV-at-it-and-hope-it-sticks, scatter-gun approach, was that someone, somewhere, would spot her potential.

Sighing in exasperation, she closed the computer down, and went to check on the chicken. Even if she did say so herself, it looked and smelled delicious. Maybe she could be a chef?

She was in the middle of steaming some fresh vegetables (Zoe had things in her salad drawer that Daisy wouldn't recognise even if they introduced themselves), when Zoe made an appearance.

'I've been thinking,' her sister-in-law said.

'While you were asleep? Good trick,' Daisy said.

Zoe had the grace to look sheepish. 'I haven't been sleeping, but I have been resting on the bed,' she added, before Daisy could tell her off.

'Thinking?' Daisy asked. 'Do I want to know what about? Is it about my being sacked, because you're not supposed to be doing any kind of work, and you said you wanted to wait until you'd read my contract.'

'No, not that. I've been thinking about what you can do.'

'About what?'

'A job, silly.'

'Go on then, what can I do, because I've been on the internet and every job out there either asks for some kind of qualification no one's ever heard of, or experience which I haven't got.'

'Then work for yourself,' Zoe said, calmly.

'Doing what?'

'What are you good at?'

'Nothing.'

'Yes, you are. Think about it.'

Daisy thought. She still came up with nothing, so she shrugged.

'Verses, cards,' Zoe prompted.

'Been there, done that, designed the bloody tee shirt.'

'But that was working for someone else,' Zoe pointed out.

'You mean, freelance?'

'That's exactly what I mean.'

'There isn't the market for it,' Daisy replied, without hesitation. 'The big boys have got it all wrapped up.'

'They haven't though, have they? I'm thinking about personalised verses, where your customer gives you snippets of information about who they want the card for, and you write a verse suitable for them.'

Daisy pondered the idea. 'It could work,' she admitted, 'but I can't simply send a verse without a card.'

'You can if it's done online,' Zoe countered. Her sister-in-law had clearly been giving this a lot of thought, and Daisy was grateful to her for taking the time, but Daisy simply didn't see how it would work.

However, Zoe did. 'If it's images you're worried about, there are loads of companies on the net which provide royalty-free images for subscription, companies like *Dreamstime*, *Shutterstock*, and *Getty*. You can pick a suitable image to reflect the occasion and the person who is receiving the card.'

Zoe looked so hopeful that Daisy didn't have the heart to disillusion her. 'It'll take a lot of organising,' she said instead, hoping the answer sounded keen enough, but not too keen. It was a lovely idea, but it simply wasn't possible. She wouldn't have the faintest clue where to start.

Zoe had that covered too. 'My nephew is great at website design. He could set you up, and I could help you with the logistics until the business was up and running,' she said. 'Research and organisation are my thing.'

Daisy didn't doubt it for one second, but she did doubt everything else, including her own ability to make it happen. She wasn't a businesswoman, she was a worker bee, and she liked the security of a job with a wage at the end of every month.

'What have you got to lose?' Zoe persisted.

'My savings, my sanity?' She was sure she could find many more objections if she put her mind to it.

'Look, I'm not saying you should give up a well-paid job to do this, but you've not got a job to give up at the moment, have you?'

Thanks for reminding me, Zoe, she thought.

'You could try it until you found something else, give it a go,' Zoe persisted. 'And you won't lose your savings because the costs would be minimal to start off with.'

What did Zoe consider minimal, because Daisy was pretty sure Zoe's minimal and Daisy's wouldn't be the same thing at all.

'Website hosting is, I don't know, maybe ten pounds a month, plus a bit more for a subscription to one of the image sites,' Zoe said.

Her sister-in-law was stubborn, wasn't she? But those costs sounded good. Hmm.

'Have a look tomorrow,' Zoe said. 'I've written the web addresses down for you. You can always work on verses until your own site is up and running, and even if it went nowhere, the worst you'd be doing is keeping your hand in.'

Daisy still wasn't convinced. She'd be better off spending her time job hunting. Then there was looking after David and Zoe – that wasn't going to happen by magic. David would be semi-mobile at best. The worst-case scenario could involve someone having to bath him, and she was damn sure it wasn't going to be her. Zoe had to take it easy, so that particular job was going to fall to their mother, by default. Sandra had seen his bits and pieces enough times, so a couple more wouldn't matter. But there was still the task of helping him move around the house, and someone had to do the cooking, the laundry, the cleaning, and the other hundreds of domestic household chores, and that was without taking him to his physio appointments. Daisy anticipated being very busy indeed.

What she hadn't had anticipated was her sister-in-law's dogged determination, and a refusal to take no for an answer.

Chapter 20

Outrageous plans or not, everything went on the back burner the following day (New Year's Eve) because David was finally discharged. The hospital had lent him, in no particular order, a wheelchair, a Zimmer frame, a pair of crutches, and had also arranged to have one of the beds from upstairs moved into the dining room, and the table relegated to the garage by two burly men, because David wasn't yet able to negotiate the stairs.

And if that wasn't enough, Daisy was expected to share the spare bed with her mother tonight because Daisy had arranged to go to a party with Sara, which she had forgotten about in all the excitement over the past few days. Sandra had insisted on staying over for the night to babysit David, who, she maintained, needed a good wash. David, in pain and very irritable, wasn't best pleased to be called a baby, or to be told he could do with a bath.

'You're being a baby now,' Sandra insisted. 'I've seen it all before, you know.'

'I don't want a bath.' David glared at his mother.

'That's just as well, because you can't climb the stairs. What you need is a proper bed wash. I bet those nurses didn't give you one.'

'I'll give *you* one in a minute,' David muttered under his breath.

Daisy, sitting beside him on the sofa, giggled. Her brother bared his perfect teeth at her.

'I've borrowed one of Mrs Danson's chairs as well,' Sandra said.

'Mum,' David sighed. 'We've got plenty of chairs, four in the kitchen, six in the dining room, two in here and a three-bloody-seater sofa. Will you just stop fussing!'

'But this one is electric. You sit in it and press a button and it lifts you back out. You can't expect our Daisy to manage you. She's got fewer muscles than a slug, and Zoe isn't allowed to lift anything.'

'Oi!' Daisy cried. 'I'm planning on going to the gym, I'll have you know.'

'Why bother? You're allergic to exercise,' her mother replied. 'It brings you out in a rash,' she added, giving Daisy a hard stare. 'Look what happened the last time you went for a jog; you had a red rash all over your backside.'

'It was a heat rash.'

'If you say so,' Sandra retorted. 'Now, David, about that wash.'

Daisy fled, but not before she heard David yell, 'You can stick that flannel where the sun doesn't shine,' and their mother's determined reply of, 'I intend to, son. It could most likely do with a good scrub.' Zoe's soft laughter followed her up the stairs.

Daisy was still chuckling to herself when she did a final check in the mirror: sparkly black dress? Tick. Strappy, impossibly high heels? Tick. Flashy gold necklace and bracelet to match? Yep. Lipstick on, hair done, and false eyelashes in place. All she needed was a quick squirt of her favourite perfume, grab her black, beaded clutch, and she was ready to go.

Her mood had lifted considerably since her useless internet search. She knew it was all down to the prospect of a good night out, a new year ahead (out with the old, and in with the new) and that maybe babysitting her younger brother would be more entertaining than she'd first thought. At least staying at David's house got her out from under her mother's nose, except for tonight.

'I'm not driving at that time of night, and I'm not paying for a taxi either,' Sandra had stated. 'Those New Year's Eve rates are daylight robbery. I'll get into bed with you, Daisy.'

'I can drive you back home, I don't mind,' Daisy had offered, but her mother was having none of it.

'You'll be as pissed as a fart, if I know you, Daisy Jones. You won't be in any condition to be driving anyone anywhere, except me up the wall.'

Daisy certainly hoped she *was* drunk, so she could ignore the fact that her mother was going to be sleeping inches away from her, because her mother snored. Daisy could hear it through two walls and across the landing. Goodness knows what it would sound like from less than a foot away.

She'd arranged to meet Sara in a bar in town, and she asked the taxi driver to drop her at the top end of Friar Street, an ancient cobbled street with buildings going back to medieval times, which had a lively atmosphere with many trendy pubs and restaurants. They'd arranged to meet in a pub called *The Cardinal's Hat*, and it was packed with revellers dressed in their finery, and already well on their way to being three sheets to the wind, despite it being only eight o'clock. It was going to be a long night indeed, for some people.

She fought her way to the bar and ordered two white wines.

'Making up for lost time?' a voice asked in her ear.

'Pardon?'

The man at her elbow wore a suit, no tie, shirt undone to the second button, and his dark hair was gelled back. Designer stubble coated his cheeks and chin, and his skin looked suspiciously bronze for the time of year.

'Been anywhere nice?' she asked.

'Eh?'

'The tan.'

'The new salon up the road. I was going to offer you a drink, but I see you've got everything in hand.'

'They're not both for me,' she said, taking a swift swig of hers, and thinking that if Sara didn't put in an appearance in the next five minutes, they very well might be. After the week she'd had, she needed a couple of stiff ones.

'Where's your friend?'

'Not here yet.' Daisy checked her phone. No messages. She checked her watch: ten past eight. Plenty of time. Sara was renowned for being fashionably late. Daisy would give her another twenty minutes before sending a "where are you?" distress call to her friend.

'I'll keep you company until she arrives, if it is a "she",' the stranger offered.

'It is a she,' Daisy confirmed, 'and she's late.'

'Typical woman.'

'*I* was on time.'

'You're obviously not typical. You certainly don't look typical to me. In fact, you look like a very special lady indeed.'

Smarmy, but she'd take it all the same. It was an awfully long time since anyone had chatted her up, and she was in the mood for some male attention, even though she wasn't looking to take it any further. After the dent Freddie had put in her confidence, she was happy for this strange man to have a go at bashing it back out.

'Married? Boyfriend?' he asked.

'Blimey, you don't hang about, do you?' she said.

The man was just under six-foot-tall (she took an educated guess) and she had to tilt her head back to look at him. She liked what she saw, even if he was a bit too smooth and cocky. He was good-looking enough to carry it off.

'You can't blame a man for wanting to know where he stands,' he said. 'I'm not aiming to tread on anyone's toes.'

A man with morals? Refreshing.

'No husband, no boyfriend,' she said.

'Bloody hell, Daisy. Leave you alone for five minutes and you've already bagged yourself a fella.' Sara appeared at her side in a flurry of fuzzy brown hair and Gucci Rush.

The two women hugged and kissed cheeks.

'Uh… I'm sorry, I don't know your name,' Daisy said to the stranger.

'Art. And you're Daisy.' He held out a hand Daisy took it and they shook. 'Nice to meet you,' he said.

'Nice to meet you, too,' Daisy replied, then turned back to Sara. 'Art was keeping me company until you decided to show up.'

'The bus was late,' Sara said, and Daisy rolled her eyes. Sara had probably been the type of school pupil who used the line "my dog ate my homework" – she always had some excuse for her tardiness. It was part of her charm.

'I can carry on keeping you company if you like,' Art said.

'Er…'

As tempting as the offer was, three was most definitely a crowd. He let out a whistle, designed to be heard above the loud music, shouty voices, and raucous laughter.

'Meet Ted,' he said, as a man pushed through the crowd and joined them.

'I don't mind if I do,' Sara breathed in Daisy's ear. 'This one's mine, you've got your own.'

Far from being polished and smooth like Art, Ted was an uncut diamond, with long hair and loads of tattoos. He looked as though he should be in a pair of shorts and a t-shirt with a surfboard under his arm. Just Sara's type.

'I prefer the other one anyway,' Daisy muttered out of the corner of her mouth as the introductions were made.

'Sorted!' Sara clapped her hands together.

'Is it? What about Andrew?'

'I can pretend, can't I?' Sara protested. 'I don't have to touch.'

'You'd better not. Andrew would be devastated.'

'I've no intention of breaking his lovely little heart,' Sara retorted, 'but you've got to admit, Ted is one damn fine piece of man.'

Daisy looked. The evening had the potential of having disaster written all over it, if Sara wasn't careful. How Andrew put up with such a flirt for a wife, she couldn't imagine. Sara's wedding and engagement rings twinkled on her finger, and Daisy consoled herself with the thought that Ted could hardly miss them.

'Where is Andrew tonight?' Daisy asked.

'He's going straight to the party. We'll meet him there later. In the meantime, I'm going to have a couple of drinks and a bit of fun.'

Sara downed her wine in one long swallow and plonked her glass on the bar. 'Another please, barman,' she said, and the barman duly obliged. Daisy, not to be outdone, finished hers and ordered a second. Already she could feel the alcohol sinking in, soothing her ragged nerves.

'Any gossip?' Sara asked, when the two men had their attention caught by the big screen on one side of the bar.

'Hell, yeah! You're not going to believe it,' Daisy said. She hadn't spoken to Sara over Christmas, so she hadn't had a chance to fill her friend in on the series of disasters which had befallen her and her family.

'I've been sacked, then Zoe announced she's pregnant, or rather, David did, then she saved my life and—'

'Woah, back up lady and slow down. Sacked? Pregnant? Lifesaving? I need details.'

Daisy leaned against the bar and began her story. 'It all started with the sixpence,' she said.

'A sixpence? What's that?' Sara asked, before Daisy could go any further.

'Old money, before decimalisation. It's a coin about this big.' She held her index finger and thumb a half an inch apart. 'Smaller really, made of silver. Apparently, it equalled six old pennies. Gee-Gee got me to make a Christmas pudding and put it in.'

'Why would anyone want to do that? Someone could choke on it.'

'Someone did,' she said dryly. 'Me. At about the same time David told us Zoe was pregnant. Zoe had to thump me on the back because I seriously thought I was choking to death.'

Sara's face was alight with astonishment. 'Then what happened?'

'I swallowed it,' she replied.

'Oh, God. Are you ok?'

'I'm fine, but I've got to wait for it to come out.'

'You mean—?' Sara clapped her hands to her cheeks. 'It's still in there?'

'Shush. Yes, but I don't want the whole world to know.'

'Can't they operate?'

'Apparently, it will come out on its own.'

'How will you know if it has?'

'Every time I go to the loo I'm supposed to check.'

'That's effing hilarious,' Sara shrieked, and Art and Ted gave the girls an amused look.

'Shut up!' Daisy hissed.

'Then what? You said you were sacked. Poor you.'

Poor me indeed, Daisy thought, trying not to think too hard about her unemployed status. 'I went into work the day after Boxing Day, and Grumpy Simon told me they were going to make me redundant soon.'

'They can't do that!'

'They can.'

'So you've not been sacked then, but made redundant. That's a relief because it's hard to get another job once you've been sacked.'

Daisy was beginning to realise that. How could she have been so stupid. But then everyone in work used the internet for their own personal business, it wasn't just her. That bitch, Melissa, had well and truly screwed her over.

Daisy explained what had happened.

'The cow!' Sara exclaimed. 'What a lying, treacherous, two-faced...'

'I know, but did you know that Zoe is a paralegal? You'll never guess what her firm specialises in.'

'Yeah, employment law, or something,' Sara said.

'How come you know more about my family than I do? First Freddie, now Zoe.'

'Your mum told me.'

'She never told *me*.'

'I bet she did, but you probably weren't listening. You were probably thinking about the next round of Valentine verses, I expect.'

Sara had a point. Daisy often had been known to go off on a tangent and think about work stuff if an odd comment or a throwaway remark started the creative juices flowing. But she also tended to tune her mother out, too.

'Anyway,' she said, finishing up the second part of her story. 'Zoe said I might have a case for unfair dismissal.'

'It's worth a shot,' Sara agreed. 'You've got nothing to lose. You've certainly been through the mill, haven't you?'

'That's not all.'

'Isn't it?'

'Zoe was pregnant with twins, but she lost one,' Daisy continued, and Sara let out a small cry of sympathy. 'Then David had a car accident on the way to the hospital and broke his leg in three places. He had to have an operation and has got a pin in his leg. Now he'll bleep every time he goes through airport security. And to top it all off, I'm staying at David's house to care for both of them, because Zoe has been told not to exert herself.'

'Effing hell!'

'Oh, and—'

'Not more bad news?' Sara yelled, forcing Daisy to tell her to shush again.

'No, but the doctor who treated me when I went to A&E after I swallowed the sixpence, thought that David was my husband, and that I was the one who was pregnant. Then Zoe was rushed in when she miscarried one of the babies, and the doctor realised David was married to Zoe, but thought David had gotten both of us pregnant, and that I was David's mistress.'

Sara collapsed against Ted, who manfully caught her and held her up as she dissolved into giggles.

'I'm glad someone finds all this amusing,' Daisy said, grumpily.

'I'm sorry, but you couldn't write this stuff,' Sara gasped, dabbing underneath her eyes with the pads of her fingers.

'Someone has had too much to drink already,' Ted said.

'No, someone hasn't,' Sara retorted. 'But someone intends to.' She straightened up, and smoothed down her incredibly short dress. 'Whose round is it?' she demanded, and Daisy steeled herself.

Here goes, she thought. Party time.

Chapter 21

'He wasn't!' Art spluttered, and whatever he was drinking dribbled down his chin.

'He was. Tell him, Daisy,' Sara said.

'He was' she said, wishing Sara hadn't aired Daisy's dirty laundry for all to see. But now that she had, Daisy wanted to make a bit of a joke out of it. It was better than letting the world see how hurt and ashamed she felt.

'And you never guessed your boyfriend was gay?' Art persisted.

'No.' Daisy's reply was short.

'I can't imagine how you must be feeling,' he said, raising his hand to catch the barman's attention.

Daisy could tell him exactly how she felt, but she didn't want to sour the mood, or scare Art away. He and Ted were proving to be surprisingly good company, and Ted really was a surfer. He'd come back to the UK from Australia to visit his family and catch up with old friends. Art was an investment banker, which was not particularly interesting in itself (at least not to Daisy), but he had a whole raft of stories about wealthy clients which had her and Sara in stitches.

Which was why Sara had felt obliged to share Daisy's misfortune with the two men, as a way to balance the scales. At least she hadn't told them about the sixpence and what Daisy had to do every day to look for it, though get a few more drinks inside her friend and Sara may very well tell all.

'We've got to be leaving soon,' Sara said, her voice slurring ever so slightly. 'I've got a husband and a party to go to. Do you want to stay here, Daisy?'

As pleasant as the evening had been so far, and as good as the company was, Daisy wasn't looking for romance in any of its forms, whether it was a quick kiss on the way to the taxi stand, or anything longer lasting. She needed to give herself some emotional space from Freddie, so she shook her head.

The flash of disappointment in Art's eyes was gratifying, and she wondered fleetingly if she should invite them along.

Ted, probably the most sober of the foursome, solved the problem for her.

'It's just as well you're going, considering you're hitched,' he said to Sara. 'Stay here much longer, and I won't be responsible for my actions.' He gave her friend a slow smile. 'You're one sexy lady.'

Daisy wouldn't invite Art on his own, so she kept her mouth shut.

Sara giggled, and looked away, blushing, then her eyes widened. 'Don't look now, but isn't that Melissa?' Sara nudged Daisy in the ribs.

Daisy looked, and it was.

'Want me to go over there and give her a piece of my mind?' Sara offered. 'She doesn't look all that strong. I reckon I could take her in a fight.'

Sara took a step in Melissa's direction, and Daisy grabbed her arm. Sara staggered back. Boy, was her friend drunk. Daisy, for all the alcohol she'd consumed, remained annoyingly sober. Just as well, considering. She didn't relish the thought of being arrested for bitch-slapping, however much the bitch in question deserved it.

'What's up, babe?' Ted had noticed their little exchange.

'See her over there?' Sara pointed at Melissa, and Ted and Art turned to stare.

One of Melissa's friends noticed, and said something to Melissa, who turned towards them. She waved, tinkling her fingers at Daisy. Daisy waved back.

'What are you doing?' Sara hissed.

'I don't want her to suspect anything,' Daisy answered.

'Why the daggers?' Ted wanted to know.

'She's the reason Daisy was sacked,' Sara said.

'You've lost your job?' This was from Art. 'What did you do?'

'You know those cheesy birthday cards with the cringey verses inside?' Daisy said.

Art nodded.

'I write those.'

Art looked a bit startled – a common reaction from most people when she told them what she did for a living. Anyone would think folk expected those verses and poems to appear inside their greeting cards as if by magic.

'And that woman got you sacked? How?' he asked.

'It was all my own fault really. I gave her the ammunition, and she put it in her lover's gun.'

'Hey, that's quite poetic,' Ted said.

Art was frowning. 'I don't understand.'

Daisy said. 'I'm not surprised. I didn't until I heard her talking to the MD in the toilets.'

'The managing director was in the toilet?'

'No, silly. Melissa Two-Face was having a conversation with Mr Dearborn on the phone, telling him all about Grumpy Simon sacking me, and that I wouldn't cause any trouble.'

'I still don't understand.' Art, the poor man, looked really confused.

'Grumpy Simon is – was – my manager. Mr Dearborn is the MD. Melissa is having an affair with him, and from what I can gather, because I only heard one side of the conversation, the MD promised Melissa a promotion. It can't be a coincidence I was sacked.'

'You say you only heard one side of the convo, so maybe you jumped to the wrong conclusion,' Ted suggested. He looked uncomfortable and had inched away from the two women slightly. Daisy suspected he thought she may be about to launch herself at Melissa, and he didn't want any part of it.

'I heard her say she was wearing stockings and suspenders, and that they could play bosses and secretaries. Ew.'

'She said that to him?'

'Yup. Nasty, innit?'

Ted shuffled further away. At this rate, he'd be out of the door in the next few minutes.

'Don't worry,' Daisy said. 'I'm not going to knock her teeth out, and neither will Sara. Will you, Sara?' It was more of a demand on Daisy's part, than a question.

'Oh, alright, but I still think you should let me at her.'

Daisy watched Melissa finish her drink and shuck her bag on her shoulder, her eyes narrowing as her former friend and colleague prepared to leave. Daisy and Sara stood between her and escape, and Daisy put a warning hand on Sara's arm.

'Behave,' she warned, as quietly as the noise level in the pub would allow.

Sara made a zipping motion across her mouth.

'Daisy, darling, fancy seeing you here!' Melissa exclaimed, when she came close enough. 'Having a good time?'

'Lovely, thanks, and you?'

'The best. Oh, sorry, that was thoughtless of me, considering the troubles you've had recently,' she said, then Art turned a little, and Melissa saw him face on. 'Oh, maybe things are looking up for you already?'

'They certainly are,' Daisy agreed. Her words, though spoken pleasantly, were forced out between gritted teeth. The cheek of the woman!

A hand wrapped around her waist, and a strong arm pulled her close. When she breathed in Art's masculine scent and felt his lips on her ear, she almost lost her composure.

'Play along,' he whispered, then turned her towards him and kissed her soundly on the lips.

Oh, my!

For a heartbeat, Daisy didn't respond, then she snaked her arms around his neck and kissed him back. When they came up for air, it was to see Sara with a huge smirk on her face, and Melissa with a look of astonishment on hers.

'It didn't take you long to get over Freddie,' Melissa said, her tone catty.

Daisy produced what she hoped was an enigmatic smile.

'Aren't you going to introduce me?' Melissa added.

'This is Art,' Daisy said. 'He's an investment banker.'

'Lucky you! He'll be able to invest all your savings once you get on your feet again. How *is* the job hunting going?'

The cow! 'Really good, thanks.'

'She's been offered a job in my bank,' Art said, and Daisy almost snorted in surprise and delight.

'Quick work,' Melissa said. 'Though maybe having a boyfriend as a colleague isn't such a good idea.'

She could talk! A number of expletives ran through Daisy's mind but she bit down on them.

'Anyway, must dash, I've got a hot date later,' Melissa smirked.

Yeah, I bet you do, Daisy thought.

They exchanged false air kisses, and Daisy watched Melissa sashay to the exit, her hips swinging in her too-tight dress, and all the while, Art kept his arm around Daisy.

As soon as the other woman was out of sight, he released her.

'Thanks for that,' she said.

'My pleasure. What a nasty bit of work.'

'Yeah, she is. I wish I'd realised sooner.'

'We've got to get going,' Sara said, checking her watch. 'Andrew will think I've been abducted. Nice meeting you Ted, you too, Art.'

'I enjoyed it,' Art said. 'Immensely.' He gave Daisy a meaningful look and she blushed to the roots of her hair.

Her blush deepened when she glanced around searching for the sign for the ladies' loos, and saw who was watching her – Dr Hartley. He lifted his glass in acknowledgement, and Daisy smiled back.

'You know that doctor I was telling you about?' she said to Sara as the pair of them made their way to the toilets. 'He's standing over there. Don't look!'

Sara looked. Dr Hartley was still staring in their direction, and it made Daisy feel a little uncomfortable, and a bit tingly. She couldn't read his expression, but it didn't appear to be particularly friendly.

'He's scrummy,' Sara said. 'Bit on the brooding side, like a medical Heathcliff, but I wouldn't kick him out of bed.'

Without warning, Daisy was grabbed from behind and lifted off her feet, and she shrieked loudly.

'Where have you been all my life, gorgeous?' a beer-laden voice rasped in her ear, and the next thing Daisy knew, she and her drunken assailant were heading towards the floor.

She landed on top of the man with an oomph, and he grunted when her elbow connected with something soft. She lay there, stunned, her dress up around her thighs, a sticky drink trickling down her forehead, and her legs wide apart showing her knickers.

Laughter and cat-calling rang in her ears.

Then a meaty hand closed around her right boob and squeezed. 'Nice tits,' the man she was lying on declared.

She elbowed him again, this time intentionally. Another grunt. Good. I hope I've broken something, she thought crossly.

A helping hand reached out of the sea of bodies and Daisy took it. The sooner she was upright the better.

And in the sudden, relative silence of one song ending and another beginning, Dr Hartley said quite clearly, 'I gather you're not pregnant, then?'

Chapter 22

Daisy eased her shoes off her aching feet and sank into the arm chair with a groan, glad the evening was finally over.

She'd been rugby tackled to the floor, had received an unwelcome beer shampoo, had been humiliated by a professional man who should know better (what about patient confidentiality?), had been chatted up by a bloke old enough to be her dad, had been bought a drink by another bloke who'd then assumed she would sleep with him, and had been propositioned by a pizza delivery driver on her way home. To top off what had been a disappointing night out, she hadn't been able to get a taxi and had been forced to walk (stagger) the two and a half miles from the city centre to her brother's house. When she'd arrived, she realised she'd forgotten to take a key. Her mother had been furious at being woken up, and Daisy suspected she would still be furious come morning. It didn't help that her brother was sprawled on the sofa in a drug-induced sleep and was snoring his oblivious head off.

And she was starving, but there was very little she fancied in the fridge. She was rooting around in it, picking up packets of unidentifiable stuff and putting them down again, when her phone rang. It was Freddie – great. A perfect end to a perfect night. Not.

'What do you want?' she sighed into her mobile. 'If it's to wish me a Happy New Year, don't bother.'

'He's left me,' Freddie said. He sounded upset, or drunk, or maybe both – she'd never seen Freddie drunk before.

'Who?' she asked absently, wondering what the weird packet of smelly circles were. They looked like some kind of sausage slices.

'Carl.'

Daisy put the packet down, and thought about what Freddie had said. A mean little voice in her head whispered, "serves you right", and she immediately felt contrite. Freddie sounded distraught.

'He packed his things and has gone back to live with his sister. He said he didn't think I was fully committed to the relationship,' Freddie wailed. 'What does he mean by that?'

Daisy had no idea, and she wasn't really in the mood to give relationship advice to the ex who'd so recently and spectacularly dumped her. Especially since she was tired and hungry, and had enough problems of her own.

'I don't know, but I'm sure everything will be better in the morning,' she said. 'Good night, Freddie.'

But things weren't better in the morning – far from it.

When her phone rang again a little after seven, Daisy struggled out from a heavy sleep (heavy because she'd not long managed to drop off, what with her mother's restless leg kicking her every five minutes, and the steady snoring in her ear) and she blearily reached for the phone before it woke Sandra.

She looked at the screen. It wasn't a number she recognised. 'Hello?'

'I'm Staff Nurse Marsden from Worcester Royal Hospital,' a brisk female voice on the other end said. 'Am I speaking to Daisy Jones?'

Daisy eased out of bed, so as not to disturb snore-a-lot next to her. 'This is she,' she said. Please don't say anything has happened to Gee-Gee, she pleaded, silently.

'Do you know a Frederick Young?'

'Yes…'

'He's been admitted to hospital and has cited you as his next of kin.'

'What do you mean, "cited"?'

'Your name was the one he gave us when we asked if there was anyone who we should contact.'

'Is he alright?'

'If you could come in, someone will explain it to you. He's in the A&E department for the moment, until we can find him a bed.'

A&E? She'd seen enough of the hospital's accident and emergency department over the past few days to last her a lifetime, but what else could she do, she'd have to go.

'I'm on my way,' she promised, and for the third time in a week, Daisy found herself standing at the hospital's accident reception desk.

'Freddie Young?' she enquired and a different receptionist consulted her computer and told her to take a seat. This was becoming a bit of a habit. If she kept this up, she would be spending more time here than the staff.

This time she waited over an hour before a nurse took her through the same security door and asked her to take a seat in a very familiar corridor.

Daisy sat.

'The doctor is with Mr Young now. I'll let him know you're here,' the nurse informed her.

'Is Freddie okay? What's wrong? Has he had an accident?'

'The doctor will be able to answer your questions,' the nurse said firmly, before bustling off.

Daisy waited, and as she waited, she ran through all the possible scenarios in her mind.

Freddie's voice came from a cubicle at the far end of the corridor. 'There's no point in going on without the love of my life!,' he cried.

Daisy strained to hear any response, but the distance was too great, and the blip of a machine opposite made eavesdropping difficult.

'I want Daisy,' Freddie wailed.

More muted voices.

'I gave up everything for Carly, and this is how I'm treated. My life is ruined!' Freddie yelled, and Daisy had an awful, sneaking suspicion she knew the reason why her ex-boyfriend might be in hospital.

'Daisy! Daiseeey!'

'I'm here!' she shouted. 'Freddie? Can you hear me?'

The cubicle curtain was yanked open and Daisy's favourite doctor strode out, his face like thunder.

'Will you be quiet – this is a hospital, not a nightclub,' he called, probably making more noise than Daisy had.

'Sorry,' she muttered, as he came closer. 'But I heard him yelling for me.'

'If it was up to me, I wouldn't let you anywhere near him, but he wants you and no one else, though lord knows why,' the doctor said.

'Has he…? Did he…?' Daisy didn't know how to phrase it.

'Tried to take his own life?' The doctor's tone was harsh and unforgiving. 'Yes, he did.'

'How bad is it?'

Dr Hartley's expression softened a little. 'He's fine – physically, at least…'

'Thank God,' she breathed. 'I'd never forgive myself if he'd…' She trailed off, remembering Freddie's phone call to her last night, and her dismissal of him. If she hadn't been so tired, pissed off, and grumpy herself, she might have realised how out of character her ex was behaving. She'd never seen, or heard, him even remotely upset before. Daisy hung her head in shame. Freddie had reached out to her in his hour of need, and she'd brushed him off.

'What happens now?' she asked, in a small voice.

'He's yet another member of your family who I'm going to have to admit to hospital.'

'Hold it there,' she interrupted. She'd willingly take the blame for Freddie, but neither Zoe nor David was down to her.

Or was it?

Oh shit! The sixpence. It was exerting its evil influence yet again. How many more people would it affect?

'I need an operation,' Daisy blurted. 'You've got to get this thing out of me.'

'Excuse me?'

'An operation. I have to get rid of it.' She pressed her fingers into her stomach, convinced she could feel a little hard disc in amongst the fat.

The doctor let out a low growl, and Daisy cringed. Surely her request wasn't that strange? And it didn't seem to want to come out of its own accord (day eight today, if Christmas Day was taken into account). What if the damned thing stayed inside her forever, wreaking havoc at every opportunity, until it finally killed someone?

'Go to your GP,' he said harshly. 'You can't just waltz in here off the street and demand something like that. There are procedures to follow, you know.'

'But you said—'

'I don't care what I said. Bloody hell, woman, no wonder you were out getting pissed last night, and making a show of yourself.'

'You'd get pissed if you had something like that inside you. It's been nothing but bad luck.'

The doctor drew himself up to his full height and glowered at her. 'You can't blame your pregnancy for everything.'

Daisy paused, remembering that she had a bone to pick with him on the subject of pregnancy.

'How dare you tell the whole world my personal business,' she began, her hands planted firmly on her hips. 'Everyone in the pub now knows that I thought I was pregnant, maybe everyone in Worcester. There should be a law against it.'

The doctor paled. 'I'm sorry,' he said, stiffly. 'It was unacceptable. I never should have said what I did.'

'Daiseeeey.' The wail was loud and plaintive. 'Daze….'

'Freddie is asking for me,' she said, taking a step towards the cubicle her ex was in, but Dr Heartless hadn't finished with her yet. 'It was unethical of me,' he was saying, 'and if you want to take it to the medical board, and put in a complaint, I fully understand.'

That took the wind right out of her indignant sails, and she hesitated. She'd not even thought about ethics, but now he'd put the idea in her mind…

No. She wouldn't be so petty, and after all, no real harm had been done, though if she really had been pregnant, she might be thinking along different lines.

'I'm not going to complain,' she said, with a loud sigh. 'I know you don't have a very high opinion of me – I've no idea why; last night was an accident, nothing more, nothing less – but I'm not the kind of woman to drop someone else in it.'

'Thank you.' He didn't sound thankful. He sounded just as irate as before. 'Tell that to Mr Young,' he added.

'Tell what to Mr Young?'

'That it was an accident.'

'He doesn't know.' Daisy was thoroughly confused.

'I think you'll find he does.'

Eh? Yet another surreal conversation with this mad doctor. The guy was a menace. 'What I do, or don't do, no longer concerns Frederick Young,' Daisy said, miffed.

How dare he! *Freddie* had left *her* (though technically she was the one who had walked out), but he'd left her in body, mind, and spirit long before that. What was she supposed to do – stay with him? She didn't think she had the necessary anatomy to be of any use to Freddie. *Mr Young* had made his sexual orientation quite clear, thank you very much. And the fact that he was now shouting for her and not his mother, served only to highlight just how badly his parents had accepted his coming out of the closet.

'Is he the father?' Dr Hartley asked.

She shook her head in confusion. 'Whose father?'

'Do you even know who it is?' Dr Hartley persisted.

'What kind of a question is that?'

'A reasonable one, considering.'

Hands on her hips again, Daisy took a deep breath. 'Look here, I don't know what's going on, or what you're referring to, but I think you are out of your tiny, little mind.'

'Daiseeeey!'

'Oh, shut up, Freddie!' Daisy yelled back, earning herself shushes and dagger-looks from an assortment of patients, their relatives, and staff.

'Freddie isn't the father of anyone's baby. Freddie is gay.' She shook her head angrily.

Sudden silence descended on the whole department. Daisy could have sworn that even the bleepy machine had stopped to listen.

Dr Hartley, his face stony, took hold of her arm. 'Let's go somewhere more private,' he suggested, leading her down the corridor.

'Daiseey?'

'Give it a rest, Freddie,' she called through the curtain. 'I'll be with you in a minute.'

Dr Hartley shut the office door with a soft click, turned to face her, and leaned against it, folding his arms. 'I want to see if I've got this right,' he said. 'David is your brother,' he stated.

Daisy nodded.

'David is married to Zoe, and Zoe is pregnant?' he continued.

Another nod.

'Freddie is your…?'

'Ex-boyfriend,' Daisy supplied.

'And he's an ex because…?'

How many times was she going to have to tell this story? 'Because I came home from work early and caught him in bed with someone else.'

Dr Hartley no longer looked like a bulldog chewing a wasp. He was beginning to look almost sympathetic. 'No wonder you want a termination.'

Daisy blinked. 'I'm not pregnant.'

'You just said you were.' He took a step towards her. 'I'm not going to persuade you one way or the other, it's not my place to do so, but let me offer you a little impartial advice – don't do anything rash. You've got time to make a decision, and the last thing you want to do is to keep drinking if you decide to go ahead with the pregnancy.'

'I told you, I'm not pregnant.'

'But you said you wanted a termination.'

'I said no such thing.'

'Okay, the word you used was "operation".'

'Yes, and that's what I want.'

'It's called a termination.'

'Not. When. You're. Not. Pregnant!'

The pair of them stared at each other for a while, before the doctor said slowly and quietly, 'What operation do you want, exactly?'

'I want to get this sixpence out of me.'

'Ah.'

'Yes, "ah".'

He took a step back, until he was up against the door, and this time Daisy had the impression he wanted to disappear through it as fast as his long legs could carry him. 'I've got the wrong end of the stick again, haven't I?'

'You most certainly have, mister.'

'Doctor.'

'Whatever.'

'Do you still love him?'

'Who, my imaginary baby's imaginary father?'

'Freddie.'

Daisy took a long time to answer. 'Yes.'

The doctor let out a small sigh.

'And, no. I thought I did. I thought we were going to get married and have kids,' she glared at Dr Hartley when she said the word "kids", 'but when I found out he was gay, I realised my pride was hurt and my femininity was crushed, but not my heart.' And why was she telling this sorry excuse for a doctor anyway?

Then Dr Hartley asked her something she most certainly hadn't been expecting.

'Will you have dinner with me?' he said.

Chapter 23

'No, yes, I'm not sure. Maybe.' *No*, because it was the immensely irritating Dr Hartley who was asking (she didn't even know his first name); *yes*, because this was gorgeous brooding Dr Hartley who was asking; *I'm not sure*, because she wasn't sure a doctor who had once treated her was allowed to ask her out. And *maybe*, because she'd have to check if her mother could David-sit. Her mother had set evenings for set activities, like bingo, flower arranging, (not that Daisy had seen any evidence of anything more substantial than a bunch of daffs in her mother's house), and her pub quiz nights, which seemed to involve more socialising than quizzing.

'Oh, I see. I'm sorry, I should have realised,' Dr Hartley said.

'Realised what?'

'The man you were kissing last night. I should have guessed you wouldn't be on the shelf for long.'

On the shelf, indeed! He made her sound like a dusty tin of forgotten peaches, hidden in the depths of an old lady's cupboard.

'I'm still on the shelf, as you so kindly describe it,' she said, then wished she hadn't as his expression became closed once more. Great – now he was thinking she was an easy lay, jumping straight out of Freddie's bed and into some other man's.

'For your information,' she said, 'I only just met Art last night. I didn't sleep with him,' she added, aware that the hole she was so busy digging was getting deeper with every word she uttered. 'It was just a snog.'

'A drunken one?'

'I wasn't drunk, not very.'

'You were lying on top of some random bloke, with your dress up around your waist,' he pointed out. 'You looked drunk to me.'

'He rugby tackled me and I fell over,' she retorted.

Dr Hartley was staring at her as if he wished he'd have been the one to rugby tackle her – all deep, and dark, and hungry. Her insides did a little roll of excitement.

'Yes,' she said, 'I'd love to go to dinner, but we'll have to confirm the date later. I've got to ask my mother to babysit first.'

'You've got children?'

Would that make a difference, she wondered, and she said, not really having the faintest idea why, 'Yes, two. Does that change anything?'

'No,' he said, but Daisy was certain she heard the hesitation in his voice, and she had no doubt that one of two things would happen now. Either he'd hedge about settling on a day and time so that nothing would ever come of their planned date, or they'd have dinner, then he'd never phone her afterwards.

Not a keeper then. This one wasn't into baggage. Her opinion of him, which had slowly been creeping out of the gutter, plummeted back down with a clang. She debated whether to simply tell him she'd changed her mind. But what the hell, it was only dinner, and she guessed she might be ready for a break from caring duties after a couple of days.

'I've got your number,' he said. 'I'll call you.'

Yeah, right, of course he would.

'Let's take you to see Mr Young, shall we?' he said, changing the subject, and she wanted to punch him in his patronising doctor's face.

'Daiseeeey.' Freddie was still calling for her, sounding more like a lost toddler than the responsible man she knew him to be. But then, she hadn't really known him at all, had she? Maybe this *was* the real Freddie.

'I'm here,' she said, pushing through the curtain, and Freddie's disconsolate face lit up in relief.

'My Daisy.'

'Not your Daisy, not anymore,' she reminded him, earning herself a "tut" from the nurse.

What was she supposed to do? Pretend they were still together and that everything was hunky dory? Freddie couldn't expect things to simply go back to the way they were before, no matter how much he might want to crawl back into his closet and forget the whole sorry mess had ever happened.

'Thank you for coming,' Freddie said, more or less normally. 'I didn't know who else to ask.'

'It's okay.' She'd expected to find him restrained or something, but he was sitting up on the bed with bandages around each wrist. He was also on a drip.

'I'm sorry about Carl,' she said, meaning it.

'He was right to leave me,' he said. 'I'm not sure I *am* committed to the relationship. I'm not ready to tell...' he swallowed nervously, the added. 'My parents.'

Daisy thought, neither was she, as she recalled the nights they'd spent together in Freddie's king size bed. 'Perhaps you're bisexual,' she suggested.

He sighed. 'Maybe I am. What can I do about it, Daisy? If I'm with a woman, I can't help thinking about men,' (she winced), 'and when I was with Carl, I couldn't help thinking about…' He hesitated. 'The hospital told me I've got to agree to counselling, and I have to see a psychiatrist before they let me out,' Freddie said, mournfully.

'That's a good thing, isn't it? Look on it as a kind of an MOT for the mind. We all need help sometimes,' she added gently, 'whether it's physical or mental.'

'Not you,' he said. 'You're the strongest person I know. You're never ill, except when you had flu once, and you're tough.'

She smiled at that. 'You think I'm tough?'

'As old boots.'

'Cheers for that.'

'Nothing ever seems to bother you,' he carried on. 'You can cope with anything.'

His faith in her was flattering, but not at all accurate, and she thought again how little they had truly known each other. Yes, she knew where he liked to buy his boxer shorts, and yes, she knew he hated apples and loved oranges, but those were superficial things. She knew similar things about Melissa, and Melissa had only been a colleague. But she didn't know the meaningful things about Melissa (clearly), and neither did she know the meaningful things about Freddie. The relationship had been surface deep – knowing how someone took their coffee in the mornings, wasn't the same as knowing what scared them in the middle of the night, or knowing their most precious dreams.

That's what had been missing, and she vowed she wouldn't settle for less in any future relationship. She wanted to know a man's heart and soul, and not just his shoe size.

'Which is why I'm asking if you'd move back in with me,' Freddie was saying.

Wait, what? Did she hear that right?

'Not permanently, just to see how it goes. We were good together once, weren't we?' he said.

Were they? She supposed they were, but it had been based on a lie, and what she'd clearly thought was good, hadn't been good for Freddie.

'Plus, they won't let me out without supervision,' Freddie continued, and Daisy realised the real reason for his asking. He didn't want *her* – he just wanted her as a guarantor for good behaviour.

'I can't,' she replied honestly. 'I'm living with David and Zoe for a while. David broke his leg and Zoe is pregnant, and has to rest.'

Once again, she felt sorry for her ex, but she couldn't help him, because she didn't want to put herself in an awkward position. It might be mean of her, but that's the way it was.

However, she would stay with him until a bed was found for him on the ward, and she would contact his parents if she felt she had to. She wasn't horrible enough to leave him without any support whatsoever, but she was determined she wouldn't be the one to provide it. She had enough on her plate already.

When she eventually checked her phone later that morning, it was to find she had twenty-seven missed calls and sixteen texts, all from her mother, each message becoming more irate until the final text was all in shouty capital letters and involved a swear word or two.

Oh dear.

'Mum?' she said, as soon as her mother answered.

'Where the hell are you, and why don't you answer your sodding phone? I've been stuck with your brother all morning and unlike you, I've got things to do, like cooking New Year's Day lunch for six sodding people. Get your arse back here now.'

'Mum—'

'I don't care if he's got buns of steel or whatever, shift your backside and get over to David's house before I blow my top.'

It sounded like she already had, Daisy mused, and thought "buns of steel"?

'I'm at the hospital, Mum,' she said, and was gratified at the immediate contrition in her mother's voice.

'What happened? Are you hurt? Did someone attack you?'

'What? No! It's Freddie.'

'Freddie attacked you? You wait till I get my hands on that little shit, I'll—'

'No one attacked me, Mum. Will you just listen for a sec?'

Sandra listened and wasn't impressed. Daisy wished she hadn't said anything.

'I'd have preferred you to be late because some man has had his wicked way with you,' Sandra grumbled. 'Freddie deserves everything he gets and more.'

That's the buns of steel comment explained, she thought, but her mother's vitriol was a little hard to stomach. Once again mankind (the male part of it) had reinforced Sandra's idea that all men were wasters and couldn't be depended on.

Just as Daisy was about to end the call, she remembered something. 'Any chance of babysitting sometime this coming week?'

'You *are* seeing someone,' her mother said.

'I don't know. It will be a first date, if it actually happens.' She muttered the last under her breath.

'I could do tomorrow, but that's it,' her mother offered begrudgingly.

Oh, well, that was that, Daisy assumed. He'd hardly likely to call before then, and even if he did the odds of him being free at the same time were slim. Resigned to never seeing Dr Hartley again (what *was* his first name anyway?) Daisy kissed Freddie on the cheek, promised to keep in touch, and headed off to resume her caring duties.

Chapter 24

Daisy didn't recognise the number, nor the voice on the other end. If it was one of those pesky "you've been involved in a car accident" phone calls, she might be tempted to play along for the sheer devilment of it.

David was asleep in his chair, Zoe had returned to bed exhausted, and Daisy was bored out of her tiny mind. If she was going to live here for the next few weeks, she'd have to have a stern talk with her brother about the benefits of Sky. The Freeview channels were crap, unless you liked watching endless re-runs of whatever was on ITV4.

'Hello?' she said.

Heavy breathing greeted her. It was one of those calls, was it?

'Stop wanking yourself off,' Daisy said, 'because I'm not impressed, and I'm not shocked, you pathetic excuse for a human being. If you're that desperate, go find yourself a real woman, and stop annoying me.'

She took the phone away from her ear when the voice said, 'Hello? Daisy?'

Oh, bloody hell, the pervert knew her name. She shot to her feet, dashed over to the window, yanked the curtains fully closed, then pulled the edge of the fabric aside, and peered into the darkness, her heart pounding. She'd seen *Scream* – she knew what was coming next.

'Piss off,' she hissed.

David wouldn't be any help, not with him having a gammy leg, and she frantically wondered which drawer Zoe kept the knives in because she couldn't for the life of her remember.

'It's Noah,' the man on the other end said.

Noah? She didn't know anyone called Noah, but by the sound of it, she might be about to meet him. Her heart-rate went up a notch. At this rate, she'd die of a heart attack before he reached the front door…OMG! He might already be inside the house!

A sigh came down the line. 'Dr Hartley,' the voice said.

Daisy collapsed against the wall, nearly pulling the curtain rail off in her relief. 'Dr Hartley?' she repeated. 'Noah Hartley?'

'Who did you think it was? Another ex-boyfriend? Bloody hell, Daisy, you don't half attract some weirdos.'

'If the cap fits…' Daisy said, struggling to regain her composure. Why did this man have such an annoying ability to put her on the back foot? Was he born with the talent, or had he been practising?

Then her tummy did a little roll of excitement – *he'd called*. Despite everything, he liked her enough to phone her.

'About our date,' he said, and Daisy's heart sank as she waited for him to wriggle out of it. 'I'm on shift for the next two days—' (he was letting her down gently), '—but I can do Wednesday or Thursday.'

Or maybe he wasn't letting her down at all. 'I can only do tomorrow night,' Daisy said. Her yo-yoing emotions were seriously getting to her.

'Oh.' There was a whole world of disappointment in the word, and Daisy's heart threatened to jump into her throat.

'I've got an idea,' he began, and that was how Daisy found herself yet again strolling into A&E the following evening.

She gave her name to the receptionist, but this time had the satisfaction of saying, 'I'm here to see Dr Hartley, he's expecting me,' when the receptionist asked her for her medical details.

This time she waited less than five minutes before she was called by Dr Hartley himself (she still couldn't think of him as Noah). He ushered her through the door and took her into an office.

'Quick, put this on,' he said, handing her a white coat. 'Hi, by the way.'

'Hi, to you, too.' She slipped her arms through the sleeves and buttoned it up. 'Can I have a stethoscope?' she asked.

'Only if you promise not to play with it.'

'I promise.'

He draped the instrument around her neck and it was at this point that Daisy started to wonder whether Dr Hartley was into kinky games of doctors and er... doctors.

It was as though he'd read her mind. 'Staff canteen,' he said. 'No one will look at you twice if you've got a white coat on.'

'Thanks,' she said, wryly.

'I don't mean they won't look at you because you're not worth looking at – you are, you're gorgeous – what I meant was—'

Daisy laid a hand on his arm. His babbling was endearing. 'I know what you meant.'

Their eyes met and Daisy was suddenly lost, the blue in them was so blue, and he had long dark lashes, and was staring at her, staring *into* her, making her knees tremble.

'Shall we?' He gestured to the door.

Do we have to? she wanted to say. She could spend the rest of her life gazing into those eyes, losing herself in them.

Get a grip, Jones, she admonished herself. A cluttered office in the middle of an accident and emergency department with the prospect of hospital food, wasn't exactly romantic.

Yet nothing had been more romantic in Daisy's life, and all she could think about was that he hadn't been able to wait to see her. If *that* wasn't romantic, what was?

'I hope you've already eaten,' he advised, leading her down a myriad of corridors and around so many corners she was soon lost.

'I thought we were having a meal, here?' she replied, confused.

'Exactly!'

Daisy hadn't eaten, but she wasn't hungry either. Her tummy was full of small insects jumping about, and the last thing she felt like doing was eating. The first thing? She certainly wasn't going to think about that in public.

The food was everything he'd inferred it would be, and Daisy only picked at her dry shepherd's pie. Noah, on the other hand, wolfed his down.

'I haven't eaten since yesterday lunchtime,' he said, 'and besides, you get used to the food. Kind of.'

Every so often his pager would ping, Noah would take it out, glance at it, and put it back in his pocket.

'I was surprised to see you working on New Year's Day after being out in the evening,' she said, pushing a fork full of greyish brown mush around her plate.

'I volunteered. After I saw you in *The Cardinals Hat*, I had to go into work for a twelve-hour shift. Except it turned into a sixteen hour one instead.'

'Do you often have to work such long hours?' she asked, appalled. Nine to five had been more than enough for her, thank you very much.

'It depends. I offered to swap with a guy who has a wife and kids, so he could spend the holiday with them. Then the doctor who was supposed to relieve me phoned in sick, though knowing him, it was probably self-induced.' He saw Daisy's confused expression. 'Hangover.'

'Oh.' She was curious. 'Why did you become a doctor?' She genuinely wanted to know. From what she'd seen (a documentary on TV) it seemed that the life of an A&E doctor wasn't a glamorous one. In fact, it looked like bloody hard work and long hours. 'Was it because you wanted to help people?'

'Lord, no.' Then he realised how that sounded and added, 'That was part of it, but the main reason is that I'm good at it.'

'You must have known that before you applied to medical school?'

'Nope, didn't have a clue. It just seemed like a good idea at the time, and my mum always said she wanted a doctor in the family, to save her waiting weeks for a GP appointment, so I applied. Can I ask you something,' he said, 'and I hope you'll be honest with me?'

Here goes – this was the time to confess that she didn't have two kids, and hope he forgave her for misleading him, though with their track record, one more misconception shouldn't make any difference.

'What did you want to be when you were five?' he asked, his eyes twinkling.

She hadn't been expecting that. 'A ballerina,' she replied, immediately. 'But only because I liked pretty pink tutus and not because I could dance.'

'Did you have lessons?'

'One. When I was four.'

'Only one?'

'My mother was asked to bring me back when I was toilet trained,' she said and he gave her an incredulous look. 'I got so excited, I peed in the corner,' she explained. 'My mother didn't risk taking me back again. What about you?'

'Train driver – the old-fashioned steam ones, not those modern contraptions.'

She wondered whether he had carried that enthusiasm through to adulthood, and had a train set bigger than London in his attic, or worse, he was a train spotter. She'd rather watch paint dry.

'I grew out of that, in fact, I don't really like trains much, I discovered, and then I wanted to be Spiderman. That didn't work out either.'

'I suppose the job's already taken,' she said, putting her fork down.

His pager bleeped. He looked at it, but didn't move. 'I also found out I didn't like spiders,' he admitted, then asked, 'What's your favourite colour?'

'Red, because it's sexy and sassy, and no one argues with you when you've got red on. It's a fact.'

'It is?'

She nodded. 'You?'

'White.'

'White isn't a colour.'

'No, it's an absence of colour,' he said. 'But it symbolises light and life.'

'Not in some religions,' she argued.

'Are you religious?'

'Not really, but my mother used to make me go to church on Sundays when I was really little. I hated it. I wanted to go horse riding instead, like my friend Jayne. But we couldn't afford it.'

'Do you ride now?'

'Never been on the back of a horse in my life, unless you include a donkey ride on Weston beach.'

'What would you like to do that you've never done before?'

Where should she start? The list was endless. 'Visit New York, snorkel off the Great Barrier Reef, swim with sharks, own a tortoise—'

'A tortoise?'

'They're cute. Don't judge me,' Daisy said, feigning indignation, before carrying on with her list. 'Draw something that doesn't look like a very bad cartoon, win a medal at the Olympics. I could go on.'

'That's quite an eclectic list you've got there, Miss Jones. I'm intrigued about the Olympic medal thing. Which sport?'

'The one hundred metres.'

Daisy admired him for not glancing down at her less-than-trim bod, even if it was mostly hidden by the white coat.

'Do you run?' he asked.

Aw, that was so sweet of him, letting her think she looked as though she could. 'No, not a step.'

'That might make winning a medal a little hard,' he teased, and Daisy melted at the way his voice softened and his eyes sparkled.

'What about you?' she asked.

'Space,' he replied.

'Do you need some?'

'I want to go up into it. Imagine what weightlessness must feel like – and the view.' He sighed.

'Anything else?' she asked.

'I want a sister.'

'Is that a possibility?'

'My parents are both in their late fifties, so I doubt it.'

'Why a sister?'

'Because brothers are a pain in the arse.'

'Tell me about it,' Daisy replied.

'How *is* David?'

'Annoying.'

'It's only to be expected,' Noah said.

'He was like that *before* he broke his leg,' Daisy pointed out. 'Now you can add miserable and frustrated to the mix. And don't forget, demanding.'

'Your sister-in-law?'

'Sly.'

Noah raised his eyebrows.

'She keeps trying to do things behind my back, as if I'm not going to notice a duster in her hand.'

'She's not confined to bed, you know,' Noah pointed out.

'She is if she's under my watch,' Daisy said, grimly. 'If I've got to strap her to the bed I – oh!' She suddenly remembered Freddie.

'He'll be okay,' Noah said, when Daisy asked about him. 'He'll receive the help he needs.'

'I would like to help him too, but I can't, not physically nor in any other way. I don't want to go down that path again.'

'Freddie is an adult, and he has to take responsibility for his own actions and his own life. He can't expect you to do that for him, and counselling will help him to work his problems through by himself.'

Daisy knew Noah was right, but it didn't alleviate the guilt.

'Do you like—' Noah began, when his pager beeped again. This time, when he glanced at it, he swore. 'Gotta go,' he said, jumping to his feet and pushing his chair back. 'Emergency.'

A few long strides took him to the door, where he paused and mouthed, 'I'll phone you,' then he was gone, leaving Daisy to wonder if the previous half hour had been a figment of her imagination.

She was trying to find her way to the exit (and wondering where she should ditch the coat and stethoscope) when her stomach gurgled.

Not now, she sighed, as another cramp hit low down in her bowels.

'Nurse, excuse me,' she called, spotting the familiar blue uniform. 'Where are the nearest toilets?'

'Go to the end of this corridor, doctor, turn right and they are on your left.'

Doctor! Daisy felt a pride she didn't deserve, then another warning cramp hit her.

'Thank you, nurse. Oh, and is there any chance of borrowing a pair of rubber gloves, a bowl, and a wooden spoon?'

Chapter 25

Daisy, nose wrinkling in disgust, held up a soiled silver coin in between a blue-gloved finger and thumb. All that trouble for one little sixpence, but at least she'd not have the revolting job of prodding through a bowl of poo ever again.

She tidied everything up, disposed of the tongue depressor and cardboard sick bowl in the waste bin, before using nearly all of a bottle of antibacterial gel to thoroughly clean the coin, her hands, and anything else in sight.

Then she took a couple of sheets of paper hand-towels and wrapped the now-clean but still disgusting sixpence. Her great-gran was welcome to it, though if it was up to Daisy, she would have thrown it away along with the rest of the rubbish. Fancy Gee-Gee wanting it back!

She put it in her bag, wishing she didn't have to, left the coat and the stethoscope on the hook behind the toilet door, and made her escape.

Already she felt lighter, is if the sixpence had weighed far more than a gram or so. She imagined the bad luck which had been dogging her for the past eight days had finally left her, so it was with a spring in her step that she skipped back to her car.

It wasn't where she'd left it.

Daisy stamped her foot crossly, preparing herself for another game of hunt-my-car. It wasn't the first time she'd managed to lose her own car in a car park; the supermarket was usually her favourite location of choice, and she'd lost count of the number of times she had to go searching for it with a trolley full of weekly shopping, only to find that she'd thought she'd parked it in row C, when in fact, she'd left it in row F.

But after one fruitless hunt, then another, Daisy had to admit that her car had been stolen.

'Bugger, bugger, fuckit!' she yelled.

Now what was she supposed to do? For once, she did what any normal person did and phoned the police.

'It's been towed,' she was informed.

'Towed? They can't do that!'

'They can and they did.'

'Aren't I supposed to get a ticket first?'

'Not if you park in a bay reserved for ambulances.'

She'd parked close to the entrance to A&E and she remembered how she had done a mental "Yes!" at finding a space that wasn't a mile away. She'd even thought that was lucky...

Oh, how that effing sixpence must be chuckling to itself. Daisy never knew she could hate an inanimate object as much as she hated this one. But it wasn't inanimate, was it? It was alive, and intent on causing her as much trouble as it possibly could.

'I'm going to melt you down and make a pair of earrings out of you,' she threatened.

'Excuse me, madam?' the operator on the end of the phone said.

'Oh, sorry, I was talking to myself. How do I get my car back?'

The operator gave her the address, along with the very unwelcome news that she'd have to pay two hundred and fifty pounds to have her own car released to her. The damn thing wasn't worth much more than that, and she was sorely tempted to leave it there. If she still had a job, she just might have simply gone out and bought another car. As it was, she'd have to dip into her savings to get the vehicle back, and she could see the chances of having her own place anytime soon drifting further and further away.

Damn and blast it all!

Before she collected her car, Daisy was determined to rid herself of the sixpence. She wasn't going to have it in her possession one second longer than was necessary, so she headed to the bus stop.

The Grange was a sprawling series of interconnected buildings two bus rides away from the hospital, and it was pouring heavily by the time she was dropped a street away. As luck would have it (ha!) she had left both her coat and her umbrella on the back seat of the car, and so she resembled a soaked kitten by the time she entered the sliding front doors of the old people's home.

She left a trail of soggy footprints behind her as she squelched towards her great-gran's room, though she did manage a word and a smile to the various residents she passed. Some smiled back, and some were lost inside themselves, not registering Daisy's existence, and she felt so incredibly sad for them.

She felt even sadder when she reached Gee-Gee's room, only to see another old woman in her great-grandmother's bed.

Daisy glanced around the room and noticed that all her great-grandmother's things had gone.

Daisy's eyes welled up; she'd only seen her great-grandmother yesterday when she provided the taxi service for the (very) late lunch. She'd kissed the old woman's cheek less than twenty-four hours ago, before handing her over to one of the staff.

They hadn't wasted any time in moving someone else into her great grandmother's room, had they? She realised spaces in these homes were in demand, but couldn't they have waited a couple of days? Her bed couldn't even be cold yet.

Daisy wondered if her mother knew, and quickly checked her phone. If Sandra did know she hadn't passed the information on yet. She debated calling her and Nan, but decided this was the sort of news she needed to break to them face to face.

Daisy spied a member of staff. It wasn't someone she recognised, but then the staff turnover here was quite high, and she never usually visited during a week day. She was normally in work.

'Why didn't you tell us?' Daisy demanded without preamble, drawing the girl (she was only about eighteen) away from the door, in case the new occupant overheard.

'Tell you what?' Her jaws worked a piece of gum, and Daisy found she couldn't take her eyes off the steady chewing.

'About…' Daisy pointed to the new occupant of what was formerly her great-grandmother's room.

'Are you a relative?' the teenager asked.

'Not of this lady, no.'

'Then I'm afraid I can't share anything with you. Do you have a relative at *The Grange*?'

For such a young thing, the girl didn't half have an attitude on her. 'Not anymore,' Daisy replied.

'I'm sorry, but I must ask you to leave,' the girl said.

Daisy's hackles rose. 'Not until I've spoken to the manager,' she countered.

The girl considered her request. 'Wait here,' she said eventually, and Daisy waited.

By the time the nursing home's duty manager of the day appeared, Daisy had worked herself up into a fine old temper.

'I think it's disgraceful that the family weren't informed immediately it happened,' Daisy said.

'Miss Jones, isn't it?' The woman was unflustered and didn't appear at all apologetic. The girl lingered behind her boss, watching the show.

'Yes, I'm Mrs Reynolds' great-granddaughter.'

'I'm sorry,' the manager continued, 'but we didn't realise it would cause this much of an issue.'

'Issue! What did you think it was going to cause? She's my great grandmother, of course it's going to cause an issue.' Daisy spat the last word out.

The woman drew herself up to her full height, a portly five foot three. 'In future, we will inform you of any such changes before they happen,' she declared.

'You *knew* this was going to happen?'

'Yes, course. It was planned a week ago.'

Daisy spluttered, the splutter quickly becoming a coughing fit. *Planned?* Even Daisy, who didn't much bother with the news, knew that euthanasia wasn't legal in Britain.

'I'm going to the police,' she declared, when she caught her breath.

The manager looked thoroughly confused. 'Why?'

'It's illegal, that's why. You can't just murder someone and get away with it.'

The girl had retreated halfway down the corridor and looked as if she intended to make a run for it at any minute.

'I think we should discuss these allegations somewhere more private,' the manager said, thin-lipped.

No way. Daisy had no intention of going anywhere with that woman, and certainly not into some little room where the psychopath could do anything to her. God knows what drugs they had in a place like this. A piece of old rag saturated with chloroform? A needle in the side of the neck? Anything!

'Or do you want me to call the police?' the woman added, eyeing Daisy with all the caution she'd give a rabid dog.

'Yes! The police. Good idea!' Daisy declared. 'They can hear all about how you planned my great grand-mother's death.'

The manager did a comedic double take. She looked behind her, signalling to the chit of a child to come closer. The girl sidled a few steps nearer.

'No one told me Mrs Reynolds had passed on,' the manager said. 'When did this happen?'

The girl shrugged. 'I dunno. She was fine when I left her.'

'When was that?' The older woman asked.

The girl glanced at her watch. 'About ten minutes ago. I just took her a cup of tea.'

Daisy looked from the one to the other, and back again, like a spectator in a weird verbal tennis match. Something didn't add up. This must be a ruse to make her lower her guard.

'You said you planned it a week ago,' she said, accusingly.

'Yes, I did. Mrs Reynolds has been complaining that this side of the building was too noisy, but we couldn't move her until a room in Willow Wing became available.'

'Hold it there.' Daisy held up a hand. She needed a second to think.

The penny dropped for Daisy at the same time as it dropped in the duty manager's mind.

'You thought Mrs Reynolds had passed away?' The duty manager asked. 'And that we had failed to inform you?'

Daisy nodded, mortified.

'And you thought we'd *murdered* her?' The other woman's expression swung from outrage to incredulity, and back again.

Daisy didn't blame her.

'Did you check in at the front desk, like you're supposed to?' the woman asked, crossing her arms.

Daisy shook her head.

'If you had, you would have been informed that Mrs Reynolds had moved rooms.'

'Oh.'

'Let me tell you, Miss Jones, *The Grange* is not in the habit of failing to inform relatives when their loved ones pass on. Neither are we in the habit of killing off our clients to make room for others. Do I make myself clear?'

'Yes, miss.' Daisy's response was instinctive. She'd been told off in a similar manner by Mrs Bowles, her former headmistress, and right now she felt exactly like a school-girl who'd been caught cheating in an exam.

'Right, then, mystery solved. We'll say no more about it,' the duty manager said.

Daisy finally recalled her name – Mrs Right. How appropriate.

'Take Miss Jones to visit her great-grandma, would you, Apple? Then go and see if Mrs Pastor needs changing.'

Daisy hung her head as she trotted behind the teenager. She could have sworn the girl's shoulders were shaking in mirth, and she thanked her in a quiet, chagrined voice, as the girl indicated Gee-Gee's new room. Daisy scuttled inside.

Her great-grandmother was sitting in her armchair, as large as life, watching TV.

'Why aren't you in work?' the old lady demanded, seeing Daisy at the door.

'Hi, Gee-Gee, nice to see you too,' Daisy griped. 'I've lost my job, remember?'

'I remember. I'm old, not stupid. I assumed you would have found yourself another one by now,' she said.

'It's only been five days!'

'Long enough,' Gwenda said. 'What are you doing here, anyway?'

'I've brought you your sixpence back.'

'What sixpence?'

'The one we put in the pudding.'

'What pudding?'

The Christmas pudding. You said it was for luck.' Yeah, but she hadn't specified what kind of luck, had she?

'Oh, that. It's an old wives' tale,' Gee-Gee said.

Little did her great-grandmother know…

'Anyway, I brought it back,' Daisy said.

'Why don't you keep it and put it in next year's pudding? Carry on the tradition.'

God, no! Not after where it's been, all the trouble it's caused. Daisy couldn't wait to give it back to its rightful owner. 'You said you wanted it back,' Daisy pointed out.

'Did I?'

Daisy nodded emphatically. 'You said, it was the last sixpence your father ever gave you.'

'He never gave me any sixpences. Now, if you'd have said, thruppeny bits…'

'Here.' Daisy handed the coin over. Or tried to.

Gwenda pushed it away. 'I don't want it,' she said. 'You keep it. Anyway, I don't think there's anything remotely lucky about it.'

You don't say…

Daisy left it on the table on the way out, glad she'd never have to set eyes on the damned thing ever again.

Chapter 26

A soft knock on the door relieved Daisy of her despondent job-hunting session.

'Come in,' she called, shutting down the site. There was simply nothing else out there to apply for, darn it.

Zoe stuck her head around the door. 'I've had a look through your contract,' she said. 'It clearly states that the use of the company's IT equipment and internet is strictly for company use only, and any breach or disregard of this may lead to disciplinary action, and then it refers you to the company's disciplinary policy.'

'That's that, then,' Daisy said. She'd not really expected anything else.

'Not necessarily. I really need to get my hands on the company's disciplinary policy, but regardless of what it says, they don't appear to have followed the correct procedure for the dismissal of an employee.'

'Which is?'

Zoe came into the room, and Daisy sat up, scooting across the bed and patting the covers next to her. Zoe sat and cleared her throat.

'When an employee contravenes a company's rules and regulations, there are set procedures which should be followed, otherwise the company might leave itself open to challenge, or appeal. Some actions, or failure to perform actions, can clearly be seen to be gross miscon-duct, and this often, but not always, leads to instant dismissal. But even in those instances, there are procedures which should be followed. The list of reasons why an employee would be subject to dismissal under the gross misconduct umbrella, includes things like theft, fraud, drug or alcohol misuse, but it is also subjective. For instance, a barman drinking alcohol at the workplace would probably not be treated with the same level of severity as, say, a taxi-driver.'

'Are you saying, that even though I contravened the company's policy on the use of the internet, I shouldn't have been sacked?'

'Again, not necessarily. If it can be proved that other staff members have accessed the internet for their own personal use and benefit, and the company was aware of that, *and* they weren't dismissed, then you have a case for unfair dismissal. Or if you can prove the company was aware of other instances, and dealt with them using their disciplinary policy, up to, but not including, dismissal, then you also have a case.'

'Basically, you're saying that I need to prove that either they knew and did nothing, or they knew, but the other employee only got a warning, or something?'

'Exactly!'

'I don't think I can prove that,' Daisy said, thinking hard.

'That remains to be seen. You have a right to appeal, and you have a right to ask for any records the company holds which might be pertinent to your appeal. Or rather, in your case, your solicitor will do this for you.'

'I don't have a solicitor,' Daisy said, with a frown. This all sounded very serious and grown up.

Zoe gave Daisy a pitying look. 'You do.'

'I do?'

'One of the perks of working for my law firm, is that employees and their families are able to apply for pro-bono work.'

'Pro-bono?'

'Free, to a certain point, and under certain circumstances. Hazel Holmes has looked at your case, and has agreed to take it on. She wouldn't do that unless she thought you had a good chance of winning.'

'You mean, like going to court, in front of a judge and jury.'

Zoe laughed, and Daisy realised how seldom she'd heard her sister-in-law do that recently. 'Not court, an industrial tribunal,' Zoe explained.

'Okay,' Daisy was apprehensive, despite the little glimmer of hope. 'Where do we go from here?'

'You meet with Hazel. She'll be able to give you more details and better advice than I can. Before that, though, you need to write a letter to *Caring Cards*, advising them that you are appealing their decision to dismiss you without warning, and that you have retained the services of a solicitor, who will be acting as your representative.'

'Okay...'

'I'll help with the letter. In fact, I'll type it out for you, and all you'll need to do is sign it and stick it in the post.'

Zoe was as good as her word, and before the hour was out, the letter was written, signed, and clutched in Daisy's hand as she headed to the corner shop for a stamp, then into town to meet Hazel.

Ms Holmes was a smartly-dressed, slim woman in her late forties, with the demeanour of a Rottweiler.

'Sit,' she barked.

Daisy sat, twisting her hands, nervously.

'Don't fidget. I won't bite.'

Daisy wasn't so certain.

'I hope you're taking good care of Zoe,' Hazel growled. 'I need her back here, sharpish.'

Daisy nodded, her head bobbing up and down so fast she thought her neck might snap, and she wondered how Zoe put up with the woman.

'She practically runs this place. Keeps me on my toes,' Hazel was saying, and Daisy's respect for her sister-in-law grew yet again.

'I hate employers who think they can ride roughshod over the law, and people's rights,' Hazel began, getting down to business. 'I'm not going to guarantee we'll win this,' (Daisy liked the way she said "we") 'but there is a chance the company has been underhand. Tell me everything.'

Daisy did. She was too scared not to!

'Have you got proof?' Hazel demanded, when Daisy finished her story, ending with the eavesdropping episode in the ladies' toilets.

'No, but I could get some, I could follow Melissa, and—'

'Hold your horses, detective. Say you did obtain proof of this affair, what then?

'It would prove—'

'Nothing. Nothing relating to your appeal, anyway. They could claim that their affair began *after* you were dismissed.'

'But what about Melissa's promotion?' Daisy cried.

'Again, circumstantial. They could argue that if you had still been employed by them, you would have had an equal opportunity to apply for the role.'

'So, we're back to square one,' Daisy said, sighing. This was turning out to be a total waste of everyone's time.

'No, we're not. I've handled many such cases and often, if there's the slightest hint of malpractice on behalf of the employer, then these things are usually settled out of court, or does not progress as far as a tribunal. It will cost the company to defend a precarious position, if indeed this one *is* precarious, and even if it's not, I believe you still have grounds for appeal.'

'What do we do now?'

'I'll start the appeal process, then we wait.'

Daisy wasn't very good at waiting, but with no other choice she was forced to accept.

'Will they have to re-employ me?' she asked.

'Reinstate you? That depends on a number of factors, which I won't go into now. Do you want to be reinstated?'

'I don't know.' With her job prospects as low as they were, she didn't know if she had much choice, but the thought of walking back into that office, with all eyes staring at her, and with Melissa as her line manager, filled Daisy with dread.

'Leave it with me,' Hazel instructed, showing Daisy out. 'I'll be in touch once I have some information for you.'

Back at David's house, Zoe was waiting for her. 'Well?' she demanded.

Daisy told her about her meeting, slumping onto the sofa and resting her head against its squishy back. 'I don't know if I can work there again,' she confessed. 'It would be horrible.'

'Have you thought any more about my idea?' Zoe asked.

In all honesty, Daisy hadn't. As exciting as it sounded, Daisy didn't think she had the skills, the drive, or the experience to carry it off. She wasn't even sure if she wanted to try.

'I've got a confession,' Zoe said, after listening to Daisy's excuses.

'You haven't started on it, have you, because I honestly don't think I'm up for it,' Daisy asked.

'I haven't, but what I have done, and please don't hate me, but I've sent an email to the CEO of *Rosebush*.'

'The *Rosebush*? Why?' *Rosebush* was the biggest, most successful greeting card manufacturer in the UK. The CEO wouldn't be interested in a CV from a nobody. He had an HR department (a proper one, not merely a woman called Joyce) to do the recruiting on his behalf. Somehow Daisy couldn't see him, or her, sifting through random job applications.

'Because the idea is a good one,' Zoe said.

'If it was so good, and I don't mean to be horrid, but they'd have thought of it themselves.'

'They haven't. Or, if they have, the idea didn't get as far as the CEO's desk. He likes it.'

'How do you know?'

'He said so.'

Daisy was speechless, but Zoe wasn't.

'I took the liberty of setting you up with a new email account,' she said. 'You honestly couldn't have *Daisy-*

DoLittle@butterfly.com, not if you want to appear professional.'

'I don't know what to say.' Daisy really didn't. It was very kind of Zoe, but it was too much like your mother stepping in to sort out your problems because you can't — embarrassing.

Zoe must have guessed what Daisy was thinking, because she added, 'I pretended to be you. I hope you don't mind.'

Daisy suspected Zoe might do a better job at being Daisy, than Daisy was at being herself. She certainly had, so far.

'His name is Emmett Carstairs, and he wants to set up a meeting with you. He, or his secretary I expect, will be in touch.'

'But *Rosebush* is based in London. I don't want to move,' Daisy pointed out, and a pair of deep blue eyes and the man they belonged to, popped into her mind.

Chapter 27

'Wear trainers,' Noah had said. 'And something old, and warm, and you will need gloves.'

Daisy had no idea what he was planning for their second date (if a hasty, interrupted meal in a hospital canteen could be called a date), but she did as she was instructed, fervently hoping he didn't expect her to walk up a bloody great mountain or something.

He picked her up from David's house, and gave her a slow, sexy smile. She had done her best, but old warm clothes weren't exactly the height of sexiness, though he told her she looked lovely, and she was grateful for his kindness, even if it wasn't the truth.

At least her hair looked nice. She hadn't yet drummed up the courage to have her long locks chopped off, and she'd spent ages in front of the little mirror in David and Zoe's spare room, pinning it up into a loose chignon. It didn't go with the old coat she was wearing, but at least it showed she'd made some kind of an effort.

'Where are we going?' she asked.

'You'll see,' was all he said, and he refused to be drawn any further.

As they headed out towards Malvern, leaving the city behind them, Daisy was certain he intended to drag her up the famous Malvern Hills. She'd walked up them before, and though the view from the top across the wide Severn River Valley was spectacular, the steep climb wasn't. She'd been breathless and knackered by the time she reached the top on her one and only trek up the hill, and she'd been a fitter, younger version of herself. Twelve years old, to be exact. Goodness knows what state she'd be in this time! She'd probably need mouth to mouth.

But the car didn't take the Malvern turning. Instead, Noah eased the vehicle into a narrow lane, and drove up the twisty winding road for a mile or so. The countryside was pretty, admittedly, even though the trees were bare and the day was grey and overcast.

When the car pulled into a farm yard, Daisy gave him an odd look.

'Are we there yet, or are you lost and wanted to find somewhere to turn?' she asked.

'We're here.'

'And where is *here*?'

'*Coldbrook Farm*.'

'What's in *Coldbrook Farm*, except cows?' she asked. She didn't need to see their black and white backsides, she could smell them through the closed car windows.

'Horses,' he replied, a huge grin on his face.

Was that supposed to mean something to her? 'Horses,' she repeated.

'You said you wanted to go riding, so we are going riding.'

Daisy didn't know whether to hug him or slap him. She couldn't believe it – not only had he remembered her saying it, but he had taken the trouble to do something about it. He was either very considerate, or very silly. The next hour or so would decide which.

She got out of the car in a daze. Her – riding? What if she fell off? What if she made a total arse of herself?

'My mate's parents own the farm,' Noah was saying, as he took her hand and almost dragged her around the back of the farmhouse. Her heart lurched at his touch, but it almost jumped out of her chest when she saw what was around the corner.

Two horses, both of them enormous.

There was no way she was getting on one of them. No way!

Five minutes later, she had one foot in the stirrup and another braced on Noah's hands as he hoisted her into the saddle.

'His name is Killer,' Noah said, as she balanced precariously at what she felt was about a hundred feet off the ground.

'Killer!' Daisy shrieked, and the horse's ears flicked back menacingly.

'Just kidding, he's called Max.'

Oh, that's alright then, Daisy thought sarcastically, as Noah gathered up the reins and showed her how to hold them. Then he adjusted her stirrups.

'Comfy?' he asked.

'No.'

His chuckle sent shivers down her already shivery spine.

Dinner would have been nice, lunch even. In a pub or restaurant where there wasn't a hairy, smelly beast in sight. She could happily have coped with a play, or a concert, something indoors, where it wouldn't matter if she fell off her chair…

'How do you steer it?' she asked. 'More to the point, how do you get it to stop?'

'To stop, you pull back gently on the reins, and to steer you use your legs and your hands to tell him which direction you want him to go in.'

'I don't want him to go anywhere. I'm quite happy here,' Daisy stated.

Noah winked at her. 'You'll love it,' he promised.

I won't, she thought.

Noah mounted the other savage animal, who whuffled through its ginormous nostrils at him as he clambered on board, and Daisy nearly wet herself in fright.

Noah clicked his tongue, dug his heels into the animal's side, and the horse began to move, one huge foot in front of the other. Daisy cried out when hers lurched forward, and she grabbed at his mane to stop herself from toppling backwards.

Thank God Noah had insisted she wore a helmet, she thought, even though it did mess up her carefully styled hair. At least she wouldn't knock her brains out when she came off, and come off she most certainly was going to. How did people balance on these things?

Max fell into line behind the other horse, plodding slowly after it. Daisy forgot the reins existed and clutched the long, coarse hair sprouting from low down on the animal's neck, holding on for dear life.

But after a while, she relaxed enough to take one hand off the mane (her knuckles were white where she'd been gripping so hard) and pick up one of the leather straps. When nothing happened, she did the same with the other.

'How long are we supposed to do this for?' she whispered, not wanting to speak too loudly in case it annoyed her horse.

'As long as you feel comfortable.'

'Does that mean we can stop now?'

Another chuckle. It made the hairs on the back of her neck stand to attention. Dammit, but he was sexy, though all she could see of him was his broad back, ramrod straight, oozing confidence and competence as he swayed slightly to the rhythm of the horse's gait.

She was aware she was doing a similar kind of sway, but she certainly didn't feel sexy. She felt gauche and uncertain, but she had to admit she felt a thrill. She was doing it – after all these years, she was finally on the back of a horse. And this was no pony; this was a full-sized animal, chestnut in colour with darker mane and tail. Noah's horse was a dappled grey, even larger than hers, and she admired the way he controlled it with ease. The slightest touch from Noah's hands or feet, she noticed, had the animal instantly obeying him.

He turned in the saddle, twisting to look at her. 'You okay?'

Actually, she was. 'I'm fine,' she called, and was rewarded by a wide smile. He was simply gorgeous when he smiled – his whole face lit up. He should do it more often.

They cut across the farmyard, and through a field, Daisy marvelling at the way Max stopped obediently while Noah angled his mount sideways on to the gate, then Noah leaned down (her heart was in her mouth at this point, scared he would fall off) and opened the gate, his horse stepping backwards.

He'd clearly done this before, and Daisy felt a twinge of envy and curiosity. Had Noah grown up around horses, or had he learned to ride later in life? There was so much she wanted to learn about this man, so much to discover. She was looking forward to it immensely.

'Well?' he asked.

'Eh?'

'Are you going through, or what?'

Or what, because she had no idea how to get her horse moving.

'Gently kick your heels into Max's side,' Noah instructed, 'else he won't know what you want him to do.'

Kick him? Daisy was appalled. Surely the animal cruelty police would have a field day if she did that.

'Better still, squeeze your legs together,' he added. 'He'll respond to that, too.'

Daisy's treacherous little mind wondered if Noah would respond in the same way, and she blushed furiously, her cheeks feeling very hot indeed.

She squeezed and Max walked forward through the gate.

'I can't stop him,' she called, as the horse kept going. She was conscious of Noah falling further behind as he closed the gate.

'Pull gently back on the reins and lean back ever so slightly in the saddle,' he called back.

Daisy did as she was told, surprised when the tactics worked and Max ground to a halt. He soon started moving again once Noah's horse drew level and pulled into the lead.

'I didn't do anything,' Daisy said in confusion.

Noah twisted around again – she wished he'd watch where they were going and keep his eyes on the road, so to speak. 'Horses are herd animals,' he explained. 'Trigger here, is the dominant horse, so Max will automatically follow him, unless you tell him not to.'

'Will he listen to me?'

'Try it. I'll keep walking and you ask Max to stop.'

Daisy remembered what Noah had said, and pulled gently back on the reins.

Nothing happened.

She pulled harder and Max plodded to a stop, swishing his tail.

I can do this, she thought, triumphantly, and she felt immensely proud of herself.

'I haven't thought about riding since I was little,' she said, when she caught up with Noah, 'but Jayne used to have lessons in an arena. I remember her telling me about it.'

'That's one way of learning to ride,' Noah responded, 'but this way is so much more fun. Fresh air, beautiful scenery, and no going around in endless circles.'

Daisy had to agree with him. After she realised that she didn't have to keep her eyes glued to where they were going, and her heart didn't jump into her mouth every time Max kicked a loose stone, or faltered as he picked his way over the uneven path, she settled down and looked around her. Never in a million years had she imagined going on a date like this. It was thoughtful, and also very different to what she'd been expecting.

When Noah judged she'd had enough, he cut through a field and headed back to the farm. By this time, her behind was numb, and her knees and thighs were becoming a little tender where the leather rubbed. She was also getting cold, and her hands were beginning to stiffen up, both from the chill air and her death-like grip on the reins.

In comparison, Noah looked as though he could keep going for hours. His one hand (just the one) held both reins and rested on the pommel (she'd learned a new word), the other rested on his thigh. She couldn't help staring at it – his thigh, not his hand. As the horse moved, she could see the play of muscles beneath his jeans and it did funny things to her, and she wondered if *his* thighs ached.

'Well?' he asked, when they rode into the yard in a clatter of hooves, the horses with their ears pricked up, the pace slightly faster once they were on the home straight.

'It was wonderful,' she sighed. She was cold, parts of her she didn't know existed ached, she stank of horse, and she had a feeling her nose resembled Rudolph, but she meant it. It *had* been wonderful. She wanted to do it all again, once she'd warmed up and the feeling had come back into her bum.

She watched Noah dismount and wondered how she was going to get down, when he came alongside her to help.

'Take your feet out of both stirrups,' he said, 'then lean forward and slide your leg over the horses back. Don't worry, I've got you.'

He did too. His hands were on her waist as she slid down the horse's side and landed on her feet. He held her a fraction longer than she needed for her to regain her balance. His warm breath fanned her ear, and she leaned back into him, just for a moment.

Max whickered, making Daisy jump, and the moment was lost. Pity.

'Here,' Noah said, bringing a Polo mint out of his pocket.

She took it from him, wondering if she had bad breath and Noah was trying to be tactful. She lifted it to her mouth.

'It's not for you, it's for him. Most horses love mints,' Noah said, and she went to hold it out to the horse, using her thumb and forefinger. 'Not like that, like this.'

He held a mint out to Trigger, the Polo resting on the palm of his flat hand. She watched the horse suck it up, with whiskery mobile lips.

'Always use the flat of your hand,' he said, 'otherwise they might nip. They don't mean to, but it hurts all the same.'

She gave Max his, giggling as the horse's lips nibbled at her hand, the soft hairs tickling her skin. He chomped and chewed, his mouth working as if the little mint was the size of a golf ball, then he blew down his nose at her.

Daisy was enchanted, despite the slobber on her hand. She wiped it off on his furry neck, then reached up to stroke his mobile ears. The horse accepted her caress, and Daisy felt emboldened enough to pat his long nose.

'I think a hot chocolate is in order, and a sit by a warm fire,' Noah suggested.

'Yes, please.' It sounded lovely, especially the warm bit, and they drove back down the lane and drew up outside a tiny little pub.

'This used to be a favourite haunt of mine when I was a teenager,' Noah said. 'They used to let me have a sneaky pint, even though they knew I wasn't old enough. It's changed hands since then,' he added, 'but I hope they still do hot chocolate with marshmallows.'

They did – thick, rich, and creamy. Daisy sat beside the fire, logs crackling in the hearth, with a frothy moustache on her upper lip, and slowly thawed out. Noah took a sip from his mug and the pair of them sat laughing at each other.

'Will you trust me to take you on a date again?' he asked, suddenly serious, 'or have I blown it?'

Daisy leaned forward and stared him straight in the eye. 'I've had more fun today than I've had in a very long time,' she said. 'I'd like to do it again.'

'Oh, we will,' he promised, a smile stretching across his face, 'but I don't want you to think I'm a one-horse wonder, and I've got nothing else up my sleeve. One horse… get it?' He giggled like a small boy and Daisy shook her head.

'You've got the most awful line in puns,' she said, and Noah pretended to look hurt.

'We can't all be a whizz with words, Daisy Jones. I have to work with what I've got.'

Without warning, the atmosphere sobered, and Noah leaned forward, resting his elbows on the table.

'You've got a silly cream moustache,' he told her.

She put her fingers to her face and was about to wipe it away, when he said, 'I'd like to lick it off.'

Oh. Well. Good. Daisy's thoughts leapt around in her head like a Springer Spaniel in a field.

'Too much?' he asked.

She shook her head.

'Too soon?'

She shook her head again.

'May I?'

'Please.' She tried to aim for a seductive purr, but it came out a breathy squawk.

He raised himself out of his chair, stretched right across the table and his tongue came out to gently lick away the cream.

She froze.

Never had any man done anything so erotic to her before. The tip of his tongue barely touched her, but her skin flamed all the same, and she was glad she was sitting down as her insides liquefied.

He drew back slightly, and Daisy saw a trace of white froth on the tip of his tongue, before it slipped back between his lips. Her own lips parted in naked desire, then his mouth was on hers, and she lost herself in his kiss.

'Excuse me, but we don't allow that kind of lewd behaviour in here,' a voice said, and they broke apart to see the landlord, a little round man resembling a barrel of the real ale he served, hands on hips, staring at them with a furious look on his face.

'What kind of lewd behaviour do you allow?' Noah equipped, and Daisy giggled.

Noah had one hand behind her head where he'd drawn her close, and his fingers were buried in her dishevelled chignon. He took a moment to disentangle himself, allowing time for Daisy's heart rate to return to a semblance of normality. It still beat harder and faster than it should, but at least it was no longer threatening to leap out of her chest. Her breathing was a bit heavier than usual though, and heat radiated outwards from somewhere south of her stomach.

She tried to blame it on her throbbing thighs, but she had a sneaking suspicion they weren't throbbing just because of the riding.

Noah sat back in his chair and they finished their drinks in silence. He hadn't taken his eyes off her and all she could think about was their hungry depths and the desire pulling her down into them. His lips were slightly parted and she remembered every second of them on hers, the feel of him, the smell of him.

'I want to do that again,' he said, finally.

'So do I.'

'We can't,' he replied, and Daisy almost burst into tears. Why take her out on a date at all, if his medical ethics didn't allow it.

But then he added, 'Because if we do, I won't be able to stop there.'

Oh? Oh! She didn't want him to stop either. She would have been quite happy to let him ravish her in front of the fire, if they didn't have an audience.

'I don't want you to think I'm the type of guy who sleeps with a girl on a first date,' he continued.

I don't care if you are, Daisy wanted to say. Take me, take me! her heart yelled. Actually, it wasn't her heart doing the yelling, it was something much lower down, and she realised she hadn't felt like this in a long time. Maybe never.

'I want to get to know you first,' he was saying.

She wanted to get to know him, too, but the woman part of her argued that they could just as easily get to know each other in bed, whilst they were doing unspeakably sexy things to each other, as they could by sitting in a pub talking.

'Okay,' was all she managed to get out.

Here was the type of man she dreamed of, one who wanted her mind, not her body, and all she could do was pout because he wasn't going to whisk her off to bed.

Damn him!

Chapter 28

'How did it go with Dr Loveheart?' Zoe asked, when Daisy staggered back into her sister-in-law's house, wondering if she'd ever be able to walk properly again. Who knew riding was so physical? Though maybe she was feeling wobbly because of the kiss, and Noah's instructions that she should have a hot bath and massage her thighs whilst she was in it, left her wishing he'd be the one to do the massaging.

She was about to tell Zoe, when her mother bustled into the room.

'About time, young lady,' Sandra said. 'I've got bingo to go to. Oh, and I forgot, to tell you, but some man called earlier.'

'Some man?'

'Said it was about an office junior's job.'

'He phoned *here*?' Daisy could have sworn she'd put her mobile and her mother's landline number on her CV.

'No, silly, he phoned me.'

'You? Have you applied for a job?'

'Why would I do something like that? I've got a job already – looking after you lot. He wants you to ring him back. I've got the number somewhere.'

Daisy did a quick mental search through the numerous jobs she'd applied for and came to the conclusion this one must be for the builders' merchants. She checked the time – five pm – and hoped she wasn't too late. Whenever Freddie had gone to a builders' merchants (ostensibly to pick up patio slabs or paint, but in hindsight, Daisy wondered if it had been to ogle the builders themselves), he'd always gone early because they were often shut when normal people were just coming home from work.

Daisy took the piece of paper from her mother and tried to read the scrawl.

Mr Bradley, or was it Bartley? And was that a five or a three. Mr Bradley, she decided, as she keyed his number into her mobile.

'Hi, I'm Daisy Jones. I applied for the office junior role you're advertising?'

'Bit old, aren't you?' The voice on the other end was deep and gruff, and sounded rather testy.

'Pardon?'

'I said, you're a bit old. From your date of birth, I worked out you must be thirty.'

'Yes, um, that's right.'

'Hmm. Got any experience?'

'A bit, but the advert said, "no experience necessary".'

'I was expecting school leavers to apply,' he said. 'They don't usually have any experience.'

'And have they?'

'Have who done what?'

'Have school leavers applied?'

'Yes.'

So why phone her?

'I'm looking to retrain,' Daisy said, cautiously. 'I can answer the phone, I'm used to dealing with people,' (was she?) 'and can use Word and Excel,' (she'd have to google Excel), 'and as you can see, I'm used to using email.'

'Do you know the difference between sharp sand and fine sand?' he barked.

'No, but I'm a fast learner, and I've got the advantage of maturity on my side,' she added, getting into her stride.

Was this an interview? It certainly felt like one, even if it was being conducted over the phone.

'I see you've been working for *Caring Cards*. Good with your hands, are you?'

'Eh?'

'Making cards.'

'Ah, no, I didn't make them myself, I er...' Oh dear, there was no choice, she was going to have to tell Mr Bradley exactly what she'd done at *Caring Cards*. '...constructed the verses. As well as other things.'

'Like what?'

Daisy ran through a list of the other staff member's roles. Design? Nope. Accounts? Nah, she couldn't add up to save her life, and as for stuff like VAT and tax – ug. Human resources? Hmm, all Joyce had seemed to do was send out wage slips and calculate holiday entitlement.

Ah! 'Part of my role was to explore new markets,' she said, knowing full well she was talking about visiting any new clothes shops as soon as they opened, so it wasn't strictly a lie, was it? It just didn't have anything remotely to do with her former job.

'What sort of markets?'

Time to lie. Daisy rattled off a list of supermarkets and chain stores – anywhere she could think of which sold greeting cards. Getting into the swing of it, she added, 'It was my job to ensure our stockists were kept supplied with the right cards at the right time – no point in sending them Mother's Day cards at Valentines,' she chortled. 'I also contacted new outlets and arranged a salesman to call.'

'Were you any good at it?'

'Yes,' she replied, confidently.

'Oh, all right, then. Come in on Monday for a proper interview, so I can check you over. You've got to be better than the last girl – moody as hell, she was, and she dressed like she was going to a funeral. Always crying over some lad or another. She used to put the customers off. They don't want some bird blubbing when she's weighing out a pound of nails.'

'That's my point exactly, Mr Bradley. 'You won't get any of that with me.'

'Got any kids?'

What? 'No.'

'Any plans on having some?'

Daisy was speechless. She was pretty sure that prospective employers weren't allowed to ask those kind of questions – discrimination, and all that.

'No,' she replied somewhat stiffly. Bet he wouldn't ask a man that question.

'I've got three, and two grandchildren with another on the way. You don't want to leave it too late.' How dare he make a comment about when she should have children!

'I'm sorry?' she said, her tone frostier than a bag of peas in a freezer.

'Before coming in on Monday. The earlier the better, in fact, say, eight-thirty?'

'Oh, yes, of course. Eight-thirty, it is.'

'That'll give me a chance to see to the early customers. Can you make tea?'

'Yes, I can.' At last, a question she could answer truth-fully.

'Great. See you then.' He rang off, leaving Daisy staring at her phone with a bemused expression.

'Job interview,' she said, unnecessarily to Zoe. Sandra had already waltzed out of the door. 'Um… where's David?' Daisy asked suddenly.

'Upstairs,' Zoe replied, with a tinge of pride in her voice. 'He can get up and down them now. And the wheelchair has gone back. They collected it when you were out, on your date. You've got to tell me all about it, I'm going stir crazy.'

'How did David get up the stairs?'

'On his bottom, backwards. Your mother said he used to get up them the same way when he was little.'

Things were starting to look up, Daisy thought. She'd got a boyfriend (ish), a new job (ish), and maybe she'd be able to relinquish her caring duties and move back home soon.

She hesitated. Maybe the last one wasn't quite so good. After all, who in their right mind would want to move back in with their mother and nan?

But, like the old song says, two out of three ain't bad.

Chapter 29

'A zoo?' Daisy repeated. As dates go, a zoo wasn't bad, but they'd still not managed the traditional dinner and drinks scenario yet, because Noah seemed to be working most evenings.

'I thought your children might enjoy it,' Noah said.

Oh shit!

'How old are they?' he continued. 'What are their names? You haven't said anything about them, and I realise you don't want to go introducing them to every man you go out with – not that I'm saying you go out with lots of men... Bugger! I'm doing it again, aren't I?' A low, drawn-out sigh wafted down the phone. 'Why am I only like this around you?' Noah asked. 'I'm perfectly normal with everyone else, honest.' Another sigh. 'Look, you don't have to bring them, though I would be happy if you did, but if you don't want to, that's not a problem either, but please come on your own anyway.'

'Noah, I... er... I've got something to tell you.' She had no idea how he was going to take this, but surely it wouldn't be too badly. It would be more difficult if the situation was the other way around, and she had to confess to having a couple of children hidden away at home after not mentioning them before now.

Noah was strangely silent.

'You know we keep getting off on the wrong foot...?' Daisy began.

'You don't have to say any more, I understand.'

'What do you understand?'

'You don't think I'm father material,' he stated flatly. 'And you might be right. What do I know about kids? I know a lot about their anatomy, but I don't really *know* kids, like how to talk to them, or how to interreact with them.'

'Neither do I.' Where on earth was all this coming from?

'Don't keep putting yourself down. I bet you're a brilliant mum!' Noah said.

'That's what I want to talk to you about – I'm not a mum at all,' she blurted and waited for a response. It was a long time coming.

'Do they live with their father?' Noah finally asked.

'They don't live anywhere, because I haven't got any.'

'I don't understand, you said you had two.'

'I was being flippant, and when I said I needed to get a baby-sitter, I meant for David and Zoe. To be honest, I'd forgotten I'd said it.'

'Oh.' He sounded rather put out. 'Is there anything else I should know?'

'Not that I can think of.' She hunted around for something to lift the mood. 'I don't like peanut butter or Marmite.'

'*I* have a son,' he said, abruptly.

'You do?' That was a surprise. 'I thought you said you don't know how to interreact with kids.'

'I don't.'

It was Daisy's turn not to understand.

'He lives with his mother in Brighton,' Noah went on to say. 'I only see him a few times a year.'

Had he hoped that *her* "children" would help him hone his parenting skills? And was he disappointed to discover she didn't in fact have any?

'I do like kids,' he added, 'I'm just a bit awkward around them.'

'Are you disappointed?' she asked. The time for misconstrued conversations was over. The pair of them needed to be clear and honest with each other.

'Yes, very,' he said.

Daisy scowled, trying to think back to when he asked her to go to dinner with him – it was definitely before she'd told him she'd needed to sort out a baby-sitter, so it wasn't as if he'd only asked her out to practice being a daddy on her children. She actually felt quite cross for those imaginary kids. They deserved better.

'...and when she said she was staying there permanently, I was devastated.'

'Come again?'

'When Kate said she was moving to Brighton I was upset,' he said. 'Disappointed didn't cover it.'

'Kate is…?'

'Connor's mother, yes.'

Ah, Connor must be the son, and Kate the ex. A surge of unexpected dislike and jealousy flooded through her. Then she realised what he'd been saying; it wasn't Daisy's lack of offspring which he was disappointed about, it was his ex taking his son all the way to Brighton.

'Can you come to the zoo, or not?' he asked, and she blinked at the abrupt change of subject.

'When?'

'Now, of course!'

Daisy was astounded. Talk about being impulsive.

'I suppose…' she said. With David now more mobile and able to get himself into and out of bed, (ditto the bathroom – but she really didn't want to think too deeply about that), Daisy's services weren't called on so frequently. She still insisted on doing the housework, but Zoe was gradually taking over the cooking once more, and all three of them were thankful for that, though Zoe was teaching Daisy, and Daisy was pleased with her increasing expertise in the kitchen.

'Great. I'll pick you up in half an hour.' He rang off, leaving her mystified, and slightly frantic because she only had thirty minutes to have a shower, wash and dry her hair, shave her legs, put some make-up on, find something zooey to wear… arggh!

By the time she'd rushed around like a total idiot, trying to make herself look as pretty as possible, she was all hot and bothered and felt as though she needed another shower. And all the while she kept thinking about his ex (girlfriend? wife? one-night stand?) and son, but she couldn't seem to process the information.

Noah was thirty-four, so of course he had history, but the subject of previous relationships hadn't come up, and why would it. On a first date, you don't say, "I'll have a white wine and by the way I've had x amount of boyfriends", but she could have assumed that something as significant as having a child might have entered the conversation at some point.

The bell rang, and David went to answer it. She heard them talking shop, Noah's version, as he asked her brother about his leg, then she trotted down the stairs and the two men shook hands and she was sitting in Noah's car before she had a chance to think.

She sneaked a quick look at him. He'd trimmed his beard so it was only a fraction more than stubble, and his lashes were even longer than she remembered them. His lips were firmly closed, and she noticed the tension around his jaw. Though his eyes were on the road, she could tell he was aware of her scrutiny.

'You want to ask, so ask,' he said, after the silence had stretched for several miles.

Daisy thought carefully. Yes, she wanted to know everything about this mysterious Kate, like how they'd met, what she looked like, why they'd split up, how long had they been together, did he love her... But she hoped he'd told her about his son because he wanted their relationship to go somewhere. They had a connection, didn't they? And the thought of her having two children herself, hadn't put him off in the slightest.

'What's he like?' she asked, genuinely wanting to know. She'd said that she wanted a man to open to her fully, that she wanted to know his heart and mind and soul. How could she do that if she didn't get to know his child? She tried to imagine what this son of his looked like, picturing a boy of three or four, with Noah's dark hair and bright blue eyes, and she wondered if he missed his father.

Noah raised his eyebrows and glanced at her out of the corner of his eye. He'd clearly been expecting her to ask something else.

'Connor?' His face softened. 'He's smart, and funny, and loves sport. He's got a wicked sense of humour, draws like Michelangelo, and is the tidiest kid I know. Seriously, he's a bit anal, especially when it comes to his bedroom.

I swear he's had a body swap with an alien, because he's not like any teenager I know. Oh, and he hates Ian, and wants to come and live with me.'

Slow down, mister, what was that about a teenager? 'How old is he?' Daisy asked, cautiously.

'Fifteen.'

'Right…' Mental arithmetic wasn't her strong point, but she sure as hell was able to work out thirty-four minus fifteen.

'Yes, I was young, we both were,' Noah said.

Gone were the images of a cute little boy, and in its place were pictures of a sullen stroppy teenager, with bum fluff on his face, acne, and limbs he hadn't grown into yet, and—

'Who is Ian?' she asked.

'Kate's fiancé. They're getting married in a month.' Noah smiled wryly. 'I've been invited to the wedding.' He turned his head, taking his eyes off the road for a second. 'You could come with me.'

Daisy had no idea what to say.

'Too soon?' he asked.

She shrugged.

'Okay, no problem,' Noah responded swiftly, and Daisy had the feeling she'd disappointed him.

Tough. He'd have to deal with it. She liked him, she *really* liked him, but she wasn't sure she wanted to meet his son's mother just yet, and especially not at the woman's own wedding. Besides, they'd only just met themselves, and this was only their third date.

'We're here,' he said, as they pulled into the huge carpark at West Midlands Safari Park. He checked the time. 'Fancy going around the safari park first.'

'First? What happens after that?'

'You'll see.' He had a smile on his face, but his eyes were sad.

Chapter 30

'Ooh!' Daisy squealed as the eland stuck most of its massive head in through the window, and an incredibly long tongue waved about in the air. Finding nothing edible, the antelope licked its own nostrils instead. With difficulty, it extracted its spiral horns and backed away, turning its attention to the car behind them.

Noah grimaced at the drool it left on the car door.

'I can't believe how big that thing is,' Daisy said.

'I think I can see something even bigger.' Noah pointed to the enormous grey backside. It looked like a strange, squat tank.

When it moved, Daisy realised what it was – a rhino.

'Blimey! I hope it's friendly,' she proclaimed.

'I think they're used to people ogling them, but I wouldn't want to be around if it decided it needed a bit of privacy. I don't think my car would stand a chance.'

Noah drove a 4x4 ('I need to be able to get to work whatever the weather,' he'd explained), and she had visions of how badly her own little rust-bucket would fare in an argument with such a beast. It didn't bear thinking about!

He glanced at his watch. The trail through the safari drive-through was understandably slow, as each vehicle moved at a snail's pace, and she wondered if he needed to be in work soon.

'Not until later,' he said, when she asked him. 'I've got the pub-closing shift, with its share of drunks and people off their faces.'

So far they'd been on two dates (not counting the "meal" in the hospital staff canteen) and both of them had involved animals of some kind or another. She wondered if he was planning a visit to the local animal rescue centre next. Admittedly, all their dates had been during the day, and she supposed there was a limit to what you could do on a cold, January afternoon. Lunch in a decent pub might have been nice, though.

They stared in awe at the small herd of majestic giraffes gliding past with their odd, swaying gait.

'Ooh, a baby one,' Daisy cried, pointing at a mini version. It was a fraction of its mother's height, yet was still a whopping eight foot tall. 'I wouldn't want to feed that for a week!' Its mother swivelled her long neck to stare at them with her liquid brown eyes, almost as if she'd heard.

Daisy thought this was the best part, so far. She'd enjoyed seeing the lions, but they weren't exactly the life and soul of the party, doing little else but lying around yawning, and though Elephant Valley had been impressive, she felt a little uneasy about such magnificent animals being enclosed, even though the area they lived in was a large one.

She was having a lovely time, but every so often Noah's revelation popped into her mind. What must it have been like to have a baby at such a young age, and just how close were Noah and the mysterious Kate? Not very, if the woman was marrying someone else, and Daisy was grateful for that snippet of information. She was still a teensy-weensy bit jealous, but she could easily imagine how much worse she would feel if his ex was single. And then, there was the big question of how Noah felt about Kate, and she wondered if he still loved her, or if he ever had done.

Daisy was surprised at how she felt about it all. Now the shock had worn off a little, she knew she wanted to carry on seeing him. And she knew she had been somewhat unreasonable – Noah was an attractive, thirty-four-year-old man. He was bound to have had other women before her.

'Have you ever been married?' she asked suddenly.

'No.'

'Kate…?'

'Was a year younger than me. We should have known better.' He kept his gaze on the zebra, but Daisy could tell his mind was on the past. 'We *did* know better, but we were in love,' (ouch, that hurt), 'and not as careful as we should have been, and accidents happen.'

'You didn't stay together?'

He gave a wry smile. 'It's amazing how quickly the reality of an impending baby can knock the love right out of you, for her anyway,' he said, and added, 'and she didn't want to. Our parents didn't want us to. I was nineteen, I'd just finished my A-levels and jobs weren't easy to come by. Believe me, I tried, but at that age I couldn't earn enough to keep a pet rabbit, let alone a girlfriend and a baby. I would have given it a go, though, if that's what she'd wanted.'

'What happened then?'

'She had Connor, then went back to school. I saw him as often as I could, and provided for him as best I could, but her parents made it clear they didn't want me around much and neither did Kate. When the family moved to Brighton, it made seeing my son that much more difficult. Then I got my arse into gear, and decided to be a doctor. And here I am.'

Daisy was about to ask him if he still loved her, but Noah checked his watch again and said, 'Fancy a spot of lunch?' making it clear the conversation was over.

He'd already said he wasn't due in work until later, so Daisy wondered if he was counting down the hours until he could reasonably take her home.

Lunch consisted of a chicken and mango salad for her, and a burger with chips for him. Daisy had no idea why she had chosen a salad, especially since her mouth flooded with saliva when she saw Noah's food, but she remembered her vow to lose some weight and go to the gym, so she supposed the salad was the best option.

Another sneaky glance at his watch as they rose from the table, and Daisy assumed they'd head back to the car. Instead, he said, 'We haven't seen the meerkats yet.'

Daisy loved meerkats! Who didn't? They were glorious little balls of squeaky fur with agile noses. She marvelled at the one on sentry duty, just like in the documentaries. And when he, or she, had enough of watching for danger and decided to dig and forage instead, another one immediately took its place, searching the skies and making little chirruping noises to reassure the others. And the babies! – ooh, they were *sooo* cute, hardly bigger than the palm of her hand.

But when Noah looked at his watch yet again, the mood was broken and Daisy asked crossly, 'I know you don't have to be at the hospital yet, but is there somewhere else you need to be?'

'Yes, but not me – you.' He took her by the hand and almost dragged her down a path, hesitated, looked at the sign posts, took another path, and stopped again, confused. Then he spotted what he was looking for.

'There!' he cried.

Daisy looked but couldn't see anything to get too excited about. They'd already walked through Lorikeet Landing and seen the flock of parrot-type birds flying above their heads. It had been quite spectacular but she wasn't ready to see it again quite so soon. And the Land of the Dinosaurs, which was directly in front of them, was aimed more at children than their parents. That only left Reptile World.

She'd not liked their visit to the Creepy Crawlies much – the size of some of the spiders would give her nightmares for months – and she suspected she mightn't particularly like to see most of the creatures lurking in the reptile house either, suspecting, quite rightly as it happened, that snakes would be a major feature.

But snakes weren't the reason Noah had brought her here.

They were met at the entrance by one of the park's keepers, and Daisy was taken aback slightly when Noah walked up to the man and said, 'I'm Noah Hartley, I've booked a VIP experience for my... er... girlfriend.'

Daisy's heart did a backflip, then a somersault, before it settled back down. Did he really call her his girlfriend? Did that mean she was, or was it just a figure of speech? Mind you, he could have simply called her his friend and be done with it.

And what *was* a VIP experience anyway?

'We don't usually do those kinds of experiences in Reptile World for obvious reasons, but as this is such a special occasion, we've made an exception. Just the tortoises, you say?' the keeper asked.

Noah looked at Daisy, who was beginning to guess what was going on. 'Unless you'd like to hold a snake or two, darling?'

Darling? She shot him a quizzical look, and he leaned so close his lips touched her ear.

'Go along with it,' he whispered, pretending to nibble her neck, and sending shivers down her spine. 'It was the only way I could get you in here. And do me a favour later, and say "yes".'

'I'm not going to hold any snake, no matter how often you ask,' she said, firmly. No matter how much she might like the guy, there was no way she was handling one of those horrid things.

'They won't be the poisonous ones,' the keeper informed her. 'Just a boa and maybe a python. We've got a lovely big fella by the name of Kaa. Don't worry, he won't eat you. Are you sure you wouldn't like to try holding him?'

Daisy grimaced and wondered if she was supposed to say yes to this, but Noah shook his head and mouthed, 'Not that.'

So, what was she supposed to say yes to, if it wasn't the offer of holding a snake?

'Follow me,' the keeper said, and Noah took her hand. He probably thought she might make a run for it, and she was sorely tempted. The smell in Reptile World was acrid and not at all pleasant, and after the freezing January air outside, it was also very warm and stuffy.

'Here.' The man stopped in front of a large glass window, and for a second Daisy thought it was empty. Then a movement caught her attention, and another, and more still, until she realised they were everywhere – tortoises! Loads of them, and one very big one indeed. It was larger than the footstool her nan used to put her feet on, to ease her bunions.

'Come on, then,' the man said, unlocking a door hidden in the shadows and off to the side. He held the door open, and beckoned her inside. Noah followed.

The keeper walked over to the most enormous tortoise Daisy had ever seen, and gave it a friendly pat on the shell. 'This here is Warren,' he said, 'an Aldabra Atoll giant tortoise from the Seychelles. He's sixty-five years old. You can stroke him if you like. He won't bite. Here, give him this, and he'll be your friend forever. Follows me round like a puppy, he does, but not as lively, like.' He laughed at his own joke.

The keeper gave Daisy a bunch of leaves, and she took a tentative step towards the massive reptile, who elongated his neck in anticipation, his black button eyes staring right at her.

She bent down and held the vegetation out to him. Warren chomped at it, and she watched in fascination, taking in every wrinkle and every fold, and marvelling at the sheer ancientness of him. Not only was he old in human years, but his species was old in earth years. His ancestors had walked alongside dinosaurs.

'They've been around since the Triassic,' the keeper said. 'That's about two hundred million years ago,' and she listened, enthralled as the man talked.

'That's enough from me,' he said after a while, and he picked up a small reptile, no bigger than a tennis ball and gave it to her to hold.

It was really sweet, not magnificent and awe-inspiring like his giant cousin, but small and round and scared. The tortoise had pulled his head back into its shell, and Daisy held him up at head-level so she could see his cute little face peeking out. He reminded her of one of the old men in Gee-Gee's home. After a while, when he realised she wasn't going to eat him, he poked his head out.

She was so engrossed in her new friend, she wasn't paying any attention to either Noah or the keeper, until the keeper coughed loudly, and she looked away from the tortoise to see Noah down on one knee, with an awkward smile on his face.

What was he doing down there? If he wasn't careful he'd get tortoise poop all over his clean jeans.

The keeper stepped forward to relieve her of her shelly charge, and Daisy caught a quick glimpse of Noah's face over the other man's shoulder. He was frowning and shaking his head, and mouthing, 'Say yes.' She frowned at him. What the hell was he playing at?

As soon as the keeper stepped away from Daisy, Noah smiled and held out a box.

The keeper removed a camera from his pocket and began taking photos. Daisy was about to ask him to stop (she wouldn't have minded if she'd still been holding Percy, as she nicknamed the little fella), but taking photos of her on her own was downright weird.

'Daisy Jones, will you marry me?' Noah asked.

Daisy, shocked, could only stand there, speechless.

Noah flicked his eyes to the keeper and back again, a pleading look on his face, and she suddenly realised what he was doing and why.

'Yes,' she said, throwing herself at him so he was forced to jump to his feet to avoid being bowled over backwards. 'If you try to hold me to that you're a dead man,' she hissed in his ear, wrapping her arms around him, and smiling for the camera.

'That photo will look lovely in our gallery,' the keeper said, snapping away, and Daisy couldn't help but chuckle to herself – Noah Hartley was one mad, but very lovely, man.

A round of applause had her stumbling out of his arms and staggering backwards. Seemed like they'd drawn quite an audience, and a crowd had gathered on the other side of the glass.

'Put the ring on her finger, mate,' a middle-aged woman called. 'Do it properly.' She was trying to corral three lively youngsters, who clearly wanted to enter the enclosures now they'd seen someone else do it. 'You can play with a tortoise when you ask a girl to marry you,' she said to the youngest boy, who was hanging off her arm, begging to have a go. 'It's this man's turn today.'

'Will you marry me, Nanny?' the child asked. 'Say yes, then I can pet a crocodile. Tortoises are too slow and silly.'

Daisy felt like tossing Noah into the crocodile enclosure right at this very minute, and she hoped there was no one among the watchers who knew her. It would just be her luck...

He was still clutching the box, and she wondered what was in it, gasping when he opened it. The ring was beautiful.

He took it out and waited until she realised he wanted her to hold out her hand, then he slipped it onto her finger. It was far too big, but she pretended it fitted and let him kiss her, melting against him as her treacherous lips met his.

Another round of applause.

After thanking the keeper, he took hold of her elbow and guided her out of the tortoise enclosure, then they made a run for it.

By the time they reached the car, the pair of them were giggling like fools.

'Sorry about that,' Noah said, when they got their breath back, 'but it was the only way I could talk them into letting a member of the public pet the tortoises. It's not one of their usual VIP activities, though you could have fed the penguins instead, or the lions.'

'Thank you, but I liked the tortoises just fine.' She held up her hand. 'Whose ring is this?'

'My mother's, but it's not real. It's something called cubic zirconia?' He glanced at her for confirmation.

'Fake diamond,' she said. 'Did you tell her why you wanted to borrow it?'

'Not exactly.'

'You didn't ask her at all, did you?'

Noah hung his head sheepishly. 'She'll never know, as long as I put it back where I found it.'

'Doctor Hartley, I'm appalled. First you pretend I'm a doctor, then you steal a ring. What's next?'

'This.'

He lowered his head and their lips met, softly at first, then more insistently when she opened her mouth to him, letting him taste her. When he moaned a little, deep in his throat, her insides turned to liquid heat. Then he wrapped one arm around her waist and buried the other in her hair, and she gave herself up to the pleasure of it.

Finally, after long, wonderful moments, he pulled away. His eyes were so dark they were almost navy, and the desire in their depths hurt to look at. Daisy suspected she had the same hungry, lustful expression on her own face.

Chapter 31

Monday morning arrived and the rain hadn't stopped for the past two days. Daisy shot out of her car and dashed into the builder's merchants, Bradley and Son, brushing the water off her shoulders and hoping her hair didn't look too much of a fright and that her mascara wasn't half way down her face. She had emphasised her maturity during the rather odd telephone interview, so she didn't want to look like a teenager who'd been out on the town all night for her face-to-face meeting with Mr Bradley.

'Yes?' the bloke behind the counter asked, his tone belligerent.

'I'm here to see Mr Bradley.'

The man looked her up and down, and harrumphed. 'Ken, a woman for you,' he shouted over his shoulder.

One of the customers snorted and Daisy glanced at him, nervously. Dressed in a battered old fleece with stained jeans, and dusty, scuffed work boots, the builder (she assumed that's what he was) winked at her. 'Probably the best offer Ken's had all weekend, eh, Ken?' This last was directed at the elderly man emerging from a back room.

Ken, a.k.a. Mr Bradley, grunted. His turn to look her up and down. 'Through here,' he muttered, jerking his head towards the door behind the dusty counter, and he turned his back on her and went inside, leaving Daisy to try to figure out how to follow him, because the counter stretched right across the width of the shop.

The bloke behind it, sighed, and flipped a section up, then stood to the side to let her through, before slamming it back down again.

She sidled past him, and walked nervously to the half-open door, tapping on it.

'Come in, what are you waiting for?' Ken called.

No wonder the previous office junior hadn't been up to much, if that's how he treated his staff, Daisy thought, edging inside, careful not to brush against the dirty door-frame. She was wearing her best black coat – her only black coat – and the way her luck was running at the moment, she didn't want to get muck on it because dry cleaning wasn't cheap, and if she failed to get this job, then she wasn't sure she could afford the astronomical price to get it done.

Ken Bradley was sitting behind his desk (though over-flowing, grubby table would be a better description) and peering at her over the top of a pair of reading glasses held together by some kind of grey tape. Daisy estimated him to be in his late sixties. His grey hair was thin, and his grey face was even thinner. His shirt was grey, and missing a button, and he wore a pair of grey cord trousers, which might well have been black about thirty years ago.

Everything about the man was grey, and Daisy had to hold her lips together to prevent a smile from escaping as the thought *Fifty Shades of Grey* popped into her mind. Though having never read the book, or seen the film, she had a fair idea what it was about, and she didn't think the author had a rather grimy pensioner in mind when she wrote it.

'Hope you got better clothes than those,' Ken said, pointing to her.

What was wrong with them? They were perfectly respectable for an interview, weren't they? She'd made sure she wasn't wearing anything too short, too tight, or too revealing, and she crossed her legs self-consciously, hoping she didn't have a ladder in her tights.

'You need old clothes in this job,' he said, putting her mind at rest.

'If I'd had turned up in a pair of track-suit bottoms and an old jumper, it would hardly look professional, would it?' she retorted, with a forced smile on her face.

'Depends what job you're going for,' was Ken's reply.

'I've got plenty of old clothes,' she said. 'I could always go home and change.'

'Best had. You don't want to get that nice skirt of yours all covered in cement dust.'

Did he honestly expect her to hump bags of cement? She didn't think that was in the job description. But then, not much had been – it was the shortest job description Daisy had ever seen, and she'd seen a fair few. The only thing which really stuck in her mind was an ability to make tea.

'Will you carry on the interview if I come back in old clothes?' she asked.

'What interview?'

'This interview.'

'This isn't an interview,' Ken said.

Daisy must have looked as perplexed as she felt, because he added, 'I can see you've not got two heads, so you can start now.'

'Now, as in "today"?'

'Bloody hell, you're quick, aincha? Yes, today.'

'Oh, erm, I see. I wasn't expecting that. Okay, uh thanks.' She was totally and utterly off guard. 'Can I just ask, what are the hours?'

'Thirty-seven a week, Monday to Saturday. You'll be on the other one's rota, 'er what left. The yard is open seven o'clock til four.'

'The yard?'

'Aye, the shop, you know, the builder's yard. "Merchants" is just a silly name for it. It was always called the yard when it first opened.'

'I see, and uh, should I go home now?'

'Unless you've got somewhere else you need to be?' Ken's eyes bored into her.

'No, nowhere else. Right, then, I'll be off. See you in about half an hour.'

That was the quickest, strangest interview ever. Not that she'd been to any, apart from *Caring Cards*, and that was years ago, but she'd researched lots of interview techniques and possible questions, both those which might be asked of her, and ones she, herself, could ask. Like how has the big new B&Q store on the outskirts of the city affected Bradley and Son's trade and—

Oh heck, that surly man behind the counter wasn't the son, was he? She hoped not, because he was one of the rudest blokes she'd come across. And if that was his idea of customer service, then she was surprised the business was still afloat!

After a Superman-fast change, and a lightning quick dash back to Bradley's (she'd told her mum that she'd got the job, and noticed that her mum had referred to it as Bradley's, leaving off the son part – and no wonder!), she was back in "the yard" and awaiting her first instruction.

'Milk, two sugars, and none of that cat's piss stuff. I like a decent brew,' Ken yelled at her before she'd got halfway in through the door. 'He'll have the same, but he likes Earl Grey.'

"He" was Mr Surlypants, and Daisy was taken aback to hear he had such refined taste. She'd have put him down as a Tetley man. She nearly laughed out loud – if anyone should be the Earl Grey drinker, it should have been Ken, what with him being the greyest man in the world. "He", she also found out, was called Tim, and he wasn't the son. The son was in Australia, and had no intention of coming back. Ever.

Over the course of that first day, Daisy learned a great deal, indeed, and most of it had nothing to do with the job at all.

'See that one there?' Ken pointed to a man wearing a sweatshirt with *A★ Electrical* emblazoned across his chest. He'd come in for some "one mill, grey" (funny that) "three core, on a one-hundred metre cable". Apparently, he was in the middle of rewiring a house, and apparently, he was also screwing his best friend's wife, who also shopped here.

'The friend, not the wife,' Ken explained. 'She wouldn't be seen dead in here, the stuck-up madam, so she sends her husband in instead, though by rights it's her business. She only likes the swanning about and meeting new clients bit. The husband, poor bugger, has to do all the donkey work. And him over there,' Ken had his back to the shop and was trying to waggle his eyebrows in the direction he wanted Daisy to look. 'He starts a business, makes a cock up of it, winds it up, and starts another one. Let me give you a word of advice, if he offers to do your roof, run a mile.'

Daisy wondered if "do your roof" was builders' euphemism for something, until she overheard the man in question on his phone regarding taking delivery of a pile of slates.

All the while Ken was talking, Daisy watched Ted. He was gruff and short with the customers, but then, most of them were gruff and short with him. A typical conversation went something like this:

Customer: Four lengths of two by four, and a bag of cross-head screws.

Tim: Treated or untreated?

Customer: Untreated.

Tim: Planed?

Customer: Yep.

Tim: Size?

Customer: Number tens.

Tim: Five by seventy-five.

Customer: Yep.

Tim: £36.43. VAT receipt?

Customer: Yep.

Daisy had hardly understood a word, and she realised she needed to learn fast if she was going to be answering the phones.

'What exactly is it that you want me to do, Mr Bradley?' she asked.

'Call me Ken. Sort out the office.'

Wow, that was a rather large job, especially since she had no idea where to start, what was important, what could be filed, and what could be thrown out.

'Um, okay,' she said and disappeared into the office, feeling she may not come out for a long time, if ever.

She wanted to start with Ken's desk, but wasn't sure she should. It was an absolute tip, but maybe Ken was the type of person who seemed to work in a pigsty, yet knew exactly where everything was, so she gave the filing cabinet a go first, figuring that if she knew what was in there and the order things were supposed to be in, then she could work out if anything on the desk could be filed. But first, she had to clear the stacked tops of each filing cabinet, and she removed each precarious pile with care and placed it in order on the floor.

Within minutes her hands were filthy and she'd breathed in enough dust to wreck her lungs for a lifetime, yet strangely, she found she was enjoying the challenge, especially when she discovered an unused tin of furniture polish at the back of one of the drawers and an unopened pack of dusters.

Working methodically, she first cleaned the outside of each cabinet, then took out the contents of every drawer, wiped the inside of the drawer, and replaced the contents exactly as she found them, giving each file and folder a quick once-over with the duster before she put it back. And all the time she was cleaning, she studied what was kept in each of the little hanging thingies. Surprisingly, the filing system was remarkably good, though she noticed one drawer which was labelled "Trade Catalogues" was stuffed full, and most of them were years old.

'Can I throw any of these away,' she asked, the next time Ken shuffled back into the office, ostensibly to check something on his desk, but in reality, Daisy thought, to check up on her.

'No.'

'But they're so old!'

'We use 'em for reference,' Ken replied, haughtily.

Daisy lifted one out at random. It was more than eleven years old. 'Can you still get...' she flicked through the pages, '...a Bosch cordless, chuck-free hammer drill, item number P354672D, priced £39.99?' she asked.

'Doubt it, they don't make that model anymore. The nearest one they got to that, is the—'

'So, what are you keeping this for, then?' Daisy waved the catalogue at him.

'Reference. I said so.'

'But you said they don't make this model anymore,' she pointed out.

'They don't!'

'I'm going to refile it,' Daisy said, making a decision. 'In the round filing cabinet.'

'Oh okay.' Ken glowered at the now-gleaming row of filing cabinets. 'Keep up the good work.'

Daisy waited until he left, and promptly threw the ancient catalogue in the bin. Then she stared at it for a minute, before fishing it back out again, and going in search of some black rubbish bags. She had a feeling she was going to fill more than one.

By the end of the day, she was possibly the dirtiest she had ever been in her life (she was going to have to have a long soak in the bath with a body scrub to shift the grime from her pores), but she felt a certain satisfaction from a job well done. The office was far from pristine, and she had yet to touch Ken's desk, but she now had a feel for where things went, and even if Ken's filing system was a bit haphazard, she was getting to grips with it.

To her surprise, she'd enjoyed her first day, and as she drove home, she found herself, for the first time in a long time, looking forward to tomorrow.

Chapter 32

Daisy fingered the letter cautiously, turning it over yet again to examine the franking mark. It was from *Caring Cards*, posted yesterday. A part of her didn't want to open it, guessing what it would contain. She'd already received her P45 and final wage slip, so it couldn't be either of those, and she felt a little sick.

Should she phone Hazel Holmes? She checked the time – too late, the solicitors' office was probably shut by now. Besides, what if it wasn't what she thought it was, she'd look a right idiot phoning when it might be nothing to do with her appeal.

Taking a deep breath and bracing herself, she tore open the envelope and pulled the letter out. The top was embossed with the *Caring Cards* familiar logo and she ran her thumb across it, feeling an odd mixture of nostalgia and regret. She'd enjoyed working there, she really had. The job had been easy and had appealed to her creative side, and she'd liked her colleagues – most of them.

She wished none of this had happened, and that she could walk back into the office and sit at her desk and do what she was good at. She might have had a good first week at the builders' merchants, but the euphoria had sluiced away, along with the dirt and dust in the shower, and she'd been left feeling a little flat.

Stop faffing about and read the goddamn thing, she told herself. How bad could it be? It was probably just a letter of acknowledgement anyway.

It wasn't. Far from it.

> *Dear Miss Jones,*
>   *Further to your recent letter of appeal, regarding your dismissal from Caring Cards for gross miscon-duct, the company is prepared to offer you a settlement figure of £9,860.00. This offer is without prejudice and is non-negotiable…*

…blah blah blah.

Daisy didn't read any further, letting the letter slip from her numb fingers in shock. They were paying her off!

Amazed, she wondered how they had arrived at such an odd figure. Perhaps they'd calculated her earnings for so many months, or something, and had taken off the tax. Anyway, it didn't matter – she'd won. She realised that "without prejudice" meant *Caring Cards* wasn't admitting it had done anything wrong by dismissing her, but she felt vindicated all the same. Besides, if they'd thought they had a solid case against her, they would have fought her all the way.

Now she'd phone Hazel Holmes.

'Should I accept it?' she asked the solicitor.

'My advice would be, yes. Well done, Miss Jones!'

'I didn't do anything,' Daisy said. 'It's all down to you.' And Zoe – she'd take her a bunch of flowers later. 'Thank you so much.'

'No need for thanks. I'm just pleased the case has been settled amicably.'

Amicably wasn't the word Daisy would use, because she still felt very raw and upset, but she knew what the other woman meant: no tribunal, no having to stand up in front of a judge (or whoever ruled on such things), no having her character dragged through the courts. Okay, the last might be a bit of an exaggeration, she acknowledged, having no real idea what might have happened if the company hadn't been willing to settle.

Never mind, it was all over now, and she could put the whole sorry mess behind her.

'I can finally think about a home of my own,' she said to Noah, later that evening. Yes – *evening*! A proper after-eight-pm dinner in a proper restaurant and everything, like a *real* date. And he didn't have to go to work until tomorrow. Her heart did a little jig. They had all night…

'That's wonderful news.' Noah reached across the table to squeeze her hand. 'A new job, a new house – your luck has certainly turned.'

It had been nearly a week since she'd last seen Noah, because they simply hadn't been able to match their work schedules. It felt a lot longer, and though they'd spoken on the phone every day, and Noah had begun a habit of texting her good morning and good night, it didn't fill the need inside her.

And as for luck – yes, she believed she had eventually shaken off the bad and was now on the receiving end of some good luck. It also helped that people had finally taken down their Christmas decorations. Never had Daisy been more pleased to see the back of Christmas as she was this year.

Her mother had insisted on leaving them all in place, right up until the sixth of January, despite Daisy pleading for them to be taken down.

'At least, get rid of the hanging foil things,' she'd urged, but Sandra had shaken her head.

'It's bad luck,' her mother had said.

Wrong, Daisy thought. It's silver sixpences in Christmas puddings that were bad luck. Thank goodness the tradition had more or less died out, and if her great-gran suggested it next year, Daisy would pass the pudding bit and stick the coin straight where the sun don't shine – up Gee-Gee's backside, not her own! She'd had enough of those kinds of shenanigans to last her a lifetime.

Daisy had been dragged into putting the tree up the attic, but first, every decoration and every ornament had to be carefully wrapped in newspaper. If it was up to Daisy, she'd simply have shoved the tree up through the hatch, without removing a bauble, working on the theory that it would save time and hassle when the tree was brought down again next year.

'I've had some of these decorations since before you were born,' Elsie had said. 'You be careful with them.'

They looked older than Methuselah, too, but Daisy did as she was told. Then she'd gone into work and did the same thing again, except this time she was allowed to shuffle the complete thing into a corner of the storage room and throw an old sheet over it to keep the dust off. If she could have done the same with December, she would have. It had been the worst Christmas ever, but it was all behind her now, and she had a totally new year to look forward to and a new man to share it with.

The new man in question was staring at her intently. 'Where did you go?' he asked. 'You looked miles away.'

'I was thinking how hard this past month has been, what with Freddie and *Caring Cards*, and Zoe and David, and that bloody sixpence. And now it's all turned around and the future is looking so much brighter.'

'What did happen to that coin? I'm assuming it must have put in an appearance, because you haven't mentioned having it surgically removed since New Year's Day.'

Daisy blushed. She seriously didn't want to talk about the mechanics of the coin's reappearance. 'I took it to Gee-Gee. She said she wanted it back, but when I gave it to her she changed her mind, so I left it on the table. I never want to set eyes on the damned thing again!'

'You don't intend putting it in next year's pudding?' he joked.

'No way! Besides, it brought me nothing but bad luck.'

'Isn't that Freddie?' Noah asked.

Daisy looked at the table Noah was staring at.

Damn, so it was.

Freddie waved to her, and Daisy waved back, trying to hide her dismay. Was that…? Yes, it was – Freddie was dining with Carl. She was also astonished to see that they were holding hands. She tried to grab a look at Freddie's wrists, but his sleeves were pulled right down, but at least he was out and about and looking much better than the last time she saw him.

After a few minutes, Freddie sauntered over to their table.

'Hi, Daisy.'

'Freddie,' she said, cautiously. 'Do you remember Doctor Hartley?'

Freddie nodded sheepishly. 'Sorry about all the trouble I caused,' he said.

'No trouble,' Noah replied with a smile. 'How are you feeling?'

Freddie pushed his sleeves back to reveal two plasters. 'Much better, thanks to you.'

'Just doing my job,' Noah said.

'You're back with Carl, I see,' Daisy said, and Freddie beamed.

'We're good. Carl was right, I wasn't ready then, but I am now. Coming out was all a bit much, but doing what I did opened my eyes and made me realise that I have to be true to myself.'

'How do your parents feel about that?' Daisy asked.

Freddie grimaced. 'Mum is okay, but it'll take Dad a while yet.' He brightened. 'He's invited Carl to lunch, so he must be coming around to the idea. I hope.'

Daisy was glad she wouldn't be there. Lunch at Freddie's parents was hard enough as it was. Good luck, Carl, she thought, you're going to need it!

She smiled at Carl, and Carl smiled back, a nice smile this time, not the sneer Daisy remembered from the last (and only) time they'd met.

'I'd better get back before Carl comes to find me,' Freddie said. 'I just wanted to say "hello".' He took a step back, then glanced at Noah and back to Daisy. 'No hard feelings?' he asked.

'No hard feelings,' Daisy confirmed, and she meant it. If it hadn't been for Freddie, Daisy wouldn't have met Noah, and she simply couldn't imagine not having this wonderful, sexy man in her life.

Freddie returned to Carl, and Daisy realised Noah was staring at her again, and she put her fork down, suddenly no longer hungry. Or rather, she *was* hungry, but not for food. Did that make her a hussy? She gave a mental shrug. If it did, she didn't care. This was technically their fourth date. If things went a bit further than kissing, then so be it.

At the thought of exactly how far things could go, Daisy's tummy lurched, and so did other bits of her. What would Noah look like naked? His open-neck shirt was slim-fitting, the breadth of his chest and the flatness of his stomach clearly visible. His bum, though she couldn't see it right now because he was sitting on it, had appeared firm and decidedly pinchable in his dark blue trousers. She'd had difficulty taking her eyes off it as he'd led her into the restaurant, and the trousers also showed off his long legs. Noah Hartley was all in proportion – she hoped! The wicked thought made her catch her breath.

Unspoken agreement saw them hastily finishing their meal, and Noah asking for the bill. When he'd paid (after a brief tussle, when she insisted on paying next time), they fled the restaurant.

'Wanna come to mine for a coffee?' he asked, his voice hoarse and throaty.

If they went back to his place, coffee would be the last thing on the agenda and both of them knew it.

'Yes, please,' she said, and he opened the car door for her, giving her a sultry smile.

She went all weak and decidedly girly.

'I really do mean "coffee",' he said, unlocking the door to his flat, after a tense and sexually charged drive back to Worcester, during which she'd kept stealing glances at him, and he'd kept shooting her meaningful looks loaded with promise. 'I'm not going to jump on you as soon as I get you alone.'

'How do you know I don't want you to jump on me?' she asked, and her tongue came out to flick over her top lip, without her asking it to. It seemed to have a mind of its own, and so did the rest of her body.

'Oh, God,' he said, kicking the door shut behind her as he pulled her into the small hall, and pressed her up against the wall.

His mouth claimed hers with an intensity that drove all coherent thought out of her mind, and she met him passion for passion, as his hand found the buttons of her warm winter coat and began to undo them. Still kissing him, Daisy unwound the scarf from around her neck and let it drop, and his lips went straight to the soft flesh under her ear, and nuzzled her until she thought her knees were about to give way.

She'd not been idle either, unzipping his jacket and sliding her hands inside, feeling the solid muscles of his back tense as she stroked him.

He groaned, his tongue probing her mouth, one hand slipping inside her coat to caress her breast.

My God, she wanted this man more than she had wanted any other man before. Just a simple touch from him made her tremble from head to foot and—

She opened her eyes.

Noah was staring back at her from where he was standing in the doorway to the living room. A much younger Noah, a teenage version, and he looked seriously pissed off.

He opened his mouth and one word came out. 'Dad.'

Chapter 33

Noah and Daisy sprang apart, Daisy hastily pulling her jumper down, and praying the boy hadn't seen his father's hand all over her pink lacey bra.

Noah ran shaking fingers through his hair, and cleared his throat. Still facing away from the living room door, he said over his shoulder. 'Connor, what are you doing here?' and winced as he adjusted himself, taking a deep, steadying breath.

When his excitement had diminished (his jeans *were* quite tight), he turned to face his son.

'No wonder you don't want me here,' the boy spat. 'You're too busy shagging *her*!' He swivelled on his heel and stamped to the sofa, throwing himself down on it and folding his arms.

'Connor, watch how you speak, please, and it's not that I don't want you—'

'Yeah, right.'

Noah sighed. 'This year and the next are important years for you,' he said, and by the tone of his voice Daisy guessed it wasn't the first time that father and son had explored this topic.

'I don't care.' The boy was the picture of a sulky, disgruntled teenager.

'Connor,' Noah sighed. 'You're in year ten. You have your GCSEs next year and—'

'I told you, I don't care. Why doesn't anyone ever listen to what I want?' Connor glared at his father, then turned his attention to me. 'It's *her*, isn't it?' he sneered. 'She's the reason you don't want me here. I hate you!'

'If you hate me so much, why do you want to come and live with me,' Noah responded.

Not good, Noah, Daisy thought. No wonder he said he had trouble relating to kids. That wasn't what Connor wanted to hear right now. She was tempted to chip in, but thought better of it, and picked up her scarf instead. 'I'd better go,' she said.

'Don't,' Noah said, at the same time Connor snarled, 'Yeah, go, we don't want you here.'

Daisy hovered in the doorway, uncertainly, and Noah grabbed her hand. 'Daisy is my guest and I won't have you speaking to her like that,' he said to his son.

'Guest? Is that what you call her?'

'Okay, girlfriend,' Noah said.

Connor shot Daisy a filthy look and said to his father, 'Nobody wants me, not you, not mum.'

It was unadulterated emotional blackmail, but Noah fell for it. 'Of course, we want you. Your mother and I love you very much.'

'She loves Ian now,' the teenager retorted, and Daisy saw the unshed tears in his eyes, which he dashed angrily away with the back of his hand.

'She loves you, too,' Noah said. 'She'll always love you.'

'Why is she marrying Ian then, when she knows I don't like him?'

Noah clearly had no answer for that. He rubbed a hand across his face and shook his head. 'Does your mother know where you are?' he asked.

Connor shrugged. 'Dunno.'

'She doesn't, does she, because she wouldn't have let you come all this way on your own.'

Another shrug.

'Where does she think you are?'

'A friend's.' Connor still refused to look at his father, his attention on the carpet.

'I'd better ring her,' Noah said, reaching into his pocket for his mobile.

'Don't,' Connor said, finally looking up. 'She'll kill me.'

'You deserve it,' Noah replied, thumbing the number in. 'Running away isn't going to help.'

'This isn't running away. This is coming to live with my dad.' For a second Connor was a small, confused, upset boy.

'Kate? It's Noah.'

Connor leapt up, strode towards Daisy and pushed past her rudely, before stamping into another room off the hall, and slamming the door. The sound of running water came from behind it.

'Listen, don't worry, but I've got Connor with me.' A pause. 'No, I didn't encourage him. He turned up out of the blue.' Another pause. 'What do you take me for? Of course, I'll bring him back personally. I'm hardly going to stick him on a train and send him off all by himself, am I?' A sigh. 'I don't know. Perhaps you should look at his relationship with Ian.'

Daisy tried not to listen, but it was hard not to. Anyway, she was curious about how Noah interreacted with his ex. Spikily was the word which popped into her mind. Was that because he still had feelings for her, or because she'd taken his son so far away? It couldn't be easy for Noah to find the time to visit – Daisy knew first-hand how many hours Noah worked, and the unsociable shift patterns. The two of them had enough trouble getting together, and Daisy only lived a mile or so away.

'Don't blame me! I didn't ask him to come. He came because of Ian.' Noah held the phone away from his ear. Even at a distance of several feet, Daisy heard the high-pitched voice on the other end. Kate was clearly having a bit of a tantrum. 'Maybe you should ask him yourself. It seems our son doesn't like him much. I wonder why that is?' There was a hint of a threat in Noah's voice, and Daisy hoped, for Ian's sake, that this unknown man was treating Connor right, and that the boy's dislike was something as normal as simply not wanting to share his mum.

Daisy sensed a presence behind her and turned her head. Connor's face was ashen. Noah noticed his son seconds later.

'Con, I didn't mean it like that,' he said. 'I meant—'

'I know what you meant. You don't want me here, messing things up with your new girlfriend. You've never wanted me. And now Mum doesn't either.' The boy's shoulders sagged under the weight of his hostility and anger.

'Con, Con, look at me.' Noah strode into the hall and Daisy backed up as far as the main door. She needed to leave. This was between father and son, and she realised her presence was only inflaming things.

'We *do* want you – both of us,' Noah insisted.

'Why are you living here, then? A hundred and eighty miles away?'

The question gave Noah pause. 'I'm not going to get into the blame-game, Con. You know the story.'

'Yeah, yeah.' This kid did a good line in sneering, Daisy thought, as he added, 'She moved to Brighton when I was little – I know all this, but you could have come with us.'

'My home was here. It still is.'

Daisy guessed no one had told Connor that Noah hadn't been invited.

'It doesn't have to be though, does it? You can work anywhere,' Connor correctly pointed out.

Noah sent Daisy a helpless glance. 'Look, Con, let me run Daisy home, then when I come back we'll talk. Yeah?'

The boy narrowed his eyes, his shoulders hunched somewhere about ear level, but he nodded. He clearly wanted Daisy gone about as much as she didn't want to be there.

'Don't leave the flat,' Noah warned. 'I'll be about twenty minutes. And don't touch anything.'

'I'm so sorry,' he said, once they were outside. 'I had no idea he was here.'

'I gathered that. It was nice meeting him.'

'Ha!'

'No, really, it was. He's a big part of your life.'

'Not as big a part as he should be. I wonder what this is all about. I know he's not keen on Kate getting married, but for him to act out like this, it's out of character.'

Was it though? Daisy hadn't had much experience with teenagers, except for being one herself and watching her younger brother go through the joys of puberty, but she had a feeling that if Connor didn't see his father all that

282

often, then maybe he was usually on his best behaviour when he did. Unable to think of anything constructive to say, she resorted to platitudes. 'It's probably a teenage boy thing,' she said. 'Everything will work out in the end, you'll see.'

'I hope so.' Noah pulled over into the kerb and turned the engine off. 'I'm sorry about tonight,' he said, leaning across the gearstick and cupping the side of her face with his hand. 'We never did have that coffee.'

'Coffee being a euphemism for...?' She fluttered her eyelashes at him.

Noah smiled. 'Exactly!'

But the smile didn't quite reach his eyes. They were sad and slightly wary. No wonder, Daisy thought, not envying him what he had to face when he returned home.

'I'll call you,' he said. 'But I've no idea when that'll be. I'll have to take him back to Brighton in the morning. His mother is going mental.' He checked the time on the dashboard clock. 'It's too late now, so he'll have to stay with me tonight.'

Noah didn't look particularly pleased at the thought of either of those things. 'I'm sorry,' he said again. 'I wanted you to meet him under better circumstances than this.'

'Look on the bright side,' she replied brightly, not feeling bright at all. 'I've met him now, warts and all, and I'm still here.'

'Are you?' he asked softly.

'I am.'

'Good.'

This time his kiss held a hint of the passion they'd shared earlier and when he finally drew back, some of the sparkle had returned to his eyes.

'I think I'm falling for you, Daisy Jones,' he said and a bolt of electricity shot through her.

'Me too,' she said, a hitch in her voice.

'I'll call you when I get there,' he promised, running the pad of his thumb across her lips.

Her tongue flicked out and desire flamed deep inside her. It was answered by the expression on Noah's face.

'I'd better go, Connor will be wondering where I am.'

She wanted to beg him to stay for a few minutes longer, but she knew she had to let him go. His son needed him now, and after all, she and Noah had all the time in the world.

Chapter 34

Time was going so slowly, and even though she had loads to do, sorting through piles of dusty, old invoices and putting them in date order ready for filing, it didn't keep her brain occupied enough to prevent her from worrying about Noah. She found herself checking her phone every five minutes.

When it finally did ring, Daisy almost jumped out of her skin.

And it wasn't Noah, either.

She answered it cautiously, seeing a London number on her screen. She wasn't supposed to take calls in work, but she'd never been able to resist answering her phone, except when it was her mother calling, and especially not now, when it might be Noah.

'Am I speaking to Daisy Jones?' an unfamiliar female voice asked, and Daisy was gripped with a sudden dread. The last time she'd been asked that question over the phone, it had been a nurse calling to tell her that Freddie had been admitted to hospital. What if something had happened to Noah – a car crash, a fight with Ian?

'Yes, I'm Daisy,' she gulped.

'I have a call for you from Mr Carstairs. Please hold, while I transfer you.'

'Who?' Daisy asked, but the line had gone silent.

'Miss Jones? Emmett Carstairs.'

'Oh, hi.' She still had no idea who this man was.

'I liked your idea very much. I'd like to meet with you to discuss it.'

Oh, Emmett Carstairs, from *Rosebush*. 'Great,' Daisy croaked, leaning against the wall for support.

'I'm in Birmingham this evening. Are you available tomorrow?'

'Yes, no.' Damn it, she was working, and though she was tempted to throw a sickie, her conscience wouldn't let her. She hadn't been in this job long, and Ken had been nothing but nice (in his own gruff way) to her, so far.

'That's not a problem,' Mr Carstairs said when she explained the situation. 'You're based in Worcester, aren't you?'

Daisy nodded, realised he couldn't see her and forced out a, 'Yes.' It sounded squeaky, and she cleared her throat.

'Yes,' she repeated, now sounding like someone who'd been smoking forty fags a day for the past twenty years.

'I'll take a detour on the way up from London and meet you somewhere. Wait a minute.' He must have placed a hand on the receiver because all she could hear were muffled voices.

'My secretary tells me there's a decent pub in Norton, just off Junction 7 on the M5, called *The Cripple Creek*. Do you know it?'

She didn't but she wasn't going to say so. 'I do,' she replied.

'Say six-thirty?'

'I'll be there,' she promised, her head swimming, and so she found herself sitting at a table later that evening, clutching a glass of white wine in her hand, and feeling vaguely sick.

Mr Carstairs was late, and the later he was the more anxious Daisy became. She was already fraught with nerves because Noah still hadn't contacted her, and was worrying herself silly about it, and she was sure she was about to throw up.

She'd chosen a table not too far from the door and sat facing it, so when a man in his late forties, slightly balding and with a paunch approached the table, she was about to tell him she was waiting for someone, when she spied his briefcase. If he'd been wearing a suit, she might have twigged earlier, but he wore an open-neck shirt and jeans and didn't look like her idea of what a CEO should look like.

'Daisy Jones?' he enquired.

Daisy rose and breathed out a sigh of relief as she took his outstretched hand, and shook it.

'Let's order first,' he suggested. 'I could eat a scabby cat. Sorry I'm late, but the traffic was diabolical.'

Diabolical, was it? Maybe it was diabolical all the way to London and beyond. Maybe Noah and Connor had stopped off for something to eat and they hadn't got there yet. Maybe—

Mr Carstairs stuck a menu under her nose and Daisy picked the first thing she saw, not really caring what she ate.

'Tell me about this idea of yours,' he said after the waitress had taken their order. 'I've read your email, but I want to hear it from you.'

Zoe's email and Zoe's idea, Daisy mused, but she took a deep breath and began.

'I know there are companies out there who already do personalised cards,' she said, when she'd finished explaining the concept (and not very well, because she wasn't totally sure how it would work herself, and she wasn't convinced it was such a good business idea anyway). 'But my plan is to take things to a whole new level of personalisation, by offering tailored verses and images, aimed at the individual the card is for, and no one else. It would mean more interaction with the customer, but the card would be considerably more meaningful.'

'Hmm.' He leaned back, allowing the waitress to place his meal in front of him.

Daisy didn't so much as glance at hers. She desperately wanted to check her phone again, and she was far too uptight to eat.

'Can I just say before we go any further, that I don't want to relocate,' Daisy said. Not only did she not want to, she couldn't afford to – she'd read enough in the papers to know that London house prices were way out of her league. She'd be lucky if she could afford to live in a cardboard box under a flyover!

'You're getting ahead of yourself, Miss Jones,' he said, tucking into his steak with gusto.

Daisy hadn't picked up her fork yet, and she waited impatiently for his response.

'Okay, here's what I think. We already have a person-alised card facility. I'd have to check some figures, but I'm pretty sure your idea won't be cost effective. At present, the customers themselves do the majority of the work, choosing from a variety of styles, verses and images. The start-up costs were significant, but the running costs are minimal. What you are suggesting would make the card to cost ratio prohibitive to most of my customers.'

Daisy drooped a little, but not too much. Her heart wasn't really in it.

'Have you got any work you can show me?' he asked.

'Personalised stuff? I didn't think to bring any.' She hadn't actually written any, was nearer the truth. 'I didn't think there was any point because you wouldn't know the person the card is referring to.' Phew, got out of that one!

'What about your regular work?'

'Um.' Actually, she did have some with her, and she dragged a sheaf of paper out of her bag and handed it to Mr Carstairs.

He was silent while he read them, and Daisy risked a quick glance at her phone. Nothing.

'They're good,' he said. 'I could use you. Are you sure you won't consider relocating?'

'I'm sure.'

'Pity. If you change your mind, drop me an email. I don't usually do any recruiting myself, but you intrigued me. Good luck with your business proposition,' he said as they made their way to the exit.

'Thanks.' She shook his hand again, and made her escape. It had been worth a shot, she supposed, and if *Rosebush* had taken on all the difficult stuff and left her to construct the messages and verses, then it might have worked. Oh well, nothing ventured, nothing gained, and it wasn't as if she didn't have a job, was it?

When she got home she flung herself on her little single bed and checked her phone for the umpteenth time, to make sure she hadn't missed his call or that her phone hadn't run out of juice.

He must be there by now. A four-hour drive, he'd said. Allowing for them not setting off until late-morning (teenagers were notorious for not being able to get out of bed before at least eleven o'clock), and even allowing for a couple of pit-stops along the way, they should have arrived hours ago.

Unless, she swallowed convulsively, thinking of her initial response to Mr Carstairs' phone call earlier, they'd had an accident.

How would she know? No one would think to tell her. Itching to phone him to make sure he was okay, Daisy sat on her hands.

Not yet. Give him time. Connor was his priority right now. He'd said he'd call, so he would. She just had to be patient. Or maybe he'd dropped Connor off at Kate's, and had done an about-turn and was on his way back at this very minute.

Her phone buzzed.

No call, but a text instead.

> *Arrived safely. Going to stay the night. Speak tomorrow.*

She stared at the screen, willing it to say more. Talk about bare – brief, emotionless, saying nothing except the bald facts. No inkling of how the meeting with Kate went, or whether things had been sorted out with Ian. Or even, if Noah had to drag Connor into the car and tape him in his seat in order to take him back home.

And where was Noah sleeping? Kate's house?

The green-eyed monster roared in Daisy's head and jealousy so strong it hurt, swept through her.

'She's marrying Ian,' Daisy muttered aloud. 'She doesn't want Noah.'

But what if *he* still wants *her*, the nasty, insistent little voice muttered back.

Chapter 35

Daisy spent the rest of the following day not really with it, too worried about what might be happening with Noah. When he finally did phone her later that evening, she was almost at the end of her tether. She dashed upstairs to speak to him, away from the pricked ears of her mother and grandmother and their sideways glances.

Containing her anxiety with difficulty, she asked, 'How is Connor?'

'Fine, I think.' Noah sounded distant, and Daisy didn't mean in terms of physical miles. He seemed to have withdrawn from her a little (okay – a lot). Gone was the easy banter which had peppered their previous phone conversations, and in its place there seemed to be a wary reluctance to talk, on his part anyway.

'Are you okay?' she asked.

'I suppose.'

What did that mean?

'Daisy, we – I – have had a chance to think, and I don't believe that me living nearly two hundred miles away is doing Connor any good.'

"We", as in Noah and Kate? And why should him living so far away bother Noah so much now? He'd lived in Worcester for years; Connor had grown up with the knowledge that his dad lived a four-hour drive away and that he couldn't simply pop round the corner to see him. What had changed? Connor or Noah? Daisy suspected the latter.

It could be a mixture of things, like Noah finally realising that Connor wasn't a child anymore, that his son was heading rapidly towards adulthood, and perhaps Noah wanted to have more of a relationship with the boy than the current distance would allow. Or maybe, like Connor, Noah didn't want Kate to marry, either. Seeing her again (and Daisy had no idea when Noah had last seen his ex), may have rekindled feelings Noah had thought long extinguished.

Hope flared briefly in her as she considered another possibility. There was a chance that Noah had offered to have Connor stay with him. It might suit the newly-weds better not having an inquisitive teenager in the house. Though that scenario mightn't bode too well for Noah and Daisy themselves, in that they hadn't even slept together yet. What would their chances of making love be, when there was another person in the house, one who was most likely attuned to every touch, every kiss. It would certainly make things awkward, but it wasn't impossible.

'What are you saying?' she asked.

'I'm thinking of moving to Brighton.'

'Oh.'

'It's not definite, just a thought we've been bandying about.'

'We?'

'Kate and I.'

Bloody hell, the way he said that, it sounded as though they were back together already. A hole formed in Daisy's chest where her heart used to be, and the pain of it made her gasp.

'Daisy?'

'I'm still here.'

'It won't be for ages yet. I'll have to sell the house, but the first thing is to get another job, and things like that don't happen overnight. I'll still be living in Worcester for a while yet.'

But your heart won't be, Daisy thought. It'll be in Brighton with the woman you still love, and your son.

'I'll be back tomorrow,' he said. 'We can talk then. Fancy dinner?'

Did she?

She desperately wanted to be with him, but she wasn't sure if she could stand seeing him, knowing that he didn't really want to be with her. And she also wasn't sure if she wanted to talk anymore. What was there to discuss? Which estate agent he was going to use? What hospitals were within travelling distance? How seeing Kate again had reminded him of how much he'd once loved her, and possibly still did?

This was going to hurt (her, not him) but she had to decline.

'I don't think it's wise,' she said with a hitch in her voice. She tried to hide it by turning it into a cough, but the cough became a sob, and she abruptly ended the call, not wanting him to guess how much she was hurting.

Bye, Noah, my love.

She stared at her phone, thinking about what she'd just called him in her head – "my love". And she realised that she actually did love him. It wasn't just a figure of speech.

Her feelings for him had crept up on her and caught her unawares, ambushing her when she hadn't been expecting it. She had no idea when it had happened. One minute she'd been normal and not-in-love, and the next she realised exactly how much he meant to her.

And now she'd gone and ended it.

How was she supposed to carry on, going to work, sleeping, having drinks with friends, when the man she loved was no longer in her life. If he ever really had been.

No, he had been, she was sure of it. The connection, the spark between them, had been real. There was no faking it, and it hadn't simply been lust, either. Not on her side, though it might have been on his. If Kate hadn't come back into the picture, they might have stood a chance; but she had, and Noah had laid his cards on the table.

She had no idea how to deal with this. These feelings were nothing like she'd experienced when she'd walked in on Freddie with another man. Looking back, she knew what she'd felt had been more like hurt pride and shock, rather than a shattered heart and savaged soul. Both heart and soul had been a bit battered and slightly bruised, but they had mended soon enough. If she'd really loved Freddie as much as she'd assumed she did, she never would have recovered from his betrayal so swiftly.

She didn't think she'd ever recover from this.

How had she been so stupid as to fall in love? Her mother and nan had warned her enough times about the risks of giving your heart to a man. Look what had happened to them! Daisy really was destined to end up a lonely old spinster, and to her dismay, the thought actually appealed to her.

'If I can't have you,' she sang forlornly, tears trickling unheeded down her face, 'I don't want nobody, baby.'

Then the sobbing started in earnest, and she threw herself across the bed, giving in to her despair.

When the knock came some time later (maybe minutes, maybe hours – she'd lost track of time), she ignored it. If her mother said, 'Plenty more fish in the sea,' or 'He's not worth it,' or, her favourite, 'All men are bastards and can't be trusted,' Daisy was going to deck her.

The knock came again.

'Go away,' she said, her words muffled by the pillow she held to her hot and clammy face.

'It's me, Zoe.'

Bugger. She didn't want to speak to Zoe either, but after what her sister-in-law had done for her, Daisy felt she couldn't ignore the other woman; it would simply be too rude, so she sat up, wiped her throbbing, swollen eyes on the edge of her duvet and called, 'Come in.'

Daisy expected Zoe to ask what was wrong, to be surprised to see that Daisy had been crying, but all Zoe did was perch next to her on the bed and put her arms around her. The touch of another person, someone who cared about her, was enough to set Daisy off again, and she cried until her sobs turned to hiccups, and she felt weak and drained. And still the tears trickled down her cheeks unchecked.

Finally, taking a tremulous breath, she gently extricated herself from Zoe's embrace. Her sister-in-law hadn't uttered a word the whole time, and now Daisy's meltdown was out of the way (though she suspected it was the first of many), Daisy expected her to speak.

But Zoe remained silent, until eventually, haltingly, Daisy told her what had happened.

'He still loves Kate,' Daisy concluded, after a long, drawn-out, rambling explanation.

'You don't know that,' Zoe pointed out.

'I do, I can feel it here.' She jabbed herself in the chest. Zoe stared at her.

'Okay, I know I was wrong about Freddie,' Daisy admitted, 'but I didn't love him. We didn't have that special something, so I wasn't as attuned to him as I am to Noah.'

'If what you say is true, then you still don't have that special something with Noah, because he loves someone else,' Zoe stated.

'That's harsh. Kick a girl when she's down, why don't you.'

'I'm not doing any kicking. You're doing it to yourself, by assuming that because he wants to be nearer his son, he's still in love with this Kate.'

'He more or less said so. He kept talking about "we".'

'It doesn't mean he loves her,' Zoe said calmly. 'It simply means they are parents together.'

Daisy heaved a large sigh. 'It doesn't matter anyway, because he's moving to Brighton.'

'You could always go with him.'

'There's only one little problem with that idea – he hasn't asked me.'

'Did you give him a chance to?'

Daisy shrugged.

'I thought not.' Zoe stood, and Daisy noticed how rounded her sister-in-law's stomach had become. Her pregnancy was now obvious to anyone who knew.

'We've only been seeing each other for a few weeks. Why would he ask me to move to another city when we hardly know each other,' Daisy said.

'If the connection is there, then time is immaterial. You can fall in love in a heartbeat, or you can be with the same person for years and not experience true love. Take you and Freddie…'

'Okay, I get it, but Noah still hasn't asked me,' Daisy said.

'Why don't you call him back?'

Daisy shook her head. If he wanted her, he'd ring her. 'What are you doing here anyway?' she asked, changing the subject.

'Your mother asked me to come.'

'Why?'

'Duh! Because you were crying your heart out.'

'She knows?'

'The whole street probably knows. Do you realise, you wail a lot when you're crying?'

'Great.' Daisy managed to produce a small smile. It felt fake, and she wondered whether smiles were always going to be like this from now on – a pretence at happiness, a sop to persuade the world she was okay when she was, in fact, never going to be okay ever again.

'I've got to go,' Zoe said. 'I need to go shopping.'

'It's eight o'clock in the evening. Shouldn't you be taking it easy?'

'That's a laugh! David's leg is still in plaster, and we've got no food in the house, and with me being back in work, the only time I can go is in the evenings or the weekends.'

Daisy felt awful. Since she'd started work and had been seeing Noah, she'd let her caring duty slide a little. 'I'll come with you,' she offered.

'You don't need to.'

'I want to.' She didn't, but she also didn't want Zoe lugging carrier bags full of groceries around, either. She'd never forgive herself if something happened to the baby. 'Give me a minute to make myself presentable.' Splash cold water on her face to try to hide the fact she'd been crying, was what she meant. When she saw her reflection in the bathroom mirror, she winced. Red and blotchy, she looked hideous.

Oh, who cared! It wasn't as if she would see anyone she knew – who else went grocery shopping on a weekday evening?

Melissa, that's who.

Daisy spotted her in the chilled section of Sainsbury's pushing a half-full trolley, and her already low spirits sank even further. If Daisy ever did the shopping (not that her mother trusted her to bring back what was on the list) she usually went to Tesco, and she'd never shopped at Sainsbury's when her and Freddie had been together, because Tesco had been nearer. If she had even so much as an inkling that she might bump into her former friend and colleague she would never have offered to accompany Zoe. Melissa was the last person on earth she wanted to see, especially since she knew she looked like something the cat had dragged in.

She did an about turn, hoping she hadn't been spotted, and high-tailed it to the other end of the store, where she hid in the household section and pretended to examine the toilet cleaning products.

'You've got a nerve,' a voice hissed in her ear.

Daisy jumped. 'Melissa,' she said, flatly.

'You bitch!'

'Excuse me?' Daisy had no idea why the other woman was calling her names. Melissa still had a job and a nice little promotion to boot. By rights, if anyone should be name calling, it should be Daisy.

'Homewrecker!' Melissa shouted.

'Who me?' Whose home was Daisy supposed to have wrecked?

'I saw you with him.'

'With who?' Did Melissa mean Noah?

'Aaron's brother. Don't try to deny it, you were all over him.'

'Aaron who?' Daisy didn't know anyone by the name of Aaron. Did she? Oh, hang on, was Noah's brother called Aaron? She didn't think he'd mentioned his name… She'd have to ask him. Wait, no she couldn't ask him anything ever again, because they weren't together anymore.

'His wife knows, thanks to you,' Melissa cried.

'Whose wife?' Daisy blinked, trying to work out what Melissa was on about.

'You know perfectly well who.' Melissa made no attempt to keep her voice down, and Daisy simply wanted to die of embarrassment.

'No, really I don't,' Daisy insisted.

'You expect me to believe that?'

'It's the truth!'

'I could lose my job because of this.'

'Eh?'

'Who told you? Was it Joyce?' Melissa demanded.

'I haven't seen or spoken to Joyce since I left *Caring Cards*,' Daisy protested, having absolutely no idea what she was being accused of. 'What was Joyce supposed to have told me?'

'About me and Aaron. Don't play dumb. I know it was you, I *saw* you talking to Aaron's brother.'

'Look, Melissa, I don't know what you're talking about or what you think I've done—'

'Are you calling Art a liar?'

Art…? Art…? Who…? Ah! *Art* – the nice guy from New Year's Eve. She hadn't given him a second thought, until now.

A curious crowd of shoppers had gathered around them to watch the unfolding drama. Daisy spotted Zoe amongst them, and she was holding up her mobile and miming "police" at her. Daisy shook her head. She could cope with the likes of Melissa by herself.

Now everything was starting to make sense. Art and Aaron must be brothers. Well, well, well, it's a small world, she thought. Worcester wasn't a particularly large city, as cities go – it was more like an oversized town, and the chances of bumping into an acquaintance whenever you stepped outside your front door was quite high.

'Are you saying that Art is Mr Dearborn's brother?' Daisy was pretty certain he was, but she had to check.

'As if you don't already know,' Melissa spat.

'He never mentioned his surname,' Daisy said.

'You had your tongue down his throat and he practically admitted he got you a job in his bank.'

Oh, yes, that. 'It was one kiss, and there was no job.'

'Like his brother, is he? Says anything to get into your knickers.' Bitterness saturated every one of Melissa's words.

'Art only said what he did because he knew you'd helped to get me sacked.'

'How did he know that, unless you told him?'

'Yes, I told him,' she admitted, 'but only because he wanted to know why Sara was threatening to knock your brains out. I had no idea who he was.'

'Who's Sara?' Melissa frowned, then waved a hand in the air. 'Never mind, I still want to know how *you* knew. Thanks to you, Aaron has been forced to leave the company and his wife is out for my blood. I hope you're happy!'

Strangely enough, Daisy wasn't. She was shocked and surprised, but not happy. Though Melissa had got her comeuppance and Mr Dearborn had hopefully learned not to mix business with pleasure and to keep it in his trousers when he was at work, it was a pity that Daisy and the unknown Mrs Dearborn had been the hapless victims of their sordid little affair.

'No, I'm not happy,' Daisy said to her former colleague, 'but you've brought all this on yourself. If you hadn't been so eager to get promoted at any cost, then this wouldn't have happened. And for your information, Joyce didn't tell me. You did.'

'I never!' Melissa paled and Daisy bet the other woman was frantically going through every conversation she'd ever had with Daisy, wondering if she'd let anything slip.

'I heard you talking to your lover the day the pair of you got me sacked,' Daisy said. 'I was in the toilets.'

Melissa's already pale, pinched face turned the colour of "oh, shit!".

'And by the way,' Daisy added. 'I'm not a meek lamb. I got myself a solicitor. Thanks to you and Aaron Dearborn, *Caring Cards* has awarded me a substantial sum in compensation for unfair dismissal.' And with that, Daisy rammed Melissa's trolley out of the way and stalked past, her head held high. A cheer went up from the watching crowd.

But all Daisy could think about was Noah.

Chapter 36

The bed was too small and the mattress was too lumpy. Daisy turned over, wriggling to try to get more comfortable. The sheets were scratchy too, and the duvet just didn't cover her properly, and her pillow was nastily damp from the tears which trickled from the corner of her eyes in a steady stream.

And she wished that annoying noise would stop. It was coming from her mother's room, and sounded like something was tapping the window – a bird, or… eek! A vampire! "Let me in", that's what that boy vampire had said in *Salem's Lot* when he hovered outside the window. The film had given her nightmares for weeks.

She lay rigid in her uncomfortable single bed, listening for the next tap.

There it was again.

Was someone trying to break in?

Oh, God, that was it! Burglars.

If she didn't get up and make sure, they could all be murdered in their beds. The sound of her mother blissfully snoring travelled across the landing as Daisy crept out of her room, and she wondered how the woman could sleep through such a racket. Her nan hadn't stirred, either.

The noise came again, and Daisy almost shrieked.

Against her better judgement, she padded down the stairs, freezing when she got to the last step, and wondered if she could risk peeping through the living room curtains. If a burglar saw movement it might scare him off. On the other hand, it may encourage him to stop arsing around and get on with breaking in.

She sidled across the hall and into the living room as silently as she could, easing the curtain aside.

At first, she couldn't see anything, then a movement caught her eye.

A shape shifted in the darkness, curiously hunched and bent in on itself, then it straightened, and she thought it was a man. One of its arms went back and catapulted forward, and immediately after there came the sound of something solid hitting glass, not hard enough to break it but hard enough to make that disconcerting tapping noise.

Then a voice hissed, 'Daisy!'

Bloody hell, whoever this was, he was coming after her!

'Daisy,' it said again, louder.

This time she recognised the voice and her heart constricted, missing a beat.

She hurried to the front door and unlocked it. 'Noah?'

'About time! I've been trying to wake you up for hours. You sleep like the dead.'

'That's not my bedroom window,' Daisy said, stepping into the little front garden, and looking up.

'It isn't? That explains it.'

'It's my mother's room, and you're lucky you didn't wake her up.' She tried to make out his expression in the orange-yellow light of the streetlamp. 'What are you doing here?' she asked, hope lifting her treacherous heart.

'I had to see you.' He came closer, but halted before he reached her.

'At two-thirty in the morning?' she asked. Her mouth was dry and her insides churned unpleasantly.

His shrugged.

'You could have rung,' she said.

'Your phone was off.'

Her phone certainly wasn't off. It was on her bedside table where she always left it at night, and she distinctly remembered putting it there after that awful phone call from Noah when he'd told her he was moving to Brighton. It felt like ages ago, and that she had been estranged from him for days, and not just a few hours. If this was what the rest of her life was going to be like, she certainly wasn't looking forward to it.

'We need to talk,' he said.

No, they didn't. Talking would only make things worse, drag it out. A clean break was much better. She shook her head.

'Please, Daisy, I don't want it to end like this.'

Daisy didn't want it to end at all, but she didn't have much choice, did she? 'How *do* you want it to end?' she asked, bitterly.

'I don't want it to end at all,' he replied, confusing her even further.

'You don't? But what about—'

'Kate? You've jumped to the wrong conclusion, my love.'

'How do you know what conclusion I jumped to?'

'Zoe told me. Look, can I come in? I've been out here ages, and I'm bloody freezing!'

'Where's your car?'

'Over there. Why?'

'There's no way I'm going to risk waking Mum or Nan. We can sit in your car and you can turn the heater on.'

'I've got a better idea. Let's go to the drive-through. I could murder a coffee.'

'I'd better get changed.' Daisy raced upstairs, pulling her pyjamas off even before she got to her room. Grabbing the closest things to hand (yesterday's jeans and fleece) she hastily dressed and checked the bedside table for her mobile. She'd better take it with her, because knowing her luck, her mother or her nan would be bound to need her for something. They never had woken her in the middle of the night before, but Sod's Law dictated that the one night she wasn't soundly asleep in bed, was the one night when she would be called upon. Her phone wasn't where she normally left it.

Daisy had a quick scout round for it, then shrugged. She'd have to go without it, and hope that the house wouldn't be visited by aliens, or burnt down, or be engulfed in a gigantic sinkhole (she'd read about these kinds of things). Skittering back down the stairs, the only thought in her head was, he'd called me "my love".

Had it been a slip of the tongue or had he meant it? If he'd meant it, where did that leave her?

He was waiting by the car as she slipped out of the door, closing it softly behind her, and as she buckled her seatbelt, there were only two things on her mind. The first one was easy. 'What do you mean "Zoe told you"?' she asked.

'She called me. I thought it was you, at first.'

'How does she know your number?'

'She rang me from your phone.' That explained what had happened to her mobile, Daisy guessed. The sly little minx had stolen it. Daisy wondered how she'd ever thought Zoe was insipid and stupid. The woman was more cunning than a weasel, and just as sneaky. It remained to be seen whether Daisy would forgive her – it depended on what happened in the next hour or so.

McDonalds was quiet at that time of the night – morning. The late customers had been and gone, and the early ones hadn't gotten out of bed yet.

'Can we go inside?' Noah suggested. 'I've been sat in that car half the night.' He arched his back and tried to stretch out his legs.

Daisy would have preferred to remain in the car in case she failed to hold the tears back but Noah had already opened his door. When the overhead light came on, and she saw how tired and drained he looked, she agreed.

'Double espresso,' he ordered, and Daisy thought he needed the caffeine desperately.

'When was the last time you slept?' she asked.

Noah rubbed a hand across his eyes. 'Not last night, the night before.'

No wonder he looked exhausted, and Daisy had an inkling she didn't look much better herself.

'Do you have to work today?' she asked.

'No, thank goodness.'

Daisy did, and she resented him keeping her from her bed, conveniently forgetting that she'd been totally unable to sleep. 'Make it quick, because I *do* have work in the morning, so say what you've come to say, and get it over with.'

'There's no need to pretend, Zoe told me how you feel.'

The witch! After everything Daisy had done, her sister-in-law had betrayed her. Never again would she confide in her. Zoe would be lucky if Daisy told her what the time was if she asked.

'Wonderful,' was Daisy's sarcastic reply.

'Actually, it is,' Noah said, and Daisy rounded on him.

'Makes you feel good to break a girl's heart, does it?'

'No, of course not, I—'

'Look, I know Connor has to take priority, I understand, honestly I do, but it's over. There's no point in explaining how you and Kate have decided to make a go of things for your son's sake.'

To her surprise and dismay, Noah laughed. Daisy's hand gripped her cappuccino harder, and she resisted the urge to lob it at him.

'Kate is marrying Ian,' Noah said. 'Zoe told me—'

'I don't care what she told you. You're still in love with your ex, so—' Daisy said, talking over Noah, who was saying, '—you thought I still loved Kate. I don't. I love you.'

Daisy froze. 'You what?'

'I love you, you silly goose. Why do you think I drove all the way from Brighton in the middle of the night to talk to you? I mean, I was going to anyway, after you hung up on me, but when Zoe said you were breaking your heart because you thought I was getting back together with Kate, then I had to come and explain to you in person.'

'But you're moving to Brighton,' she said, her heart pattering so hard and fast, she was worried it might explode.

'I thought about it, for about half a day, when Connor made me feel as guilty as hell for not being there for him.'

'And?'

'I told you my son was a great kid, didn't I?' (Daisy hadn't exactly seen the "great" side of him, only the stroppy teenager side). 'He saw how upset I was, but before that, on the way back to Brighton, he asked about you.'

'He did?'

'He'd never seen me with anyone else before and he was curious. In fact, I'd never talked to him about any woman before, and I didn't want him to think I did this sort of thing all the time, and that it had been sheer bad luck that he'd caught me getting physical. I explained that it was still early on in our relationship, but that I thought I was falling in love with you.'

'You are?'

Noah nodded. 'Once Connor had calmed down a bit – it seems like he's getting teased at school, and a few of the other boys have been telling him weird and wonderful, and some not-so-wonderful, stories about their own stepfathers, and he'd got a bit scared. Anyway, I met Ian, and the four of us sat down and had a good long talk about how his mum marrying Ian would affect him, and that I'll always be his dad, no matter what, and after that he was much happier.'

'Was this before or after you decided to move to Brighton?'

'Before.'

Which meant, Noah still intended to move. Daisy saw no point in continuing the discussion – unless he was going to ask her to go with him? The thought made her giddy. Would she go?'

'I said Connor is a great kid, because he is. He loved the idea of me being closer. He loved the idea of being able to pop in on the way home from school, and to see me every weekend if he wanted.'

Daisy didn't take her eyes off Noah. His face was filled with an odd mix of pride, love, and sadness.

'But,' he was saying, 'he also saw how much it was hurting me to let you go. So, he let me go instead.'

'I don't follow.'

'Connor is almost a young man. He knows he won't be at home much longer. He wants to be a doctor.' Noah beamed when he said it. 'He said he doesn't want to tear my life apart and make me move to Brighton, when he could be studying medicine anywhere in the country in a couple of years' time. He's going to apply to Birmingham and Bristol as his first and second university choices, and both of them are much easier to get to from Worcester than Brighton, so hopefully we'll be able to see more of each other.'

That's all well and good, Daisy thought, but she still wasn't sure what this meant for her and Noah, if it meant anything at all.

'Which means, that I'm not moving!' he declared and waited for her response.

Daisy had no idea what to say. She was still reeling from him telling her that he thought he was falling in love with her.

'I will be looking for another job. GP maybe – the hours are much better. Daisy?' he asked, when she still didn't say anything. 'I thought you'd be happy. Zoe said you were breaking your heart because we'd split up.'

'I was. I am, but it's got nothing to do with me whether you move or not, has it?'

'Yes, it has, because I want you in my life, but Connor's in my life too and he's the child, so he's my main concern and priority. I need for you to be on board with my seeing Connor, possibly once a month.'

'Are you saying you still want me?'

'I am!'

Daisy smiled. 'I've never been to Brighton. I hear it's lovely. Do you mean it?'

'About spending more time with Connor?'

'No, about falling in love with me,' Daisy said, her heart in her mouth.

'Yes. Absolutely. One hundred percent.'

Well, that was romantic, wasn't it! She cocked her head at him, and raised her eyebrows.

'Ah, you want me to say it, don't you?' he said, and Daisy nodded.

'Daisy Jones, I love you! There, I've said it!' He sat there, defiantly, as if he expected her to laugh at him, or worse, to tell him "thanks, but she didn't love him".

'I love you too,' she said softly, and she felt as though she'd been given the best Christmas present ever.

Chapter 37

Connor made a stunning usher in his top and tails, and sage green tie, which he kept tugging at self-consciously. He'd wanted to give his mother away, but the honour went to Kate's dad.

While the congregation waited in the church for the bride to appear, Daisy whispered in the boy's ear. 'If ever me and Noah get married, not that we are planning on it and he hasn't asked me yet, and he might never ask, and he'd only do it if you are happy with the situation, because you are the most important thing in your dad's life, then you can give me away. David might want to do it, but he'll just have to suck it up. If he is that bothered, he can be a page boy.'

'A page boy? How old is he?' Connor looked so nervous, Daisy wanted to give him a hug, but felt it might be too much, too soon, for the lad. He had enough on his plate right now with sharing his mum, without his father's girlfriend trying to get all touchy-feely.

'Twenty-seven,' Daisy said, deadpan.

Connor burst out laughing.

Last night, when Kate (who was lovely, by the way, and had eyes only for Ian, and had made Daisy feel very welcome, indeed), had gone to her parents' house to sleep, she and Connor had had a little chat about the way they'd met and Connor had apologised. He really was a nice kid, just like Noah said. Gone was the belligerent teenager, and in its place was a pleasant young man. He'd been scared, Daisy had realised, that was all, and had acted out of fear of losing his mother, and of being replaced in her affections by her new husband.

Talking of husbands, Ian looked terribly nervous as he stood at the front of the church, shuffling his feet, and every so often craning his neck around to see if Kate had arrived. He seemed a nice enough bloke, and Noah appeared pleased that Kate was getting hitched.

The music started, the Wedding March (Daisy didn't know why anyone would want anything else), and Connor quickly slipped out of the pew Daisy and Noah were in and scuttled to take his place at the front with Kate's parents. Ian gave him a reassuring smile, and to Daisy's delight, Connor beamed back at his new step-father.

As Kate glided down the aisle, Daisy thought how lovely she looked in a simple sheath dress in off-white satin, which clung to her curves, and showed off her height. Her dark hair was gathered up at the back of her head, with soft curls framing the sides of her face. A simple headdress completed the picture.

Noah reached for Daisy's had and gave it a squeeze.

'She looks gorgeous,' Daisy said.

'Doesn't she just. I'm so proud of her.' Noah was staring at the bride intently, a strange look on his face, and it took Daisy a minute to work out what it might be.

Then she got it. The look was one of love.

There was a second or two when Daisy had a mental wobble but, as Noah had told her several times, he did care for Kate, love her even, but as a brother loved his sister. He was not *in love* with her, and he didn't think he ever had been (teenage crush, and all that, and if Kate hadn't become pregnant, they would have drifted apart naturally). But as the mother of his child he cared for her, and though she exasperated him sometimes, and they occasionally argued about what they thought was best for their son, he did care for her and he always would.

Daisy had accepted that. More or less. She was aware it would take more than a weekend when the bride was totally distracted by her forthcoming nuptials, to get to know this other woman in Noah's life, but then she hadn't met his mother and father, or even his brother yet, either. She sincerely hoped they were nothing like her own. Except David, she conceded – he was alright in small doses, when he wasn't annoying the hell out of her.

As she watched her boyfriend's ex-girlfriend, and the mother of their child, get married to another man, their son solemn and sombre in the pew ahead, Daisy understood this wasn't going to be a bed of roses. She knew they would have their ups and downs, and being a stepmum to an almost-grown teenager would present many challenges, but she also knew the man at her side, his hand holding hers, was worth it.

She glanced up at him as the bride walked past, and Noah turned his attention from Kate to Daisy, and the look in his eyes took her breath away.

'I love you, Miss Jones,' he whispered, and this time there was no misunderstanding but just to make sure, she whispered back, 'I love you, too.'

Epilogue

Daisy leaned away from a table which was still groaning with the remains of an enormous Christmas dinner, and undid the button of her jeans with a sigh of relief. As usual, she'd eaten her share along with someone else's. Now she was feeling distinctly uncomfortable.

Her mother stood up. 'Shall we open our presents now?' she suggested. 'It'll give us time for our dinner to go down before I bring out the Christmas pudding.'

Not that again! Hadn't everyone learned their lesson last year?

'I'm not having any,' Daisy declared, 'and you can't make me!'

'Don't be such a party pooper. I made it especially for you.' Sandra threw her a scowl.

Gee-Gee piped up, 'Your mother wouldn't let me put the sixpence in.'

'I should bloody well hope not, after where it's been!' Daisy retorted.

'I don't know what you're banging on about; I gave it a swill under the tap.'

'It needed more than a swill, it needed melting down for scrap,' Daisy replied, darkly.

'Anyway,' Gee-Gee carried on. 'There's a doctor in the house, this time.'

Noah tipped his glass in Gwenda's direction.

'Bella will have some, won't you my darling?' Sandra cooed.

Daisy rolled her eyes. 'She's only six months old, Mum.' She looked at Zoe and shook her head in mock despair. 'It's a wonder David and I survived long enough to reach adulthood.'

Zoe said, 'We'll stick to the custard, I think,' and wiped little Bella's mouth. On the opposite side of the table, Elsie mirrored her actions with Gwenda.

Sandra unceremoniously plonked several badly wrapped gifts on the table. The baby had already unwrapped hers, and was sitting in her high chair waving a piece of decorative ribbon in the air, and gurgling to herself.

'All those expensive toys, and the kid plays with the wrapping,' David muttered, but his indulgent expression when he looked at his daughter gave the game away.

'Here,' Noah said. 'Happy Christmas, Daisy,' and he placed a small square package on the table next to her plate.

Was it…? Could it be…?

Her heart in her mouth, Daisy handed Noah an envelope. She wanted him to open his present first, because once she'd opened hers (if what was inside that gorgeous wrapping paper and beautifully tied ribbon was what she hoped it was) everyone's attention would be on the third finger of her left hand, and she so desperately wanted Noah to be able to enjoy his gift for a few minutes before the shrieking started.

Noah shrugged and opened the envelope.

'Tickets,' he said, looking confused. 'To Tenerife.'

'There's more,' Daisy said, trying to keep a lid on her excitement.

He pulled another sheet of paper out of the envelope. 'What's this?'

'Read it.'

'A visit to an observatory.'

'I wanted to get you a space flight, but I don't have the same pull or earning power as Richard Branson, so I arranged for you to visit the observatory on Mount Teide instead.'

'Just me?'

'Do you honestly think I'd let you go to Tenerife for a week all on your own?' she cried, pleased at the expression on Noah's face. His grin was wider than the cracker he'd pulled earlier.

'Your turn,' he said, and Daisy eyed the box with barely contained enthusiasm. Slowly, carefully, savouring every second, she unwrapped the little box, intending to save the paper, the ribbon, and the bow. She didn't want to forget anything about this glorious day.

She placed the unopened box on the table, a dark blue velvet box, just large enough to contain a ring, and her heart thundered so loudly, she wondered how come no one else heard it. Closing her eyes, she tried to imagine what sort of ring Noah had chosen. She hoped he was a solitaire kind of guy.

Opening her eyes, and taking a deep breath, she slowly eased the lid open to reveal...

A necklace.

'How lovely,' she managed, disappointment knocking her hard. She lifted it out, hardly seeing it as her eyes blurred with tears, and she turned her back to the table.

'Put it on me?' she asked, relieved to hear the steadiness in her voice. She'd never forgive herself if Noah thought she wasn't thrilled with the gift. He twisted in his seat, and fastened the chain around her neck. She used the time to compose herself, and plaster a grin on her face.

'You haven't looked at it properly, have you?' he accused, and she realised she'd disappointed him after all.

She lifted it off her chest and pulled her chin in, peering cross-eyed at the pendant. When she saw what it was, she didn't know whether to laugh or cry.

'I had it mounted,' Noah said, as Daisy gaped in disbelief at the silver sixpence.

'Is it...?' she asked.

'Yes.' Noah grinned, clearly pleased with himself. 'Your great-gran found it where you'd left it on the table. She wanted to put it in the pudding again this year, but I told her the luck wouldn't work a second time, and I persuaded her to give it to me.'

It was a lovely gesture, but all Daisy could think of was where it had once been. And here she was, wearing the disgusting thing just above her heart. Then there was the issue of luck... She had worked hard to get rid of the damned thing once, and now it had found its way back, like something out of a horror film. It seemed bad luck wasn't finished with her yet, and she had the awful feeling that something nasty was about to happen... Again!

She got up, and planted a kiss on Noah's lips. 'Thank you. I love it,' she said, crossing her fingers to ward off the lie.

'Now that's all out of the way, I'll fetch the pudding,' Sandra said, but when Daisy began to help her collect the dirty dishes and the mounds of food still left in the tureens, her mother waved her away.

'You helped prepare the lunch.' (Daisy had cleaned the veg – that was all her mother trusted her to do). 'Let the men do some work for a change. They can help clear it away. David, Noah, help me carry these into the kitchen.'

Once they were out of the room, Zoe whispered to her, 'You did a good job, there.'

'What do you mean?'

'Don't worry, I don't think Noah could tell.'

'Tell what?' Darn it, she'd hoped no one had realised she'd thought the box contained a ring, and she was fully prepared to deny everything.

'That you don't like the necklace,' Zoe said. 'I don't think I would either, knowing where it's been. Trust a doctor not to see that. Still, it's a lovely thought, and it didn't bring you bad luck, did it?'

Daisy pondered her sister-in-law's comment. Her run of bad luck had actually started *before* she'd swallowed the coin, but it had continued right up until she'd "eliminated" it. Or had it? Actually, when she thought about it, if it wasn't for the sixpence, she never would have met Noah. And Melissa and the MD had been planning her exit from *Caring Cards* long before she'd set eyes on the sixpence. But now she had a new job with prospects (Mr Bradley – Ken – was making noises that he wanted to ease back a little and enjoy those grandchildren of his, and was giving more and more responsibility to Daisy), a nice lump sum, and the icing on the cake – Noah. Handsome, funny, loving, sexy Noah, who knew her as well as she knew herself (except when it came to certain small, silver coins).

'Ta dah!' Sandra breezed back into the dining room, holding a plate of flaming pudding. Noah came in behind her, holding the bowls, and David carried a jug of brandy sauce. Bella let out an ear-piercing shriek when she saw the flames, banging her chubby fists on her high chair.

'See,' Sandra said, 'the baby would have some, if she was allowed, so you'll have to have her share, Daisy.'

'If it will stop you going on about it, I'll have a spoonful,' Daisy conceded. 'But if I choke on it, my death will be on your head.'

'Stop being such a drama queen,' her mother said, holding her hand out to Noah like a surgeon expecting a scalpel.

Noah slapped a bowl in her palm, Sandra spooned a small amount of pudding into it, and David poured brandy sauce over the top.

'There, hardly a mouthful. Happy?' Sandra said, popping the dessert down in front of Daisy.

'Did you put the sixpence in it?' Gee-Gee asked, peering at it. Over the last year her eyesight had become progressively worse and so had her hearing. Her memory wasn't so good, either. Daisy was simply grateful the old lady was able to join them this year, because she really didn't fancy eating Christmas lunch at *The Grange*. Most of the food there could be sucked up with a straw.

'No, Gee-Gee, it's around my neck.'

'It won't do you any good there. You should have put it in the pudding. I thought you were going to, Sandra?'

'No Gran, you must have heard wrong.'

'There's nothing wrong with my hearing, I'll have you know!'

'Now, ladies, no squabbling,' David said, and Daisy shot him a grateful look. She didn't want her family to frighten Noah off; his family was so much more… normal.

In an effort to tune out what could be the start of an epic row, Daisy turned her attention to her bowl. It was only a spoonful, so she scooped it up and popped it in her mouth.

Bloody hell! The woman had put a sodding sixpence in it after all, Daisy thought, after she'd bitten down on something very hard indeed. It was a wonder she'd not broken a tooth.

'Mum!' she cried around the mouthful of gooey pudding and rock hard…

That wasn't a coin, it was the wrong shape for a start, sort of lumpy and with a hole in the middle.

She spat it out into the palm of her hand and stared at it.

There, covered in sticky, dark brown pudding, lay a diamond ring.

Daisy continued to stare at it, wordlessly.

This time she really did think she was going to die, because she couldn't breathe. Elsie nudged her in the ribs, and placed a small jug filled with soapy water on the table.

'Here, let me, seeing as you're not going to,' her nan said, snatching the ring out of Daisy's hand, dropping in the jug and swirling it around. When it was clean, she took it back out and gave it to Noah.

He went down on one knee. 'Daisy Jones, will you marry me?' he asked.

Everything and everyone were totally and utterly silent. Even baby Bella didn't make a sound.

'Yes, oh yes!' Daisy cried, when she couldn't hold her joy in any longer, and Noah slipped the ring on her finger.

'It's got six diamonds around the big one,' he said, 'and they represent every penny in that sixpence. The middle diamond represents our love.'

Daisy squealed with happiness, and threw herself into Noah's arms. As their lips met, Daisy Jones realised she was a very, very lucky lady, indeed.